Chalcot Crescent

'Reads like a first novel... it's so fresh and vibrant and funny. The funniest dystopian novel I've ever read.'   BOYD HILTON

'This legendary English author really opens up in this wickedly sharp story of her imaginary sister Frances... Riveting!'   *Look Magazine*

'A great scroll of memory, skewed history and canny observation. Wonderfully imagined, constantly surprising.'   *Saga Magazine*

'In this novel we are back to the bohemian, anarchist, feminist, audacious Weldon of old, mischievous and funny... A sparkling read, this is Fay Weldon back on top form.'   *Good Book Guide*

'It fizzes! The great thing about this book is that it isn't written by someone who's twenty-five.'   JOEL MORRIS

'Frances narrates much of the novel with a twinkle in her eye... knowingly light-hearted and tongue-in-cheek... As it careers towards a seemingly apocalyptic ending, the book reveals a healthy cynicism about men, women, feminists and the alternative.'   *Independent on Sunday*

'Wildly imaginative and satiric... We could almost be back in the land of J.M. Coetzee for the convolutions of narrative identity but for the fact you'll laugh out loud a whole lot more at *Chalcot Crescent*.'
Dove Grey Blog

'A saga that has more than a touch of the dictatorship doctrine of Orwell's 1984 about it... [Weldon's] dazzling skill in mixing her personal facts with creative fiction provides its own frolics in [this] eclectic fantasy.'   *Camden New Journal*

Fay Weldon was brought up in New Zealand. Creator of the slogan 'Go to work on an egg', writer of the first ever episode of 'Upstairs Downstairs' and currently Professor of Creative Writing at Brunel University, Fay is best known for her novels *Praxis*, *The Life and Loves of a She-Devil* and *Worst Fears*. In 2001 she was awarded a CBE. She has eight children and stepchildren and lives on a hilltop in Dorset.

CHALCOT CRESCENT

Fay Weldon

CORVUS

First published in Great Britain in 2009.

This paperback edition first published in Great Britain in 2010
by Corvus, an imprint of Grove Atlantic Ltd.

9 8 7 6 5 4 3 2 1

A CIP catalogue record for this book is available from
the British Library.

ISBN: 978-1-84887-306-3

Printed in Great Britain by
Clays Ltd, St Ives plc

Corvus
An imprint of Grove Atlantic Ltd
Ormond House
26-27 Boswell Street
London WC1N 3JZ
www.corvus-books.co.uk

Le problème avec notre époque est que le futur n'est plus ce qu'il était.

Paul Valéry

Two years after I was born, my mother had a miscarriage. Had she not, I would have grown up with a younger sister. This is the sister's story, set in an alternative universe which closely mirrors our own.

Surprises

Is there to be no end to the surprises?

I had a good friend who said to me, 'But I always thought by the time you got to forty everything would be sorted out. You'd have a husband and a home and children and there'd be no more trouble. But now look!'

Her name was Cynthia. It was her fortieth birthday. Her husband was divorcing her, not without reason; her love life was in chaos, and all three of her children were proving ungrateful. I remember replying that so far as I could see very few things in life worked out the way they were meant to. Age didn't enter into it.

'A friend's offered me a week in a holiday cottage in Turkey,' she said, 'only it would mean leaving the children. Do you think that's okay? I deserve a break.'

And I said no, it was not okay, the children were upset enough as it was and now was not the time to leave them. 'And as for deserving,' I said piously, 'there is no such thing. Just because you've had a hard time doesn't mean an easy one ought to follow. There is no automatic system out there which keeps good and bad in balance.'

But Cynthia went anyway and a plane crashed outside Paris on the day she was expected back and as I was watching the TV news I saw one of her Victorian-style buttoned boots in the foreground of the mess of charred metal and scraps of flesh and scattered possessions strewed over the forest floor. Which was how I knew she'd been on the plane.

That was a nasty surprise. I always thought perhaps there was a bit of foot left in the boot. Eighteen little leather buttons, each one to be attended to. I always marvelled at how she found the time to put them on, being a mother of three with a home to run. That was in 1974.

On the other hand the children came into a great deal of compensation money, and their lives may have turned out better for the loss of a mother. Who is to say? All is surprise and paradox. I was no better for the loss of a friend, of course, friends being rare and valuable, and not imposed by chance, as mothers are, but there was no compensation for me.

'Gran,' said Amos, 'you're shivering. Should I wriggle down on my front and fetch a blanket?' We had been sitting on the stairs for some three hours waiting for the bailiffs to finally accept that we are not at home and go away. But their persistence was extraordinary. They would knock – the peremptory knock of an authority not to be denied – only police and bailiffs have this particular knock – bang, bang, BANG de-bang – wait some three minutes and retire to their car. They would not drive away – we could hear Love Radio – and after some twenty minutes they would return and knock again. How could they know we were in the house? It was beginning to get dark. The street lights had not gone on so presumably there was another power cut: and both our mobiles were out of juice. If we stood up we could be seen: so we sat on the stairs and waited, one eighty-plus grandmother and her handsome grandson.

Mind you, Amos was not quite as handsome as he once had been, but still okay, I supposed, even impressive. Just rather less like the blond Jesus than before, with flowing golden locks and a beseeching look: now the hair was cropped and receding, and the look, though still expectant, was interwoven with disappointment, as must, I suppose, happen to everyone as the years pass. As a child he had been glorious; now, in his mid-thirties, he was strong-featured, good-looking, but a little mad-eyed. Genes will out. I was flattered that he had bothered to come to my aid. That had always been Amos' way, even as a small toddler. Stocky and blond and laughing. You felt gratified when he bothered to acknowledge your existence, come to you and shove a small sticky hand into your big one.

'Good idea,' I said to Amos, and he slithered down the stairs on his stomach towards my bedroom, now set up on the ground floor, along with kitchen and bathroom, to save my eighty-year-old knees from too much work. This is as far up the stairs as I can get. My knees will not turn the corner beyond the landing to reach the rest of my domain, where I ruled for fifty years, through good times and bad. I will be glad of a blanket. It is true Amos may be as much interested in taking the opportunity of rolling himself a spliff as in bringing me warmth and consolation, but never mind.

The Way We Live Now

The people next door at No. 5 have a generator and would be happy enough to let us plug in and recharge our mobiles, but all down the Crescent back doors have been sealed, fences removed, and back gardens combined to create a communal allotment. So now we can use only our front doors. It was a small price to pay for the vegetables we produced, or so I had thought until now, when I realized there was no way Amos could nip next door unseen. Our friendly local Neighbourhood Watch had talked about breaking through doors to connect the first floors all down the Crescent, and it had seemed to me a fine idea, though currently illegal according to the new Fire, Health and Safety Act 2013, but it seemed so drastic a step we had never got round to actually doing it. What, live communally, as people once had in Soviet Russia? It was voted out: the young people, oddly enough, were against it, the old for it.

It has been hard to accept, especially for the young, that the sudden change in the way we live is not a passing phase, a matter of a couple of years, but is going to continue, and will probably see me out. But we are getting ourselves together – the vegetable field out the back flourishes under NUG's CiviGro scheme, and ration books have finally been issued, or so the blogs tell us, though few have turned up on our doorsteps. Apparently they are hijacked by 'organized gangs' between printing press and distribution. Personally I

6

am thankful that someone somewhere is organized. Governments – we have had three elections in the past two years – have failed us until now. But the new regulations that flow from NUG – the National Unity Government, composed not of politicians but sociologists and therapists – as a tap flows water, seem finally to be softening and fertilizing the ground. Necessity makes a harsh but fair master.

'Necessity,' says Amos darkly, 'is the argument of fucking tyrants and the creed of slaves. Just you wait.'

I am glad the lad has had some sort of education and it comes naturally to him to quote William Pitt. It is more than either of my children can do. But then Amos, he went to a 'good' school, paid for by his stepfather. My girls went through the State system, not from any necessity but because my then husband Karl was socialistically inclined: a leftie, as my second husband described him.

Amos may be right about NUG but such is the pace and nature of the new legislation I suspect much of it gets forgotten accidentally on purpose.

When people complain that I am cynical, I say, but I am not cynical, I am just old, I know what is going to happen next. That is what experience does for you. Mind you, there are still surprises, like my friend Cynthia falling out of the sky. The plane broke up in mid-air, and many on board were returning from the Paris fashion shows. Beautiful girls showered down from the skies, still strapped to their seats. Cynthia was no model – indeed my mother spoke of her 'having an unfortunate face' – but it did not stop her having an emotionally tumultuous life. Some people are born to it.

There can be good surprises, in case you think I am a miserable person. I am not. This grandson of mine, Amos, the one the family had given up as a hopeless case in his teen age, a drug addict, a drop-out and a disgrace to the family, who'd even at one time joined the BNP – even though, or perhaps even because, he has a Jewish stepfather – is prepared to sit on the stair below mine and offer me help and company in this my hour of need and distress. That's a surprise. I don't see Venetia or Polly, my daughters, sitting here. Perhaps they've given me up too as a hopeless case. It is not a pretty thought. I have lived and breathed for my children, or so I tell myself. They may see it differently and probably do. 'Bailiffs at Mum's door' will not sit well with them. It smacks of mismanagement, and they are both very managing girls.

Astonishing how Karl and I, with our lovers and divorces and dysfunctional carryings-on – though I am sure we never failed in love towards our children, just each other – have produced such functional children, so ready to condemn. 'Mother, a store card? You have a store card? Nobody with any sense has a store card! A store card up to its limit?' Gasp.

Yet they are the generation, not me and mine, who have brought this country to its knees. We brought freedom of thought, sexual liberation, imagination, creativity, wealth – they just spent. Well, true, I did too but they did it worse.

On cue, bang, bang, bang-de-bang – the very stairs tremble, the paint on the porch will flake. Authority has a heavy knock. They use their fists – they do not even bother with bell or knocker, though the knocker is antique and heavy, a brass fish with a curly tail, overlooked by my husband Karl when he stripped the house of his belongings, long ago, in revenge for my daring to buy him out of a property he felt to be intrinsically his, although the law disagreed. Work that sentence out for yourselves. The memory of these events makes me breathless. I will not rewrite it.

I would normally have had the front of the house repainted this

year had the bank not decided to call in the overdraft and my mortgage not gone into arrears. Bang, bang, bang-de-bang. Come out of
there, you cheat, you wretch. Show yourself, antisocial element that
you are! Oh, I am, I am; forgive me, NUG.

'Fucking banksters,' Amos had said when we fled our lunch –
National Meat Loaf and the last of the tomatoes from my window
box – for the stairs, where we couldn't be seen. 'They still own us
and control us. NUG will never get them under. Their scabby
minions will forever be banging on the door.'

Amos has an admirable way with words, laced through though
they may be with profanity. Literacy is in his blood. Am I too not a
writer, albeit a forgotten one? Frances Prideaux, CBE? Remember?
And Amos' great-aunt Fay, though she was reduced to cookery
books, and his great-aunt Jane, the poet? And his great-grand-
mother Margaret Jepson earned the family living through writing,
and Margaret's brother Selwyn and her father Edgar as well. The
particular talent seems to have bypassed Venetia and Polly altogether, which may be why they live such settled lives. Venetia paints,
but I sometimes think it is an affectation rather than the real thing.

'It is in the leech's nature to go on sucking blood,' I respond, 'until
the last possible moment.'

The bankers serve very well as scapegoats, but what can they do
if the world turns out to be bipolar; if one day the sunspots flare
again, the polarity reverses, the nations of the world shut up shop,
put up the barriers, each looking after their own as best they can?
One day mania switches to depression; in individuals it can last
years, on a global scale how long? It doesn't bear thinking of. Our
currency under NUG is so without value not even food can be
imported; let alone oil, let alone electricity from France. North Sea
gas has finally gasped its last. And were not those whom Amos

9

insults the cream of our youth? They too are victims, lured into a world of money which represented neither toil nor value. Bound to fail: bribed, used, betrayed, and then ruthlessly discarded. I speak strongly because Ethan, Amos' young half-brother, my other grandson, with his First in History, bright and innocent, was one such. He is a Ministry chauffeur now: at least he had a father, my son-in-law Victor, well up in NIFE, the National Institute for Food Excellence, to pull strings.

Even so, Ethan was angry. He is a young man. He lost his Porsche and his string of girlfriends. He blames the bankers of the past – thus letting himself off the hook – the Bilderbergers and their kind, for setting up a universal Ponzi scheme and knowing very well what they were doing. He joined Redpeace, an angry Greenpeace breakaway group, and through its webpage circulated the facsimile of a letter written in 1838 by Amsel Rothschild to his New York agents, introducing the idea of 'the mortgage'. The letter turned up on my computer, I am on Redpeace's mailing list but do not download – it seems dangerous.

The few who can understand the system will be either so interested in its profits, or so dependent on its favours, that there will be no opposition from that class, while, on the other hand, that great body of people, mentally incapable of comprehending the tremendous advantage that Capital derives from the system, will bear its burden without complaint and, perhaps, without even suspecting that the system is inimical to their interests.

Well, well, he was right, we did not suspect. But it's not, I think, that we are mentally incapable. We would just rather not comprehend, and spent the money while we could, in our two-hundred-year patch of mania.

As it happened, Ethan's moment of anger and indignation quickly passed: he unsubscribed from Redpeace. Their missives still come through to me, but mostly I delete them unread as they arrive. I cannot bear a screen cluttered by irrelevancies. One day, one day, when I have the time to work out how it's done, I will actively unsubscribe.

Ethan likes being a Ministry driver, he tells me. You get to speed down the centre lane in cars not quite as good as the old Porsches – after the Volkswagen takeover they are not quite what they were, being more sedate and social – but good enough. The VIPs he drives confide in him. And he now has a less glossy but far nicer girlfriend in Neighbourhood Watch, whom I have not met but of whom he speaks in admiration, and only one, and so no longer has the emotional strain of juggling his affections as once he had to, checking over the Porsche for stray thongs in case one of the others found out. That kind of thing.

O, What A Noble Mind Is Here O'erthrown

Take no notice of me. I was pretty smart in my heyday, I daresay, but thinking Amos has left me on the stair just to roll a spliff is as likely to be the paranoia of old age – the carer is a thief; someone is trying to poison the cat; my metal fillings are broadcasting messages – as a rational judgment.

What continues to worry me is why the men at the door don't go away. Why are they so sure we're in here? Why should they be so interested anyway in an aged lady novelist has-been? I got a glimpse of them as they arrived and got out of their car – two guys in a grey executive Lexus – a sure sign of an authority about its righteous business. One was large, young, black and handsome, shiny as a panther, the other small and white and undernourished. They wore suits and ties – almost as if they were in fancy dress, bringing a kind of bizarre *Clockwork Orange* formality with them. But you, dear reader, will be too young to remember that prophetic Kubrick film, and the sense of menace, of frightening times to come, of a world barely in control, that it brought with it.

Bang, bang, bang-de-bang. I'll huff and I'll puff and I'll blow your house down.

My home, which I always thought so charming and so very me, so very much mine, so redolent of cultural superiority, turns out to be just a house of straw, built by selfish little pigs who once lived off the fat of the land, and need now to be brought to justice. See how

I veer between a helpless defiance and an acute sense of guilt? Mea culpa, me and mine. Amos may be right: the admen have brought us to this state, where we side with those who have taken us hostage. The Stockholm syndrome of the debtor. I am on the side of those who persecute and damage me. Many a wife, of course, is in the same state.

Outside the street lamps flicker on, and go out again. The light on the CiviCam at the end of the street stays off: that means it isn't functioning. We're meant to report it but nobody bothers: it's a concrete monstrosity, quite out of keeping with the original Victorian gas lamps – which the Crescent is lucky enough to still have, albeit converted to electricity. This is a conservation area, and posh, or at least was, until a couple of years ago. Now pavements are beginning to crack and rats come out and stare at you, and no-one bothers to hammer out the dents in the Saabs and Mercedes that still line the street. Most turn out to be in negative equity, like the houses behind them, and there are no buyers. For years pundits kept saying things would pick up, that people were postponing buying until prices came down, but the fact turned out to be that people had just lost interest in buying things they didn't need. Consumerism just went out of fashion one day, like the hula hoop – one day everywhere, the next nowhere, for no apparent reason, and after that there was no going back.

Economists presuppose a population ruled by the rational self-interest of individuals, but alas, it is not the case. Societies are no different from the individuals that compose them, and are as likely to be ruled by Thanatos as Eros, to be periodically seized by the urge to self-destruct; just as the sun is given to a plague of sunspots from time to time for no apparent reason.

There was a brief period, some three years ago, when deflation began to flatten out, hailed as the Recovery, but it was short-lived, and merely triggered off inflation.

And inflation no longer had the charm it once had in making light of what one owed. The small print at the bottom of the credit agreements, by which everyone lived and no-one ever read, gave an option to whoever bought on the debt – 'the banks, the banks,' as Amos would cry in triumph, 'the blood-sucking scum' – to index-link existing debts. A rare person it was who could live free of debt, free of anxiety, free of fear of the future. The dread of nuclear war back in the sixties and seventies was nothing to it. But perhaps every decade chooses its own anxiety.

Amos wriggles up with the blanket and tucks it round me. I had misjudged him. He loves his old gran.

'Do you think they have heat sensors?' I whisper.

'The filth do,' he murmurs, 'so these shits will be next. All the agencies are now one and the fucking same.'

Now I too had fallen for the attraction of bad language in the sixties, when the hippie classes associated it with the vital primitivism of the working classes, and envied it, and stole it as our own, along with people power, long unwashed hair, torn jeans and other accoutrements of poverty. For some reason we believed the non-thinking classes were more highly sexed than the bourgeoisie. My family complain I am foul-mouthed, and I do try not to be. A fuck or a shit when I drop something on my toe is about as far as I go. But I wish Amos wouldn't do it: it somehow undermines his cause, his complaint against society.

'But we're still all right so long as we don't open the door,' I say. 'They're not allowed to break in, are they? It's only if you let them in the first time they can come in any time, break the door down if necessary.'

'Don't fucking bank on it,' says Amos. 'Debt collectors now have powers once reserved for the police under the Prevention of Terrorism Act 2005.'

This child knows so much. He spent a year in prison for drug dealing, and was lucky it was not longer. I paid for the best lawyers, the best barristers. Ten years back I was wealthy. Now I live as others do. I can no longer protect my family. Nor could Victor at the time: he was then a scientist working with Cancer Cure and did the job for love rather than money. If he said the boy should face the consequences of his actions, it was because tough love was the prerogative of those with no money to spare, rather than from conviction, and both, I believe, were glad when I stepped in and helped. Venetia loves her son and Victor did his best to do so, though I daresay Amos was not the easiest of stepsons. We all love our children when they are born, sometimes quite passionately. I know I did. I know Venetia did. Yet so many children complain so bitterly about how their parents failed in love. I don't know where it goes wrong.

Victor is one of the few people I know who is flourishing under the new NUG regime: he is no longer a struggling research scientist but works for the National Institute for Food Excellence: his salary is inflation-linked. The rich get richer and the poor get poorer. He is in a position, thank God, to help his family face bad times, as I no longer am.

But it's no use bleating to Amos about mother love. He has resisted all society's attempts to feminize him: he is a triumph of testosteronic impulse. He was always the bad boy of the class, the one who fought in the playground, dealt in football cards, buying cheap and selling dear, for all his gentle looks. He may have a girl-friend but if he does he does not mention her.

'Amos,' I say now, or words to this effect – 'we are not terrorists, simply law-abiding citizens hiding from our creditors. A civil offence, probably, but hardly criminal. It is not as if I am a non-entity. Am I not Frances Prideaux, a declared national treasure – albeit some time ago – her plays in the West End, her popular novels translated all over the world? I am not defenceless. I have the power of public opinion behind me. I could ring *The Times* if the landline hadn't been cut off, and they'd have their people round in no time, to watch another national treasure bite the dust of bankruptcy.'

But even as I make my speech my voice trails away. I know what Amos is thinking but is too nice to say. How long since you had a play on, Gran? Twenty years? A novel published? Five? Forget it. The luxury trades are over, and that means you. You were a competent enough writer but you never rose to great heights: the world has forgotten you, as it forgets poor widow women since time began. You made a lot of money once but you spent it. Forget it.

'Power's back on,' he says, and so it is. The street lights stop flickering and glow. Kettles can be boiled, mobiles recharged, computer work caught up with, shop tills worked again. The hospitals have priority, and generators, but there is a shortage of doctors and nurses. Those who came to us from overseas have gone home, where the climate is better and the wages turn up on time.

But yet, sitting here on the stairs in hiding at this advanced age of mine, under siege, in the company of this errant, druggie, foul-mouthed grandson of mine, I am almost happy. This is the greatest surprise of all. I really do not care what happens next. *Jimmy crack corn and I don't care, Jimmy crack corn and I don't care, Massa's gone away. Massa's gone away.* History will wash over me like a tide and take me with it. I haven't so long to live: I am not so eager to stay alive, though I will miss knowing what happens next. 'They' – the forces of law, order and financial stability whose representatives are at the door – also have their kind side. Their committees will decide I am daft, provide me with a bed, warmth, a television set and even these days, I daresay, a computer. I can become a blogger whom nobody reads. I can fade away silently.

My daughters may come forward and offer to take me in, but really I would rather they did not. They have husbands and their duty lies towards them. I realize in retrospect I married my husbands mostly to get away from my mother. Perhaps they did the same to get away from me. Bang bang BANG de-bang. Nemesis at the door, and I don't care. *We all live in a yellow submarine.* The tune runs through my head.

> *And our friends are all on board.*
> *Many more of them live next door.*

As you get older, songs from your youth run through your head unbidden. You think they are irrelevant but actually they are not. They're like dreams, waiting to inform you if you will only take notice. Hymns are there a lot, these days. *See here hath been dawning another blue day, Think 'fore thou let it slip useless away*, as I wonder whether I can be bothered getting out of bed in the morning. Thus reproached, I rise and get on with this novel, or diary, or memoir, or whatever you want to call it. 'I Vow to Thee My Country' is another one. *And soul by soul and silently her shining bounds increase, And her ways are ways of gentleness and all her paths are peace.*

Where does that come from, I wonder? I'm sure I love my country. I do, though it has become a hard place to love: going through a bad patch, as they say of marriages. I'll work on it. One must not give up hope. I remember all those Marxist groups of my youth, the firm belief that capitalism must destroy itself in time, and all you needed to do was destroy the old institutions from within and, phoenix-like, the Glorious New Society would arise. A likely tale, as it turned out. But it is not finished yet. It is too early to tell the forest from the trees.

How I Come To Be Amos' Grandmother

Okay, let's get it over. There is a lot to be told in this tale of the past fifty years. I had hoped to keep myself out of the history but I see I cannot, without exempting myself from guilt, which is hardly the point of a confessional. I have become very conscious, now I am old, as I remember being when I was a young woman and sex and babies were so closely bound together, of the interconnectedness of everything – the interplay of the gear wheels and cogs of acquaintance, the pistons and levers of event, that lead to forward motion. We do not have the visual images of connectedness that once we did: a sight of the ship's engine on the Channel crossing, the polished brass, the thrusting levers, the pounding sexual power; or just how you had to wind the handle to make the car engine spring to life on a cold morning. It was obvious then how all things connected. The stray kitten that mewed on your doorstep, decades back, as you cooked fish fingers for the children's tea, would turn out to belong to your long-lost best friend and the acquaintance would be resumed and then you'd run off with her husband. Fate determined all things. What happened was meant to be. With the advent of the computer that sense faded away. Engine units are sealed: robots made, replaced rather than mended. We email rather than meet, connectedness is electronic, there are few stray kittens because the cats are sensibly neutered. It has been a relief as well as a loss.

Actually, in the last year, the kittens have begun to appear again. No-one can afford to have cats neutered, or keep them alive when their kidneys fail, and the town vets are going out of business. The country vets prosper, as once again the nation has to feed itself. But that's by the by.

And As I Was Saying

I was born in 1934 in New Zealand to Dr Frank and Margaret Birkinshaw, younger sister to Jane and Fay, whose portraits can be seen in the Wellington Art Gallery even today. (New Zealand has weathered the last five years rather well: at least it has enough food to eat, though petrol is severely rationed, air flights are limited because of cyber attacks from one militant group or another, and pirate ships from Indonesia torment the Pacific. There was even some talk that cowrie shells were to be the new international medium of exchange, but I think it was fanciful.) Rita Angus, the artist who painted my sisters Jane and Fay, decided that I was too noisy and fidgety a child to include in the picture and that I spoiled her composition. I was only two. I have always felt the exclusion, and I daresay resented it.

My parents divorced and in 1946 my mother Margaret, on the first civilian boat out of New Zealand, where the war had trapped her, brought me and my two sisters to London. She was penniless but valiant, and never put much value on fathers, or indeed men in general. The city, as my twelve-year-old self remembers it, was in pretty much the state it is today. Hungry, unpainted, swarming with grey-faced people and with weeds pushing up between paving stones. Scholarships took me to grammar school, and thence to St Andrews University, where I followed in my sister Fay's footsteps and studied Economics and Psychology. Jane went to Exeter and there, always a traditionalist, took a degree in English Literature. We girls were left fatherless in 1946. Fay and Jane had both disappointed my mother by having boy babies at an early age by unsuitable men. I followed suit, giving birth to a girl, Venetia. Fay had no option – no money, no home, too early for State help – but to have her child adopted. Jane, pregnant by a penniless artist, was at least married.

'All three of you were punishing your mother,' a psychoanalyst later told me, 'for leaving your father, abandoning him on the other side of the world, and letting him die there.'

I daresay he was right. Poor Margaret was thereafter to spend her life looking after our various offspring.

But another, simpler, version is that when I was a girl it was a common assumption that you didn't get pregnant if you did it standing up. I believed it, and that's how Venetia came to be born. So many of us are born out of ignorance, or drunkenness, or accident, so few out of considered choice. Even today's children, whose early sexual knowledge comes mostly from computer porn, assume that sexual intercourse consists of blow-jobs and anal congress, with the vagina as a mere afterthought, and scarcely a condom in sight. The sex education teacher may spout away all she likes, but is obviously talking nonsense: the child sees, the child knows, the rate of teenage pregnancies continue to rise. What happens is one thing, what ought to happen is quite another.

Venetia was conceived in one of those little alleys that run between Wardour and Dean Street in Soho, me leaning back against a wall, skirts up to my waist. It was a full black skirt with an underlay of white net petticoats. Derek was Fay's boyfriend, and he loved her, but I had sexual wiles and she did not, and she could not forgive

22

him for his fling with me, and broken-hearted he wandered off to Canada and died there skiing into a tree, some said on purpose. Poor Fay, I pattered after her like a curse, always the envious younger sibling, taking what was hers whenever I could. Chips from her plate, shillings from her piggy bank, whole paragraphs from her essays, boyfriends from her side. In the end, when I married Karl, I knew perfectly well he was the husband she should rightfully have had. Yet she never betrayed me: it was always her impulse to understand and forgive. She came to the wedding and smiled bravely; I felt a bit bad but not all that bad.

I knew something momentous had happened when Venetia was conceived if only because the outside world faded away and stillness fell: Derek and I had entered into a slow-motion existence. This hiatus, this pause in actuality, had nothing to do with love, though I assumed at the time it had, being young and romantic. But I have felt the stillness a few times since. I believe it to be when your life veers off from its expected path, like a car slowing down before taking a sharp corner: there is a kind of pause while the parallel universes sort themselves out. I felt it again today when the bang on the door first came and I decided I would not answer it, but hide. I was glad to feel it after so long. I was still in the world of possible outcomes, alternative universes, not the one I have been stuck in for so long, until now, upon the stair.

Pregnant with Venetia, a fact I did not know until Derek was well dead and there was no point in telling Fay, who was also pregnant by him, I refrained from having an abortion or considering adoption. I had a sense that what was meant to be was meant to be and fate was on my side. I had a degree, I had good friends, I was passionately in love with Venetia, unborn and born, and was never very sensitive to what the world thought of me. I attributed the pregnancy to an unknown passer-by of wealth, good looks and charm, which indeed was true of Derek. So much one must do for one's illegitimate child – leave them with an image of an admirable if absent father.

Then came odd jobs and hard times, with my poor mother Margaret helping out – how desperately she had hoped for a life of her own, free from children, but we would not let her – until Fay got me a job as a copywriter. Fay, still unmarried but with lovers aplenty, rose and rose unstoppable – and without, I may say, scruple, in the advertising industry. She could afford to be generous. And soon I too was earning well: I was even better than she was at the persuasive game. She, childless, remained a quasi-man inside the industry. I had not married – children were not seen as the items of value they are now: no man wanted a stepchild if he could help it – but I had Venetia, and she turned out to be an advantage, not a handicap. In those days it was rare for women to rise to the heights of the advertising industry, but I could look at the suited men round the boardroom table and say to them softly, 'I am a woman, a mother, I understand what women want,' and they would believe me, and trust me, and I was right, and more, I had a way with words on the page. And I got them (and kept them) good clients.

Also, as I was an unmarried mother, and therefore a bad girl, the boardroom men had little hesitation in approaching me for sex, and I was happy to oblige at a time when blow-jobs were not yet common currency. To me they seemed a simple, cheerful and kindly act towards needy married men. 'Nice' wives seemed to be mean with sex: the thought of the blow-job was peculiar and strange to the decent women of the time. Procreation was the point of marriage, not pleasure. But I will not dwell on all that. It is a long time ago, and we shed our skins every seven years. On marrying

Karl I quickly had another baby, Polly, a half-sister for Venetia, and turned into the contented wife and mother I always had the potential to be, had not my envy of Fay propelled me into other ways of life.

It was when Venetia was seven that the all-forgiving Fay took me to a party where I met her then boyfriend Karl Prideaux, artist, musician, charmer and antique dealer, and stole him right from under her nose. For once it was not because I wanted something of Fay's – not that she was ever to believe it – I just wanted Karl, on first sight, as he wanted me. Destined, foretold, all that.

Stealing Karl

I was a different person then. I look at that time from afar with a sense of awe and marvel. I am no longer me: my skin has changed too often, five times and more if you allow ten years for a complete change. I am the other Frances back then, going with her big sister Fay to a party in Hampstead, where the artists and writers gather. Fay is accustomed to such excitements, Frances not so. Were the nights different then? It feels like it: they carried more mystery, more sense of future. But perhaps that is just youth. The moon is full, it is the days before yellow lines on the road, and anyone can park anywhere, and no-one had yet stood upon the moon and explained it was a lump of rock, with film to prove it and depress everyone, not a gift to lovers from heaven, or made of green cheese either. These days Frances, looking at the moon, senses entropy, and, listening out, can only dimly hear the music of the spheres. But when she was walking alongside her big sister, their high heels clicking in unison, she a couple of inches taller and slimmer of waist, such music rang sweetly in her ears, and the very air seemed scented with promise of excitements to come.

'You haven't met Karl, have you,' says Fay. 'I met him at the launderette in Regent's Park Road. My washing machine had broken down.'

'So now of course you use his,' remarks Frances.

'He doesn't believe in domestic machinery,' says Fay. 'So now I take his washing down there as well.'

'What does he believe in?' asks Frances.

'Sex,' says Fay, and for some reason this irritates Frances very much. Her life is earnest, Fay's is all frivolity.

Fay lives in a house in Chalcot Square round the corner from Chalcot Crescent. She bought it for £6,000 cash. Women can't get mortgages from banks, but they can borrow money from friends and lovers and pay it back. Chalcot Square was run-down, the green patch in front of the houses grey, damp and littered with old prams and bits of dismantled bicycles. Rachman, the famous slum landlord of the day, frightened elderly tenants out by painting the evil eye on the front doors and employing actors to prance around as evil voodoo shamans. But she is not elderly, she is young, and not easily frightened, and has a plan anyway to move in with Karl around the corner in the Crescent, where it is lighter, and airier, and far more pleasant, and the grass of Primrose Hill is thick and green, and you can hear the lions roar in London Zoo just down the road.

This happens in 1961 when Frances is twenty-seven, and lives in a walk-up (seven flights, ninety stairs) with her mother and little Venetia. Her mother Margaret stays in with Venetia when Frances goes out to work in her advertising agency. Margaret hates it when Frances goes out to parties in the evening and she is left alone, chafing from the burden of how her daughter obliges her to live, feeling excluded. Frances feels her sister Fay should take a little of the burden of entertaining Margaret off her shoulders – Margaret declines to make friends or have a social life of her own: she was born in 1909, after all, and feels company means family: that friends should drop in their visiting cards, not themselves, and remain at a formal distance. Margaret never much liked any of her children bringing friends home, and as for lovers, seriously no.

Fay earns double what Frances does. Sometimes she feels bad about Frances' hard life, but then Frances has only herself to blame. And Frances does not have to bear the burden of guilt Fay does: she did not have an abortion. Fay rather envies her that. Abortion is illegal and you go to prison for having one if you are found out, but the police aren't looking very hard. They would have their work cut out to get round everyone. Both Fay and Frances are unusual in that they have well-paid jobs and are unmarried in an age when few women can support themselves, or want to.

'I look forward to meeting him,' says Frances.

'You might not get on with each other very well,' says Fay.

'Why not?'

'He has an artistic sensibility,' says Fay.

'You mean I haven't?' demands Frances.

'The new Chinese rug you're so proud of,' says Fay, 'is hardly the last word in aesthetic chic.'

'What's the matter with it?' demanded Frances.

'It's nylon, it's machine-made and mass-produced,' said Fay.

Frances was proud of the rug, the first household item she had ever bought for her home after years of living in cheap flats. It suggested to her that things were looking up: that there just might be a future in which possessions and pleasures were freely available. It was circular, thick, dusky pink with a giant dragon woven into it. She loved it. It was luxurious: she had achieved it by her own work and her own efforts. It was her own taste, not her mother's. She had overridden Margaret to buy it. Margaret liked only what was sensible and virtuous. Frances was proud of it. Venetia liked to sit in the middle of it and hum nursery rhymes. Frances had shown

28

the carpet off to people, and thought they looked at her rather curiously. Were they all laughing at her?

She said nothing but resolved she would steal Karl from Fay. She would have him and make his artistic sensibilities her own. She would move in, escape her mother, have this man's babies, make him buy a washing machine and not let Fay lord it over her any more, by virtue of her two years' seniority and childlessness. All sight unseen. But some passing deity – of the kind who existed in the magic London of the past – was passing by in the balmy, enchanted air of that night, heard her unspoken mind and granted her wish.

The party was at Studio House, 1 Hampstead Hill Gardens, a vast house now divided into ten luxury apartments, but then in single occupancy, owned by Professor William Empson, author of the *Seven Types of Ambiguity*, a book that many admired but few understood, and his fiercely beautiful wife Hetta, who had begun life on the South African veldt, where her father laid about her with a sjambok the better to keep her in order, but failed. The Empsons supervised the wilder shores of literary and artistic life in the sixties. Wine flowed, bread and cheese were devoured by the struggling, hungry and talented: Elias Canetti of *Crowds and Power* was there, and the young Bernice Rubens and her husband Rudy Nassauer, and Iris Murdoch – wearing slippers even then – and John Bayley. Mira Hamermesh the film-maker, and Nic Roeg and Karel Reisz, and the young Roger Graef, and Jonathan Miller and Angela Carter were all there: but not Ted Hughes and Sylvia Plath, because they were down in Devon, around the time Assia Wevill and her husband David were visiting for the weekend. Sylvia asked Assia to peel the potatoes and Assia felt herself misused and treated like the maid and went down the garden path to where Ted was, and flirted with him and kissed him just to be revenged on Sylvia, and see where that led, two dead women and one dead child later.

In just that same spirit did Frances go up to Karl at the Empson party, after having talked briefly to William himself, who remarked that 1961 was a palindrome and like a pencil; sharpened at both ends, and, when she asked him why he was wearing two ties, replied to her that he couldn't find his belt. All that energy and promise, there and then not there like a puff of smoke in the cosmos.

And then she asked around and found out that Karl Prideaux was a talented painter, that his wife had gone mad and was murderous and locked up in a loony bin, and a better painter than he was, that he'd been left money and was in psychoanalysis, that he hated his mother, that he'd come into money and gave drunken parties in Chalcot Crescent down the hill, that since his wife left – she had taken to sleeping in a dustbin before they came to take her away – he slept with anyone that moved, what was that pretty fat girl doing at this party – wasn't she in advertising –?

'That's my sister,' said Frances –

'And how about you? It's a lovely night. Would you like to come outside into the moonlight where it's a bit quieter –'

'No thanks.'

She can see where Karl stands with a group of friends, where he seems to be the natural centre of attraction, his arm around Fay, who is looking singularly pleased with herself. She catches his eye. He is not tall, but stocky and muscular, Picasso-like.

'That's my sister,' says Fay. 'She's the one with the illegitimate child who lives with my mother. She's very brave.'

Karl looks at Frances properly. She looks at him. They know each other. The powers from on high have arranged the whole thing, including her wrong, mean motive, which is now irrelevant.

'I have a child too,' he says. She hadn't known that. And then to Fay – 'No child is illegitimate. It has as much right in the world as anyone else.' It's a rebuke. She flushes.

And within two minutes Karl and Frances were out in the garden where it was quieter, underneath the fairy lights, and he was asking why she looked so unhappy, and she was telling him about the married man she was seeing, about the 'Cry Me a River' syndrome, and then before they knew it they were on the ground beneath the trees and he said, as men did in those days, 'I'll only put it in a little way,' but of course he didn't. She thought he was like the pulse of the universe, its heartbeat – that, then this, that, then this, that, then this – the steady rhythm of life itself and the sudden understanding kept her with him for years, though it did not prevent her, from time to time, when upset or jealous or simply bored, for looking for the same quality elsewhere.

When they went back inside to fetch her coat, Fay was standing there, blonde curls askew, make-up streaming down her face. She looked awful when she cried. Frances felt bad about it but not for long.

Then they were walking together down the hill towards Chalcot Crescent and he said, 'I feel bad about your sister. One shouldn't go to a party with one girl and leave it with another,' and Frances said probably not but it was too late now. Within a week they were living together.

Studio House now stands empty, dilapidated and with Virginia creeper pushing out its window frames, its garden a mixture of rubble and weeds. It held its own until 2011, when an epidemic of unknown origin and a 60 per cent fatality rate spread out from the Royal Free Hospital and crept up as far as St Stephen's on Rosslyn Hill, and down the road as far as the Vale of Health, before seeming to burn itself out – there were too few trained pathologists to find a vaccine, let alone a cure – but they reckoned it was carried by rats on a house-to-house basis. By then most of Hampstead had vacated the premises, but the rats hadn't, so very few inhabitants returned.

Becoming Amos' Grandmother

'Making love to you is like making love to the sea,' Karl said, after the second day.

'And with Fay?' I asked.

'To the village pond,' he said. What chance did she have? I didn't tell her he said that. But I treasured it for ever.

For once she pleaded with me. 'But I love him, Frances,' she bleated. I took no notice. She was too docile for him, anyway: he would have made her life hell. He needed someone like me to fight him back.

So I moved with Venetia into Karl's house and have stayed here ever since. From No. 3 Chalcot Crescent I have lived through five decades of world history: I have been living witness to the birth and death of feminism, the terror and denial of the dangers of nuclear war, the rise and fall of terrorism, the fall of first communism, then capitalism – which once we thought would last for ever – the death and rebirth of nationalism, and I survived. Now finally world history reaches my doorstep and comes the knock on the door and the bailiffs are here.

These stairs I sit upon – the carpets have been renewed from time to time, upgraded as my books sold and my income grew, from worn brown hessian to dark-patterned Axminster to avocado nylon mix to white pure wool – now feel rather thin and grubby. I cannot afford to have them professionally cleaned. Nowadays I use dustpan and brush, as I did at the beginning. (It is almost impossible to find vacuum cleaner bags in the shops: whether a genuine shortage or a government ploy to stop us using electricity, who is to say? We are all conspiracy theorists now.) Wealth changed to poverty with the passage of time. Agents rooked me, and accountants cheated me: I was never as clever as I thought. Fashions in writers change. I believed I was rich long after I ceased to be so. Another Hollywood film, the next West End musical, that I always believed were around the corner to rescue me and mine never materialized.

As for Fay, she recovered from her heartbreak soon enough, and went to be writer in residence in ANU in Canberra and there married a professor of anthropology. She writes cookbooks, which do well enough. My mother Margaret eventually joined her in that town, as did my elder sister Jane and her two boys. Jane writes poetry, and her work is well received. It is mythical stuff; I don't understand it. Jane once complained I did not have a poetic bone in my body.

'At least I write to the edges of the page, and get paid for my pains, which is more than you do,' I said sharply, and she looked at me with her cool judging eyes and dismissed me as frivolous.

So now I have Australian relatives but we are not often in touch. Shadows of various resentments remain. My father died in New Zealand, suddenly, in 1949. I scarcely remember him, and blame my mother for that. But mostly I am conscious of Fay blaming me for changing the path of her life so drastically. Vibes drift over from the Antipodes.

And it's true when Karl and I were going through hard times – we would have the most tremendous rows – he would say, 'I should never have left your sister. I must have been mad to go off with you,' and I would say, 'I should have let Fay keep you, fat cow that she was,' and he would say, 'You are so bony it hurts,' and it would all end in bed, and we would forget until next time. Sometimes I wonder what kind of children Fay and Karl would have made together, if I had not intervened. So many 'what ifs', so few answered.

Eventually Karl left me and the children for a rural life and another woman and I bought him out of the house. I say that flatly but it almost killed me. I have five grandchildren. Venetia was to become an artist and have three boys, Amos – following my example, as she is quick to point out, out of wedlock – and Ethan and Mervyn within it, by Victor, then a scientist of integrity and passion, if a trifle Aspergery. Polly, a staunch feminist, took on board as stepdaughters Steffie and Rosie, children of her partner Corey, a rugger-playing lad from Samoa: and I regard these two girls, both now at art school, as grandchildren though not of my genetic descent. So much any decent woman must do, in these days of extended families.

So that is my family: that is how Amos comes to be my grandchild. His father is unknown. Venetia, to be blunt, was always vaguely in love, albeit platonically, with her stepfather Karl. These are the complications that ensue when marriages cease to be for life, when children are born out of wedlock, when governments, out of some peculiar obsession of their own, discourage marriage by legal and financial penalties, and make the temporary bond more popular than the permanent. Partnerships split apart like seedpods, and the poor children burst out into the world and drift with the wind to take root where best they can, rather than where they were meant. I know I am in no position to talk: I too failed. I was a stupid girl, with little sense of responsibility, of the significance of marriage, of how one's actions rebound through the decades, how the lusts of the past come back to haunt us. *Hamlet*'s ghost's complaint. *So lust, though to a radiant angel link'd, will sate itself in a celestial bed, And prey on garbage*. Venetia was born of lust: so was Amos. But then perhaps they are the best children of all: the garbage ones flicker with radiance; they are the most interesting.

How Amos Came To Be Born

Some ten years into the marriage, and there was trouble between Karl and me when I found him embracing another beneath the coats at some artist's drunken party; words were exchanged. Venetia, also at the party, overheard my tears and protests, and the following week, drunk herself after the Freshers' ball – she was seventeen and had just started at St Martin's School of Art – allowed herself to lose her virginity to some passing student stranger beneath a half-finished sculpture of a frog by Paolozzi, which she seemed to think somehow sanctified the act. In Venetia's world, art was all, as it was in Karl's. And thus Amos was born, father unknown. I was shocked and concerned for her. At least I could name Venetia's father, even though I lost touch with him.

'It's all your fault,' I said to Karl, after she came home triumphant with a positive pregnancy test. 'You beneath the coats, she beneath a sculpture. She felt betrayed by you as much as I did. Why would-n't she want to get even with us by getting pregnant?' We were both in psychoanalysis at the time.

'Good God,' he said, 'I was under the impression we had an open marriage. What are you going on about? It didn't mean anything. We didn't even know each other's names. If you hadn't made such a fuss Venetia would never have known about it.'

People used to talk like that. These days the young take their sexual relationships seriously. People have a useful habit of turning disadvantages to advantages. Only when Aids made promiscuity dangerous did fidelity become fashionable, at least amongst the educated classes. Fifteen years previously, since the advent of the pill and widespread contraception, sexual adventure had been looked at favourably. Now sexual restraint turned from a bore into a virtue.

As for this 'open marriage' – I am sure I had never discussed it with Karl – it was not an age for discussion of anything other than politics. He just assumed it. We both belonged to the same Trotskyist group. Sexual jealousy was considered beneath contempt, which suited men rather more than it did women, and was one of the reasons – along with men's assumption that we would make the coffee and do the secretarial work – that we moved over into feminism, invented the concept 'sexism' – which once defined could be found and deplored everywhere – and the rest is social history and why my daughter Polly is like she is. But back to the party and Venetia's pregnancy.

'It is far more likely to be your sexual adventures,' Karl said, 'and your example, that have set her off on this path. She should have trained as a secretary. She is no kind of artist. I could wish she had better taste in sculpture, though. If the child turns out to be a frog, serves her right.'

Karl did not like Paolozzi. He was definite in his tastes and, as so many artists of that generation were, convinced that if a work of art was saleable, it was worthless. Commercial success was the sure sign of artistic failure. As I made more money, and my column inches in the papers and magazines lengthened, so I lost artistic credibility in his eyes. He acknowledged the letters of Van Gogh, the autobiography of Benvenuto Cellini and the novels of Wyndham

Lewis as acceptable literature, but very little else. My pathetic kitchen-sink novels, with their occasional inducements to the new feminism, were an embarrassment, though the money they brought in was welcome enough.

It is true that a week or so before the incident of the coats Karl had found an assignation note, half falling out of my jacket pocket as it hung upon its peg, and had read it, turned pale, stuffed it back in, and gone on up the stairs. The incident was not mentioned. And I had thought least said soonest mended, but perhaps I was wrong. Perhaps it was then that he began to fall out of love with me. I daresay I had left the note in my pocket to make sure Karl would find it – or so my analyst was determined to believe – just as he had the next week made sure I would find him beneath the coats at the party, with a scraggy-haired girl with big, dirty bare feet.

It was part of the culture at the time that any minor sexual peccadillo on either side of a partnership would be overlooked. The drugs of the day were not always as strong as they are now, but usually enough to make anyone dizzy. Karl and I were both in analysis, and understood only too well the concept of acting out – of performing an action to express, often subconsciously, one's emotional conflicts – the results of such action all too often being antisocial or self-destructive. Everything we did was under each other's, and our analysts', scrutiny, and just as we delivered dreams to fit the analyst's convenience, we would deliver our actions likewise, to fit the script the analysts were writing of our lives. We understood this in each other – or I had supposed we did.

Amos existed as a by-product of my infidelity, or Karl's, or the analysts who prompted us to discussable action, or merely the demon lust come to take possession of my precious daughter. Whatever. Or perhaps somewhere up in the *Bardo Thodol* or the

Tibetan Book of the Dead it was written that the soul of Amos should choose just such parents as Venetia and a stranger, to bring about the divine purpose of stopping the great wheel of government if only for an instant, so when it started up again, as such wheels always will, it set off in a slightly other and better direction. And why, now, Amos sat upon the stair with me, and dissembled, as people will with their old grans, whom they assume to be a bit daft but are not necessarily so.

> *Li'l David was small but oh my*
> *Li'l David was small but oh my*
> *He fought big Goliath who lay down and dieth*
> *Li'l David was small but oh my…*

> *I'm preachin' dis sermon to show*
> *It ain't nessa, ain't nessa*
> *Ain't nessa, ain't nessa*
> *It ain't necessarily so*

Bang bang bang-de-bang. They are still there. They want my worldly goods. I am not so stuck on possessions as they imagine. I could go down and open the door to them and let events take their course, and say so to Amos, but he says on no account am I to do that. The bailiffs will go away in time and then we will have the opportunity of smuggling most of the valuables out. I wonder who he means by 'we'?

It occurs to me that the men at the door may be after Amos, not me at all. This is a worrying thought, if also a comforting one. But no. If they were CiviSecure they would simply break in. No, it is my money and possessions they are after. But you can't get blood out of stone. I hear there are vast warehouses all over the country full of repossessed goods. No-one wants them any more, or can afford them even at knock-down prices. The *nomenklatura* take their pick on Sunday afternoons, or so it is said, but very quietly.

The Stairs

When I was in my early thirties I would sit upon these very stairs when Karl and the children were asleep, and write and write my novels. I used wide-spaced A4 pads and a Pentel pen. Karl was irritated by the sound of a typewriter; so many things irritated him: fox hunters, Conservatives, pop music – jazz was okay: he played New Orleans trumpet whenever he got a chance. He was suspicious of domestic machinery of all kinds; so the stairs had to be swept down with a brush and pan – not the Hoover, with its bump, bump, bump down the stairs as I dragged it down after me, or the whirr of the washing machine, with its annoying change in sound levels as it changed pace from soak to wash to spin, so in the end it seemed easier to lug the nappies round to the launderette.

The novels were popular, being a celebration of outrage at the domestic fate of women at the time, and over the years. The hessian stair carpet with the holes, which had nearly sent us to our deaths many a time, I replaced; but the nylon mix with its static electricity gave Karl a headache. Fortunately pretty soon I could afford pure wool. Mothproofed, of course – I sometimes thought this was what gave me headaches, but Karl insisted.

Otherwise I found the stairs a good place to write. I was not cut off from the life of the household, yet not quite part of it. The children were reassured by my presence there, and would bypass me deftly, and not stop to cling, or whine, or demand, or plead, but simply get on with their lives. My life in the advertising agency had trained me in instant recall, cured me of the belief that one needed peace and quiet to write. One did not – one needed only desperation and deadlines.

Sometimes early in the morning, when she was around three, Polly would come down wrapped in her blue dressing gown with the pink bobbles, ignoring me, and sit in front of the letter box waiting for the postman to arrive. When the letter box clicked open she would growl like a dog, catch the letters as they fell, wait for the sound of the postman's feet retreating, and push them out of the house again. She was always a very territorial little girl. Karl was a good father to Polly, and I saw no reason why she should become such a feminist, and continue to see all men as oppressors, long after the liberation revolution had been won and the world feminized. There are as many women being chauffeured down the centre lanes of our cities as there are men, and I am sure the women are the most draconian of all. I expect feminism is in her nature as much as in her nurture. And of course the postman was a man.

When her stepdaughters Steffie and Rosie were small she would throw out their My Little Ponies, Barbie dolls and any toy in pink, green or purple as soon as they came into the house. I regret to say I would make a point of giving them fairy castles in violet and mauve, and Cinderellas in white crinolines, carefully chosen not to quite be within the embargo but nearly. Corey their father would notice and laugh. He is an amiable man, and the laugh seems to rise from the depths of his being to embrace the whole room and everyone in it. The laugh entrances Polly, who takes the world so seriously and literally, even as she disapproves. Her bark is worse than her bite: at least I hope so. My little stepdaughters would go and search the bins after she had thrown their treasures out and retrieve them, and she didn't seem to notice. The gesture is the thing and they all know it.

For his part Karl scarcely noticed Venetia when she was growing up. The more she adored him the more he overlooked her. He was perfectly pleasant to her: she was a blonde, handsome, straight-forward, clever child, who took to painting to win her stepfather's approval, and kept it up all her life. But he believed she had no 'real' talent, and was without that personality which harboured the true artist. In other words she was not like him. She was not his. She did not look like him, think like him, or suffer like him. She would never weep over the letters of Van Gogh; but would laugh uproar-iously over comics. She might come top in maths and science, but that only made her the more suspect in his eyes. He put up with his stepdaughter for my sake, but she did not interest him. For which I suppose I should be grateful – many a mother suffers when the stepfather she chooses for her child is too admiring and noticing of the growing girl for comfort.

Bang-bang-bang de-bang. Again. What are they trying to do to us? Break our nerve?

'It may be,' I say to Amos now, 'that I deserve my fate. That I do indeed have a debt to society. The bailiffs at the door have right on their side. I lived off the fat of the land for a while: but what had I done to deserve it? For a few words on paper which if they did any-thing at all disrupted society, upset the natural balance of the genders, trained women to despise men, and so on.' But I am only trying the words out for size. I do not believe them.

A Pattern Of Surprises

That story I was telling you about Cynthia falling out of the DC10; it did not end there. Not even death is final. The past comes towards us, like the ghost of Hamlet's father, to make our futures. The aircraft disintegrated in the air and many of the bodies just fell out and tumbled down to the ground, still strapped to their seats. Did they die as they fell? Were they unconscious when they hit? Or did Cynthia float down in her seat, drifting this way, drifting that way, and have time to think on the way, 'I should never have left the children'? If she could have, she would have. That's motherhood for you. I don't suppose she bothered to think, I should have listened to my friend Frances. Now she'll be able to say, 'I told you so.' So many things we don't know, will never know. A Day of Judgment would be good, in which all things were made clear. Who was on the grassy knoll when Kennedy was killed? What would have happened had King Harold won at Hastings? What did my friend Cynthia think as she fell from the sky? And yet certain things have a way of emerging, splinters of fact working their way out from the flesh of the past. And then, like as not, one wishes they hadn't.

That air crash was all surprises. I had a letter a couple of months later from my friend Liddy in Venice, California, enclosing a death certificate, saying could I do something for her, her husband Terry had committed suicide. She had told his old parents in London he had died of a heart attack, because it seemed kinder than the truth. Who wants to know their only son has given back the gift of life? Only now they wanted to see the death certificate. Could I have it forged, so it no longer said death by his own hand, but by cardiac arrest?

That was three surprises in one. (A) Terry? Dead? How could he be? Nobody had told me: he was the love of my life; if I hadn't married Karl I would still be yearning after him day and night. Indignation mixed with grief. (B) Suicide? But why, how? (C) Why did Liddy think I was the kind of person you asked to forge death certificates? But she was right about me, because I ran straight round to a friend, a commercial artist, weeping, and asked him to do it and he did.

I wept because Terry was dead, the one who came to me in dreams – and still does, though I am in my eighties. He never made it beyond his thirties. A working-class lad, dark, handsome and chippy, lots of shiny black hair, hooded eyes, infinitely glamorous. He rode a motorbike, made me drunk on Cointreau one night, delicately removed the plain woollen dark green dressing gown my mother had made for me – he said it made him laugh, but it was all I had – and took my virginity. That was 1953. I was nineteen, and felt my virginity to be a great curse. Men until then had seemed too polite and responsible to take it away.

That was the greatest surprise I ever had – the first acquaintance with sex. Such a surprise my spirit left my body and watched from a corner of the ceiling while the act was performed. I never looked back: sex was not just a many splendoured thing; it was the only important thing in the world. He was no ardent swain, more's the pity, but I think he liked me, and I passionately and madly adored him. At the time he was having it off with my best friend Liddy (not that the phrase was used in those days: sex was a serious matter, and she had his engagement ring – just as well, contraception then being by the withdrawal method only). She was the pale, slender, doe-eyed beauty: I was the plain friend every pretty girl likes to have, to act as foil.

Whenever Liddy was out of town he would come secretly to my bed in the basement, and when he was in bed with her in the attic, which was mostly – I would weep and weep into my pillow. I suppose that by the time she sent the death certificate she knew this. I don't think she knew at the time. We all believe our sexual activities can stay secret: in my experience they never do. Someone always tells. In the end Liddy married him and I daresay in one of their rows the subject came up. And she may well have felt I owed her a favour.

I rang friends. Terry! Suicide! Twenty years out of college and we alumni had kept in touch. More surprising that sixty years on those who survive still do. It was soon after the war – families had disintegrated, homes been destroyed, populations dispersed – stuck up there in the Scotland, on the end of a long damp dishrag (so my mother described it) we students were one another's family.

'Oh yes, that Terry.' They were slightly disparaging about him, even in his death. He was never really one of them: he did science; they did humanities: never the twain should meet, except in bed. 'Oh yes, Terry. Working for the Douglas Aircraft Company. The one whose DC10 just fell out of the sky. You had a friend on that? Oh, bad luck.'

And then the next surprise. Liddy came over from California. The daughter, Florrie, came too. She was twelve. She played outside with Venetia while we talked. She looked like her father; the same hooded eyes, the same dark shiny hair. Part of me thought she should be my child. Liddy said if you're wondering why he did it, that air crash in Paris played on his mind. He blamed himself. She'd come back from shopping and found him with a bullet through his brain and a gun in his hand and a file in front of him. It contained all the memos he'd sent to the company saying their DC10 was unsafe, there was no way an aircraft should be built with the control cables running the length of the fuselage floor, when that floor was not reinforced, and loss of pressure could collapse it. They'd sat on his memos and done nothing. A lot of people were killed.

'I know,' I said, 'my best friend was on that aircraft.'

I thought if he'd been married to me he wouldn't have killed himself. I would not have let the memos go unanswered, the fuselage would have been strengthened so when the cargo door blew out its floor wouldn't have collapsed and the control cables would not have been severed and everyone would have got safely home, though no doubt a few might have been sucked out with the pressurized air as it fled the aircraft. If I had not lain around weeping and had more courage and more sense of self-worth and had any idea how to set about it, which to others seemed to come naturally, but not to me, I might taken Terry away from Liddy and Cynthia's children would still have a mother. She would have clung on and not been sucked out.

And then I lost touch with Liddy, rather deliberately. There was too much going on in my life: I was too busy being a famous author, and emotionally tossed and turned by Karl, to take on moral responsibility for a widow and child. There must be others, I thought, but I didn't check. I was too angry with her for letting Terry die. I was too jealous because she had had more of Terry than I ever did, wafting around in the attic with the smell of sex seeping down the stairs to torment me while I wept in the basement, and because in the end she let melancholy and remorse overwhelm him. But really I suspect it was because she once said to me, when I asked her why I didn't have the success with men she did, simply, 'Because you're not beautiful.' Terry really wasn't one of us, anyway, and nor was Liddy. She studied Botany. But I hope Florrie was okay. Children can get caught up in this sort of madness, and it ends in tears, sometimes death. I feel bad about Florrie. I should have been, as they say these days, 'there for her'.

The Wickedness Of Men

I remember my friend Susannah, who came over in the exodus of
mostly Jewish white refugees from South Africa in the sixties, in
flight from apartheid, to continue the fight for the ANC in Europe.
Architects, musicians, writers, poets, intellectuals all. Karl and I
were giving a dinner party – I marvel now at how much I could do
when young, up at five to write the novels, three days a week at the
advertising agency (never give up your day job), two children, four-
course dinner parties: Elizabeth David, creamy fish balls, lemon
roast veal, chocolate mousse – murderous in today's terms, all cream
and brandy but oh my! The delights – and Susannah had read one
of my novels and said it was wicked to try to upset the established
order, she would never work or earn: feminism was evil – women
existed to serve and adore men – and I argued, and she and her
husband Jonathan got up and walked out. And Karl blamed me.

But a couple of weeks later Susannah was round in tears: she
had got home from shopping to find her husband had sold the
house over her head without telling her – men could do that – and
had gone to Israel to be a rabbi. Now what was she to do? I refrained
from saying, 'I told you so,' and did my best for her: got her lawyers
and so on, and lent her some of my ill-gotten gains.

It is never sensible to put too much trust in men's continued
capacity to look after you. They get swept up in some sexual or

religious or radical fever and put you aside as trivial. And once out of your lives they forget about you altogether; their life with you is wiped from memory. You remember, they do not. It is as if you never were. Divorce baffles women, but seems normal enough to men. We are a different species, and the male of the species was devised to stick around while women are pregnant and children are helpless, and roar at the mouth of the cave – but if she'll do the roaring, and he the earning, he's off. Or if, like Susannah's husband, his wife never did Shabbat properly. Though it turned out – it usually does, men seldom go to empty beds – there was another woman involved.

'After your grandfather left me –' I say to Amos.

'He was not my real fucking grandfather,' Amos reminded me. 'He was no blood relation. We shared no genes. I was conceived under the statue of a frog by Paolozzi.'

'I did not know your mother had been so specific about the details,' I remarked. 'Karl, while he was with us, brought you up as one of his own grandchildren.'

'Until he fucking left,' said Amos. The children of warring protagonists harbour more bitterness, and longer, than do the protagonists themselves.

I had long ago worn out my anger with Karl, though it was strong and vicious enough while it lasted. He left me for a fat, plain, placid girl sculptress whom he said had more talent in her forefinger than I had in my whole body. He had by now deserted Freud for Jung, and had a therapist of the cut-the-ties-that-bind variety, recommended, I later discovered, by the sculptress herself. He had a kind of affair with the therapist – at any rate it involved a lot of massage and relief of tension, and then moved on to the sculptress herself. The divorce laws were by now such that I had to support

Karl and her, whom I came to refer to as the Dumpling, in their old rectory in the country with a good north light and a studio they could share, and occupy the moral high ground at my expense and be happy. I was angry at the time, I do admit. In fact I nearly died from rage, which translated itself into acute asthma. Karl seemed to like fat girls. He should have stayed with my sister Fay.

Venetia was reluctant to keep up the contact but Polly, then four-teen, would spend the occasional weekend with her father and new stepmother, to my disgust. She did not like the Dumpling, or politely told me she did not, complaining that she went round with bare feet, and that they were large and often dirty. I have always wondered if it was she beneath the coats at that party long ago, but I have never asked and what did it matter? I would rather not know how many years the deceit had been going on. It would be too painful. It would only obviate the good years, the years when Polly would patter down the stairs to confront the postman; it would delete more of my past than I could bear.

The Dumpling died a couple of years later of one of those rare quick cancers that sometimes follow on a pregnancy, leaving Karl with a son, Henry. Karl wanted to move back with me but I had by now bought him out of the Chalcot Crescent house and was living in it as I pleased, with a washing machine and a lover, and the Brancusi Karl had used as doorstops now on marble plinths, and my various awards – BAFTA, Society of Authors, prizes for best short story, framed and on the walls, and could give smart parties, which Karl would have found meretricious – and I would not have him back. Though Venetia and Polly begged me to.

But they wanted him back for themselves, not for me. And he would have been off again: he had the taste for it by now, and so did I, for other men and lots of them. Just as I never forgave my mother for leaving my father, so my children never quite forgave me for not having Karl back. I see it in their eyes when I go round to see them, or they come over to visit me. Mother, the one that lost them their father. Forget I gave birth to them, reared them, all that stuff: forget it was he who left me; in their minds I drove out Father.

Sometimes Karl would visit, and bring Henry round: a very dull child with his mother's placidity and large feet. These things fade into the past, but they are never over. Fate had meant Karl for me, brought us together by a stroke of magic and I had believed destiny meant us to live happily ever after, but Karl had reneged on destiny. It was all there in my books, that this would be the outcome. I wrote it over and over and over. Men are faithless bastards. I just never believed it for myself. In the end I just felt like such a fool. And the thought of him and the Dumpling in an intimate embrace was still more than I could endure and still is, decades later, long after both have died and turned to dust.

Amos' Tirade

'I thought my good fortune,' I say now to Amos, 'was like money. I thought it was a tap that flowed and never stopped. Love and marriage, mortgage and money. I should have known better.'

'No-one knew any fucking better,' says Amos. 'We have all been cheated, conned, fleeced and suckered. Why aren't you angry? You should be.'

I reply that it is not in my nature to be angry for long.

'I was angry with your grandfather for a bit,' I admit, 'but it did nobody any good and it was too exhausting to keep it up.'

'You women always reduce things to the personal,' he says. 'Don't you even see what has been going on out there? Aren't you interested?'

'Tell me,' I say. He does. He explains how the conman works. The conman says to the sucker, 'Let's play a fast one on Joey,' the sucker is tempted and colludes, and before he knows it Joey's up and away, part of the deal, the sucker is out of pocket, and the conman is laughing all the way to the bank.

'And these days the conman is the bank, and we're all of us the suckers.'

'Then I shouldn't have colluded,' I say, 'I shouldn't have been tempted. I shouldn't have bought goods I couldn't afford. I shouldn't have gambled on the stock exchange with money I hadn't earned, spending on what I hadn't got, used my credit cards, my store cards, for things I fancied but didn't need. My fault.'

'You and a zillion million others,' Amos said. 'It's been a gigantic con, the better to soften you up, aided and abetted by the admen. The friendly bank, the caring government, your flexible friend. This is a nice house, throw you out and the State can house its own. That's all this is about.'

Amos is no blood relation to his Aunt Polly but they talk the same way. The only difference is that Polly goes on and on about the evils of the patriarchy, whereas for Amos it's The System. I see myself in both of them: they must get the conspiracy theorist genes from me.

Corey, Polly's partner (she doesn't 'believe in' marriage), gets on with his muscle building and crowd-control evening classes and all Polly's indignation flows over his head. Corey once complained to me that if he was just quiet, staring at his sports shoe for a while, Polly would ask him what he was brooding about, and tell him to learn to express his feelings. 'But I haven't got any feelings,' Corey said, 'I'm just looking at my sports shoe. Why can't she accept that?'

I suggest to Corey that in the interests of a quiet life he could invent some internal agonies but he shook his head and said that would be lying. He didn't have any. They get on well enough. But who has Amos got in his life to 'share' with? He may have a girlfriend, and I don't think he's gay, but he likes to keep his personal life mysterious. I'm pretty sure he doesn't confide in his mother. Ever since Venetia foolishly asked Amos not to talk politics or religion at dinner because it annoyed Victor, he just talks small talk when he's round there. Venetia said I was always saying that to Polly – no politics or religion at the dinner table. And that is why Polly is what she is – but I'm sure I never said any such thing to the girl.

One's children are always recalling things one could swear one never said. Anyway, these days he seldom rants on.

'The elephant in the room you refuse to see is growing so large it's about to split the house itself,' says Amos. Is he some kind of a public speaker? He has the words off pat. I know so little about this scion of mine. 'The elephant is barring all the exits, trunk against the door: tail up the chimney, flanks blocking the view from the window.'

'You can see this elephant then?' I ask. I feel the need to placate and distract him as if I am dealing with a madman. We are sitting here on the stairs, an old lady and a youngish man, hiding from the bailiffs, and he, he is making a speech. At least he brought me a blanket. A thought occurs to me again that they might be after him, not me. They may not be bailiffs, and they might be secret police. They arrived half an hour after he did. But that's paranoia: they would have burst in with guns blazing. No, this lot come armed with writs and warrants. Sooner or later I am going to have to go to the loo. I will have to stand up. I refuse to crawl.

Let them see me, let them take me in charge, let them carry off all my possessions.

I hope the water is back on. It usually is, in sequence with the power supply. There is a big water shortage: one of our chief exports now is water. Freely it falls from the sky into our reservoirs, whence it is carried off to God knows where in the world, but probably to France. What we get from the taps is metered, expensive, and the supply cut for four hours a day. The seas of the world are polluted so that salination is an even more expensive business than once it was, and so our rain, once our misfortune, is suddenly now our export good fortune.

'We are owned by the banks,' Amos is saying. 'Everyone is owned and controlled, every politician with a secret, every scientist with flaky funding. Every journalist or academic who wants to keep his job – debt runs the world. They have made sure of that. Mrs Thatcher started it when she got rid of public housing. Every man his own householder: every man owned by the mortgage company, that is – and then she turned the mortgage companies, with their overtones of Social Credit, into private equity firms and the rest is history. Every proud house owner who got an overdraft to build a conservatory, every father who took out a loan for his daughter's wedding, every parent who borrows to buy a child's holiday –'

'I was thinking of getting a Stannah stairlift,' I say. 'But the house is too old, the banisters too delicate.' Still he is not to be stopped. His bright-blue eyes, I realize, are large-pupilled. Is he on drugs, or is it just enthusiasm?

'Even royalty,' he goes on. 'The highest in the land, for hundreds of years back. Those who make war, make peace, make international contracts. All in hock to the bankers. Scratch my back, and I'll scratch yours. Edward VII had gambling debts; Winston Churchill could not keep up Chartwell in style without loans. Lord Curzon was in hock to business friends, Roosevelt too.'

'The Queen?' I ask, but I cannot make him laugh. 'Is she a lizard form too?' He does not get the reference. There had been a conspiracy theorist nut in the nineties who went around claiming that the Queen was a lizard form from Sirius.

'The best in the land infected by the scum of the land.' His voice is rising. 'They deserve to die, to be strung from the lampposts. Caged in a football stadium and machine gunned. Pinochet had the right idea. Death to the banksters!'

My grandson is mad. Drugs have affected him. I laugh.

'Why are you laughing?' he demands.

'You were the sweetest little boy,' I say.

And so he was, happy and trusting and full of energy. Venetia was a single mother: I did a lot of looking after Amos when he was small, when I was in my forties, between the books and the plays and the feminist conferences and promotional tours and the cultural exchanges with the Soviet Union. I ended up a good public speaker. Or if I couldn't take time off to babysit, the country was awash with au pair girls who would, over here to learn English, or to catch an Englishman, when they were seen as desirable prey. Those were the days.

'Why do you think we have wars? Who benefits? Not the people, that's for sure. Not the peasants, the workforce, the poor: no, it's bombs and starvation for them. They don't have money, they can't be robbed, blood-sucked, they might as well die. Bomb a city and at least someone can make money seeing that it's put up again.'

'Hush,' I say to Amos now. 'If you speak too loudly they will know you're here.'

And again comes the thought that he's the one they're after, not me. But that must be wishful thinking brought on by my great age.

Are they just letting him know they're on to him? I remember that back in the early seventies, when the arts of surveillance were just getting going, how my phone was tapped. I had been employed to write 'the greatest romance in the world' for a big US TV company – the love story of John and Jackie Kennedy. In those days you knew your phone was being tapped because there was no interference on the line – no static, no missed calls, no crossed lines – all the usual imperfections suddenly wiped away. But this was a CIA tapping, because they had one of the new word-sensitive monitors – which would cut in when you said anything that concerned them, in this case the word Kennedy, or Cuba, or President, or assassination – and the tone of the background would alter pitch. I had fun with my friends trying it out. In those days no-one took 'security' seriously. They were just overgrown schoolboys, paranoiac fuckers playing games around an iron curtain.

But they had other tactics too when they wanted you to know they were on to you: a shot across your bows. The interference would increase: crossed lines would give you background conversations in which your name would be mentioned: nuisance calls with heavy breathing would get you to the phone at all times of day and night. You would mend your ways – not speak at the CND meeting, nor attend the ANC gathering – and they would go away. But you had been warned.

Perhaps this is what is happening now? Amos is being warned. It has nothing to do with the note that came through the letter box yesterday, saying that unless payment was made within the day officers of the law would be round to confiscate such of my belongings as they felt necessary to support my debt. Another surprise. One never quite believes it will come to this.

Rather, one believes that there is a guardian angel standing by who will come to the rescue when push comes to shove. When Karl says he has left me and the children for the Dumpling, the Angel will surely rewind time. When the letter from the court comes, the Angel will be there with a cheque from some film company and will hand it over and I won't even have to go down to the front door to open it. Surely the Angel will be sitting here next to me on the stairs and Amos will not be mad, but sane, and like anyone else, but there is no angel. And yet that angel was with me so much of my life. She was there when I was born and gave me good looks, health and talent. She helped me make money. She helped me meet my destiny, who was Karl. And then Karl went. And then it was as if he took the

Angel to his new place. Not that she did the Dumpling much good.

Now the surprise of this letter, of all the other letters one has had in one's life. Here are your excellent A grades from school; here is confirmation of your daughter's scholarship; your offer of a pay rise if you will only stay on at the agency; (Karl) 'I love you, darling, for ever more' – or words to that effect; will you accept a Damehood from the Queen for services to literature?; (Fay) 'I'm okay now about you marrying Karl, will you come out for a holiday?' – I never did; you have sold the film rights to D-I-V-O-R-C-E, and the opera rights, and it is now translated into ten different languages; the British Council wants you to represent your country; will you be President of our charity? And so on and so forth and now this.

How oddly authority phrases it. As if they were doing me a favour – 'supporting my debt'.

Once I would have rung my agent and she'd have the money round within the day. I was worth keeping out of trouble. But now I have no agent and the agent has no clients and there is no money. And I don't know what to do for the best. Money gives you confidence. With money you can laugh at authority. Once you could always buy your way out of trouble. If your car gave too much trouble you just bought a new one and the secretary did the boring paperwork. How were we to know what would happen next? That it would all change, and so suddenly? How the State would micromanage our lives, monitor our every transaction, tax us for making music, imprison us for a false word, oversee the legitimacy of our jokes, film our every movement, enter our houses at will, surround us with wardens, take our children from us, our cigarettes from our lips, ban the salt cellar from the table, and the wine from our glasses.

And yes, Amos is right. I am angry. If I search for anger – see, I can find it.

I am also angry at Mother Nature, who discards us after we are of childbearing age and withers us up, in spite of what we do to stop her with pills and potions, and makes our knees ache, and chill get into our bones, and gave us the ability to bear witness to our winding down. But she never had any interest in our comfort, let alone our contentment. All she ever wanted us to do was reproduce, and if we are beyond that, forget it. And of course all this stuff about the decline of the West is relevant, and dreadful, and someone needs to be punished, obviously, but what about me?

How Well We Lived Then

But how well we lived then, in the lemon veal and chocolate mousse days, when we all went to hell in our own way. How well in particular I lived. I consider this house of mine. It's just so nice, though it could do with a coat of paint, inside and out. I bought what I wanted, not what I needed, and in the back of my mind was the idea that what you bought you could always sell. The oak refectory in the kitchen, the William and Mary dressing table, the Venetian chandelier in the bedroom where once I disported myself with Karl and quite a few others since – a mass of exquisite little glass flowers, each one different; the bookshelf of first editions, the Chagall on the wall, the Worcester dinner set, or what's left of it. Investment? Never. When you come to sell it all it's not worth a dime. Nobody wants it. Everyone's selling, no-one buying. Might as well keep it and enjoy it. We are not yet at the stage when the girls are selling their honour for a bar of chocolate, or their family silver for a bag of potatoes – though some say that's not far down the road. In the Crescent we're growing our own potatoes and beans – the Neighbourhood Watch now exacts a tax of a quarter of all crops – things have gotten surprisingly feudal round here. People make jokes about Robin Hood and the Neighbourhood Watch is known as the Sheriff.

The agents of corruption at the door can take it all. I didn't really need it, didn't really want it. It was just something to do. Really I have lost interest. Possessions are for the middle aged, not for the old. What I love is the life I lived here once. It is part of me, they can't take that away from me. The house has been here nearly two hundred years. I have been part of it for some fifty of these. We are hermit crabs, we wait until we find one empty and then we crawl into it, shelter under its roof, and presently scuttle off somewhere new. I know oddly little about the people who lived here before me: why should those who live here in future think of me?

I say none of this to Amos. He believes like all his generation that he was born in the year zero and history started with him.

Amos has calmed down and fallen silent. The bailiffs are back in their car. Amos takes the opportunity to slither upstairs again. Off to find his gear and roll a spliff, I suppose. I wonder what is going on even now in his mother's house? I can guess. Obsessive as ever about keeping my hand in – unlikely though the prospect of publishing is – I lie on my front, laptop on the stair above me, elbows on the stair below, and write the following. It is fiction but based on likelihood. Bang, bang, bang de-bang. Forget them. There is just enough light through the skylight above the front door to enable me to see the keyboard. I love fiction. It is so much easier to escape from than fact.

Venetia's Lovely Home

'I had a call from Amos today,' said Venetia to her husband Victor the next day at breakfast. 'He's staying over at Mum's. Apparently she called him and said she'd had a letter from the bailiffs and he went over to reassure her.' Amos was Victor's stepson. They got on well enough, so long as Amos kept away from contentious issues.

'What does he want from her this time?' asked Victor, buttering his toast. It was National Butter, all you could get in the shops at a regulated price. It was made out of fat from many undeclared countries of origin, but with enough Chinese dried milk in it to make it look, taste and behave like butter. If you melted it, it was true, there was a degree of solid residue left in the pan, and with every batch that came into the shops there seemed to be more solids and less oil, but it was okay. Better at any rate, Victor assured Venetia, and more nutritional than the low fat-alternatives Venetia had insisted the family eat in the pre-Crisis days when obesity had been a social problem. Victor liked to look on the bright side, sometimes almost to the point of self-delusion, ever since he had stopped work in oncology research, and been co-opted on to the Committee of the National Institute for Food Excellence.

That had been three years back, when all the major charities, including Cancer Cure, had agreed to pool their efforts, in the interests of humanity, efficiency and consistency, to combine in the new umbrella organization, CiviKindness, or CK. There was really no option, private donations having fallen away to the extent they had. Almost overnight, public attitudes had changed. Let the volunteer army rattle boxes as it would, and professional fund-raisers plead and shame, giving was suddenly out of fashion. Either the public had no money to spare, having decided charity begins at home; or they suspected the various organizations creamed off too high a proportion of the takings. Or, as Venetia thought, they were simply sick of unpleasant images: women with hooks through their mouths, children with harelips, burned babies and so on. The people had given up on giving, as CiviKindness pointed out, so the State had no choice but to take over. Legacies to the various charities now went straight to CiviKindness, as did long-standing bank orders, cancellation no longer being an option. Specialist research staff were allocated to various government departments so talent was not wasted. Victor had been lucky enough to be taken on by the NIFE, where his pay was index-linked and his family covered by health insurance. No wonder Victor was cheerful: just sometimes, Venetia thought, too cheerful.

'Perhaps he doesn't want anything from her,' said Venetia, peaceably. 'Perhaps it's just to keep his Gran company.'

'Nutty old bat,' said Victor cheerfully. 'They're both delinquents. And Amos always has an eye to the main chance.'

'I wish you wouldn't talk about my mother like that,' said Venetia, 'or my son.' Victor looked surprised.

'But it's true,' he said. 'I'm very fond of your mother but she is a nutty old bat and she should have sold that house when it was worth something. And you know perfectly well what Amos is like. Sometimes I really don't understand you.'

It was a statement of fact. He didn't, and she would have to explain yet again, if it seemed worth it, that family cohesion was not best served by the facing of difficult truths. But it didn't seem worth it so she let it ride. Victor was very much a left-brain person, a scientist, logical and clear-headed, on the Aspergery side. As her sister Polly observed, when it came to emotional intelligence Victor was one sandwich short of a picnic, and it had got worse in his new job. Venetia refrained from saying that when it came to Corey the lights were on but nobody was at home, and wouldn't it be nice if he had a job at all. Venetia spent a lot of time biting back this remark or that in the interest of family unity. The task had to be left to someone and the mantle had fallen on Venetia. She was a strong, handsome woman, mother of sons, not as young as she had been but still full of fortitude and wearing well.

She could be relied upon to have candles ready in a power cut, a bath full of water when the taps ran dry and, until the UG99 wheat fungus got going in 2010 and put an end to wheat growing world-wide, a loaf of National Bread in the cupboard. Now of course she had Victor's work food card to use at any of the CiviStore Grade 1 shops, and rye bread was available. Sometimes she wondered what exactly Victor did at the NIFE to deserve such goodies, but he was not meant to talk about his work at home and she honoured that.

Indeed, life at Grand Avenue, Muswell Hill, went on much as it had in pre-Crisis days. Senior civil servants, government ministers and the meritocracy lived here, in large detached houses. They had fuel allowances: their ration books arrived, their wages were paid in Euros and were seldom late. Roads up here on the heights were not potholed. The area suffered, along with the whole country, from power cuts and water shortages, but otherwise, at least if they closed their eyes as they were driven through more dilapidated areas to their places of work by CiviSecure chauffeurs, they could imagine life was even better than once it had been: the cars varied, but most had powerful engines. Work-creation schemes had brought Soviet-style central lanes to most Whitehall streets, and were reserved for official cars, so gridlock was a thing of the past. Car sharing was obligatory, even at Victor's level, and he would travel in with three or four others from the neighbourhood. Official cars were a variety of executive makes, confiscated from the thousands which had built up in dock areas all over the world back in 2009, waiting for orders that never came.

This year the Government would be bringing in the CiviCar: a green city runaround at an affordable price, if you were in State employment and had an unblemished citizen rating. Meanwhile the chauffeurs, many of them ex-City men, put the Mercedes, BMWs, Lexuses and Jaguars through their paces, and dreaded the arrival of the dreary but practical CiviCar. Four-wheel drives were seldom seen: they had come to symbolize waste, extravagance and greed, and it had become customary for street people to attack and trash them – a practice tolerated by the authorities as a safety valve for their anger.

Another Scene From Venetia's Life, According To Her Mother, Who Wasn't There But Can Imagine

Just after Victor's transfer from oncology to Food Excellence, watch Victor help Venetia turn their mattress. He is a big solid expensive-looking man with large, bright brown eyes in a broad, slightly fleshy face. She worries that she may be colourless: dark eyeliner rings her very blue eyes, and she is seldom without lipstick. Her paintings reflect her worries: she uses acrylic paints which she applies vigorously on to white canvas. The mattress is big and expensive, and had been bought back in the days when Venetia was working for the Arts Council. They had bought it on their Selfridges store card, now fortunately at last paid off – though a £3,500 purchase had cost them £9,400 by the time the banks had assured Selfridges it could manage its customers' finances better than they could, and raised the interest rate as the small print allowed them to do. Not even Victor had bothered to read the small print.

Now of course Venetia no longer worked for the Arts Council. The Recovery had rather suddenly turned into the Bite, and she had been made redundant. No more arts funding; no more grants; no more jobs. She was not sorry: now she could spend more time doing her own work. She was like her mother in this: you might not be able to sell your efforts, but that didn't stop you working.

'What is this envelope?' Victor asks. It is a thick brown envelope stuffed between mattress and divan base.

'Oh that,' says Venetia. 'It's my severance pay.' She had forgotten about it. 'I have an artistic temperament, Mum,' she excused herself to me. 'I can never concentrate on deceit for long.' And I remembered how I had left the note from my lover half hanging out of my coat pocket for Karl to find, and could see my daughter might well have inherited the gene for inadvertent confession from me.

'But there's more than two thousand pounds here,' Victor says. 'What is it doing under our mattress? Anyone could steal it.'

'I don't see how,' says Venetia, 'unless they were turning the mattress. And robbers don't usually turn mattresses.'

'They will make it a habit,' says Victor sombrely, 'unless citizens learn to trust the banks again.'

'But they charge you for keeping your money there,' says Venetia, 'so what's the point?'

'Only a small sum,' says Victor.

'Do they brainwash you or something at your new job?' asks Venetia. And Victor says, 'No, as it happens. But one does learn something about the realities of life. If the currency were to be devalued again formally this would be worth nothing,' and he refuses to say more on the subject. He takes the cash and pays it into Venetia's bank account without any further conversation other than, 'We all have to have trust and faith,' he says, 'and pull together. Besides, it isn't good to be seen to hoard currency. It isn't wise.'

It was useless hiding things from Victor: she should have known better, or else have felt more guilty and hidden it somewhere less obvious. He looked and remembered and learned: he forgot nothing, and it was getting worse. Once he could laugh at himself and apologize for being an obsessive compulsive – but now he stomps through the house ranting about missing keys or underpants, finding them where he left them and snorting his conviction that 'someone' had hidden them. Venetia thought perhaps his new job was a strain; but he said no, he liked it, it was good to be useful.

Venetia did not protest. She enjoyed her life with Victor and as long as she did not argue they got along fine. The sex was good and that always reassured her. Steady, and unworried, once or twice or even three times a week, after more than thirty years, and somehow in tune with the rhythm of the universe. True, she preferred the light off rather than on, being conscious of a certain slackness of skin, a certain barrelness of figure in middle age, but Victor didn't seem to mind. 'It's all you,' he'd say, taking a pinch of extra flesh at her waist and squeezing it gently, 'that's all that matters.' She felt no jealousy of unknown research assistants he might meet at work, as she would have done when she was younger. They were the envy of their friends.

'But he does seems to have lost his sense of humour,' complains Venetia on the phone to Polly.

'He never had one to lose,' says Polly. 'You delude yourself. Do you think he knows something about devaluation the rest of us don't?'

'He's a scientist, not a currency expert,' says Venetia. 'And what he does is not so different from what he did before. It's still stem-cell research; what he was doing for Cancer Cure. No-one's wasting expertise these days.'

'Spoken like Victor's wife,' says Polly. 'Ask Ethan.'

Venetia's second son Ethan had been in banking and now worked for NIFE like his father, but rather down the scale as a Ministry driver. Venetia asked. Ethan said to tell Polly devaluation was obviously on the cards, now inflation had started pushing back the deflationary pressures of the last few years and the effect of quantitative easement was being felt. But not to worry: everyone should eat, drink and be merry while they could. As to the 'bottoming out', it was not going to happen. Democracies were simply not equipped to deal with a consumer society which had lost the knack of consuming, as after a stroke a man can lose the knack of speech. Ex-bankers loved gloom, Venetia had noticed.

Mervyn, Venetia's second son by Victor, was studying Politics and Economics at the LSE, and expected to get a First. Classes were large – seminars of thirty students were not unusual – but as Victor pointed out, statistically speaking, size of class and quality of education were positively correlated. And Venetia would try not to let her eyebrows rise in doubt. At the Ministry, Victor took an obligatory weekly class on 'Positive Thinking and the New Economy': perhaps that was all the change in Victor amounted to. He learned his lessons well.

Sitting On The Stairs Waiting For The Bailiffs To Go

Amos has been gone a long time. He is probably asleep. The smell of skunk pervades the house, horrible strong stuff. The sort we used in the sixties was milder and made us witty and lively – or so we thought – and this new stuff just makes you surly and sends you to sleep. Before that, in the late forties and early fifties we took Dexedrine, a form of amphetamine, to keep us awake in lectures, and to help us pass exams. Snorting drugs, or smoking them, was beyond the limits of our sophistication. A friend of mine, subject to narcolepsy, now takes Dexedrine to stop him from falling into the teapot like the dormouse at the Mad Hatter's tea party (a reference, for the benefit of you younger readers, to Lewis Carroll's *Alice in Wonderland*) and he sometimes passes spare pills on to me. But they don't work on me as once they did: they don't fill me with the wild mental excitement, the exhilaration of the mind I remember: they just make me feel unconnected with reality in a misty and disagreeable kind of way.

Amos is past the full flowering of youth. Surely he should have grown out of drugs by now: he should no longer be claiming with a boyish laugh that he was born one spliff short of a complete human being. Nor am I totally convinced by his account of his life amongst the NGOs: it doesn't quite ring true. I am not sure what he does for a living, but I imagine it to be more concerned with the underside of society rather than its open face. He is forever 'passing through'. He will turn up at the Hunter's Alley house I bought for the use of the boys back in the days of my wealth, and use there as a base for a while, and Ethan and Mervyn will fuss over him, and do his laundry, and plug in his BlackBerry while the power is on, make a million phone calls, hop over to Muswell Hill to see his mum and be polite to Victor who we must not forget is his stepdad and then move on. For some reason one never quite likes to ask where to.

When I jokingly said on the phone this morning that I expected a call from the bailiffs any minute, he came round at once. Barely had he arrived than the joke ceased to be a joke and came true. We were lunching on our National Meat Loaf and the last of the tomatoes from my window boxes, when came the banging on the door and the world turned serious.

I did not of course write the previous section about life in Venetia's lovely home exactly as you read it above. I admit I have worked on it. I have had the time to do so. I wrote it rather roughly on the stairs, in first draft, while my leg cramped and my neck twinged, so I was happy enough to stop and stretch when Amos finally came loping down the stairs with my blanket, preceded by a waft of skunk.

Amos' Genetic Inheritance

Amos' natural father, donor of the genes, was unknown – other than very briefly to his mother. It had been on my daughter Venetia's first night at Camberwell Art School, at the Freshers' ball, and the candlelight too flickery for recognition of who exactly was so pleasuring her, and when the tutors became involved whoever it was never came forward. It is not unusual for virgins to get pregnant on their first sexual encounter. Sheer surprise makes any waiting egg drop from the Fallopian tube, and bingo!

Amos is Venetia's eldest son and has over the years offered more problems than her other two boys, Ethan and Mervyn. But then the genes are different. Amos, brilliant at school, a good-looking charmer, a leader of men, worshipped by the two younger boys – and then suddenly a druggie drop-out at sixteen, and a professional drug dealer by twenty-two. 'That's what happens if boys don't have a proper father,' or so everyone said. I don't think it made the slightest difference. He had Victor as a stepfather from the age of seven and a perfectly steady, even boring life, until he decided to hot it up via the drug trade. At twenty-three he was in prison – shopped by his associates for having got too big for his boots, muscling in where the big boys – serious boys, the ones who murdered and tortured – thought they had every right to be, shocked back into sense by the company he found himself obliged to keep. By twenty-four he had turned his life around. It is dreadful having a family member in prison: there is no more innocent enjoyment to be had – it is the family's sentence as well as the child's – but inside he at least learned – as Victor put it – to appreciate his family, and give up his ghastly friends.

Since then Amos has come and gone in our lives, polite – other than for his propensity to swear, which seems ineradicable – self-supporting, affectionate, charming, but always slightly enigmatic: no fixed address that one knew of, but always contactable by email or mobile. An activist, an environmentalist, an aid worker, employed by various NGOs abroad – though one by one, as the Crunch bit and global markets vanished, these dropped off the map and left the failed countries of the world to struggle on their own. Which by all accounts they are doing quite satisfactorily – rather better without us than with us – though the accounts are unreliable as ever. Whether an eyewitness blog emanates from a genuine blogger or a government source who is to say?

Amos had no fixed address by his own doing, by the way: it was no wish of mine. Indeed, I had bought a rather mean little house at 11 Hunter's Alley in King's Cross primarily for Amos, but where Ethan and Mervyn now live, in benign young-man squalor. Amos occasionally turns up and spends the night, just passing through. I gifted the house to the three of them formally five years back, which, as everyone agreed, was amazingly generous of me, and certainly rather rash, since my last book could not even find a publisher. But as I say, it took me some time to wind down my spending habits – I had my own personal credit crunch a couple of years before everyone else. The bank manager had ceased to be a person and become an interchangeable minx in a short skirt, called my 'personal advisor'. And all she said was, 'We cannot extend your loan. In fact we are calling in your overdraft.'

The Hunter's Alley house was cheap because I had a friend – I had met her when she was producing a forensic science drama, on which I was one of the writers, with whom I had been working on a forensic science TV series – who knew someone who dealt in repossessed houses. A recluse had been found dead inside No. 11 when the police came knocking on the door because of the smell: the body had lain undiscovered for six weeks and it was summer. The house was council property: they had cleaned it up and put it up for sale. I bought it. I had no scruples.

Most houses have had someone die in them: it doesn't stop new owners in the present enjoying the property of the departed. I surprise myself by how little I care. And I wonder if my karma is suffering because of that. Mrs Doasyouwouldbedoneby comes alarmingly to mind. Charles Kingsley's *The Water Babies*. Who was the other one? Ah yes. Mrs Bedonebyasyoudid. Which was the most terrible? The latter always turned up after Mrs Doasyouwouldbedoneby had gone by, and you had ignored her and were about to be punished. The Victorians were great on retribution. These days we focus on understanding and forgiving, though we are allowed the grief now compulsorily announced from the witness box by members of the victim's family. And written, one suspects, by some mawkish policeman with a liking for the job. 'Such a bubbly girl: everyone loved her: the grief is with us every day.' 'Our fine son with all his life in front of him taken from us on the eve of his A levels' – or even the ones who say to their child's rapist and murderer, 'I am a Christian, I forgive him.' What kind of morality is that?

Why People Get Together

Actually, I suspect, as I read through my account of Victor finding the money under Venetia's mattress, that I am rather envious of Venetia and her ability to land on her feet and have her husband turn into one of the *nomenklatura* under her nose, at a time when that way survival lies. I have never been quite sure Victor was right for Venetia. She was an artist, and Victor was a scientist. The two do seem to like to get together, as do poets and scientists, the better to give each other a hard time. The scientists simply cannot understand why the poets and artists get more worldly attention and respect and headlines than they do. And the female poets and artists bow their head under the shame of it – that the scientists occupy the moral high ground, curing disease and helping mankind, and all the wives have to do is throw patterns of colours and words together and the world goes mad with delight. Yet still they insist on cleaving together. Nature, always seeking balance, chooses opposites to attain it. And the children turn out well, as the children of opposites so often do. The amiable and the morose, the competent and the incompetent.

Both parties to a union subject the other to a usually unspoken vetting process. He's got a car and a job and a high IQ but he's black and my parents hate him, but my friends approve so I will: she's got good legs but supposing she turns into her mother and she drinks too much, but she's sexually kind and my friends like her so I will. What was Venetia thinking of when she made her decision? I have a dysfunctional family and a peculiar mother and I'm an artist so I'm an outsider, but he's also an outsider, being Jewish, but he's got a regular job and a stable personality and the respect of his peers and we can just be ordinary together and perhaps no-one will notice what outsiders we are? Heaven knows what goes on in the heads of one's children.

I have a friend who writes film and TV scripts and wins BAFTAs, but her husband was a paediatrician and too busy saving babies to join with her in glory, or even be there at the ceremonies.

'I came home from a BAFTA do with an award,' she once said to me, 'and I longed to celebrate, leap in the air and kiss him and have sex. He was so handsome. Like a surgeon in a Mills and Boon novel. But he was just back from the hospital exhausted and the baby had died after a five-hour operation. It had weighed less than two pounds, such a little scrap, but they'd thought it had a hope. So we went to bed and slept on separate sides of it because he had another operation booked for the morning and had to be fresh.'

They got a divorce, on the grounds of his infidelity. Presumably their timing had never been right. He'd be rejoicing about a successful conjoined twins separation and she'd be mourning a damning review. She never remarried.

'Men want the glamour of fame at first but soon get fed up with it,' she said. 'No way a man can put up with not being top dog. They can't stand your success.' She was twenty years younger than me, well indoctrinated in the feminist cause, and seeing gender rather than human nature as the root of all ills. She never mentioned the word love: she would have been ashamed. Humiliation, boredom, embarrassment, unfairness, lack of togetherness, no reciprocity, all words which came lightly to her lips, but never 'love'. At least my children talk of it a lot.

'I know Victor can seem a bit pompous to other people,' Venetia will say, 'but I love him.'

And Polly, my other daughter, the feminist, will constantly reassure her children that she loves them. I assume my children take it for granted that I love them, that I would die for them if I thought it would do them any good.

Me, I live alone now, but I would like to live with someone I love and who loves me. It seems such a simple thing to ask, and so difficult to achieve. I managed three batches of around fifteen years' duration each – Karl, Edgar and Julian, with a few others in between, which I suppose these days counts almost as consistency. And at eighty I daresay one should give up. Though, why?

Do You Remember Florrie?

I ask, because when Amos came down the stairs again he was on his mobile.

'I thought you were out of juice,' I said.

'I tapped into next door's supply. They have a generator.'

'But how did you get next door?'

'Out the fucking back window and in through theirs,' he said. 'Don't worry. They'll never know.'

'You mean you broke in?' I was appalled.

'They're away. Or repossessed, probably. I see the signs of a hasty exit.'

'You broke their window?'

'I was very careful,' he said. 'I put a towel round my hand.'

But he'd lost interest in me. He was on the phone.

'Florrie,' he was saying, 'is Amy there? Tell her Amos called.'

I was glad he was in touch with an Amy. Perhaps he did have a love life after all. And if it was an Amy he was not gay. Which had occurred to me, and is always rather a pity because of the issue of grandchildren, or non-issue. But Florrie?

It is not so common a name. And that friend of mine, Cynthia, who fell out of the plane all those years ago. And the friend I betrayed whose name was Liddy, and whose daughter was called Florrie and she went outside to play with Venetia while we talked about forging Terry's death certificate so it read cardiac infarction rather than *felo de se*. Was it possible that Venetia and Florrie had stayed in touch? That Florrie had a daughter called Amy and that was the Amy Amos was trying to find?

The Cynthia/Liddy/Terry story had not finished there. And this is the truth of it: the world is fuller of stories and surprises than you would ever guess. The cogwheel factor of Terry who took my virginity under the influence of Cointreau and who failed to marry me so I had Venetia and he had Florrie was unstoppable. Another wheel engaged; it had just taken time to do so. Then by God it got going. Decades later I got a letter from a retired admiral who had worked with Terry on the development of visual landing aids for aircraft carriers, and it said Terry had not killed himself, Florrie had shot him. She had got mixed up with a Californian sun/drugs/occult/youth cult: this was when that sunny world was building up to the Manson Family excesses. Terry had been going to ship the whole family back to London to get Florrie away from it, and Florrie found out, waited until her mother went shopping, found her father's gun, loaded it, and shot him in the head as he worked at his desk. Patricide. Then she just sat on the floor and stared into space.

Liddy came home and with friends rearranged the scene so it looked like suicide, and the police, though they had their suspicions, went along with the version of a depressed man ending it all. The family was British, not one of theirs, on the way out of the country; who wanted a scandal, a lot of rich kids involved, and a crazy twelve-year-old locked up for life? Terry had talked of me a lot, said the Admiral, he'd want me to know the truth, and because he didn't want Terry to be thought of as a quitter, a suicide, because he was simply not. I spoke to the admiral briefly on the phone – we agreed Liddy had probably done the right thing. Terry would have wanted her to do it this way. He would want to take the blame for his child. It was nothing whatsoever to do with the Paris air crash.

And he had talked of me a lot. That made me feel real again, tied up with a kind of silken bow, like a sheaf of old love letters. It was enough.

I called up the alumni to let them know. Not suicide, murder. Remember him differently, I said, but they didn't seem much interested. He was never one of them, after all, just part of me.

'Is that the Florrie who's a friend of your mother?' I asked Amos.

'Yes, that's her,' he said. 'Didn't you know her father or something?'

'Yes I did,' I said. 'How's Amy?'

'Amy's fucking A,' he said.

'Not on drugs or anything?' I asked.

'No more than anyone,' he said. 'Why?'

'Just wondered,' I said. All this in-the-genes stuff. It wasn't quite what I wanted for Amos. But God knows what the lad had running through his veins. What had become of Amos' hit-and-run father anyway? In prison, on a whaling ship, an accountant, a politician, a designer of posters for the National United Government that now ruled us, for whom Victor worked, and Ethan drove, and who then was the righteous man?

Those outside had given up bang-de-banging.

'They've gone,' he said. 'The scum have scarpered. I think we're free.'

'But they'll be back,' I said. I was chilled and tired and felt like crying.

Amos went loping down the stairs putting on all the lights – power had again been restored. 'Not necessarily,' he said, and told me there was a note put through the door saying the bailiffs would be returning with a court order allowing forcible entry. But it would take them years, said Amos, to get round to it: the courts were backed up solid and we were safe for a while. In fact safer than usual. I'd have been ticked off a list. There were so many bankruptcies and repossessions in the offing the debt collection agencies were overwhelmed. And no-one's heart was in it, anyway, because what did you do with houses once there was no-one in them? They just grew mouldy and fell down.

Regulations now forbade anyone from owning an empty house for more than a year; property developers were out of business, and to live in a repossessed house was seen as unlucky. A hysteria of superstition had seized the nation: fortune-telling and clairvoyance were one of the few growth areas, along with debt-collection agencies and security firms. And everyone knew when a house had been repossessed: since the coalition party – National United Government – got in, posters saying *Repossessed – NUG scum did this* would be plastered over empty houses, and it could be days before anyone got round to tearing them down again.

And where did the new generation of the dispossessed go? Friends, family, the streets – though the police scooped the actively homeless up pretty quickly. People spoke of 'the outskirts' – wherever the outskirts were.

'I see the Joneses have gone, I wonder where to?'

'Oh, the outskirts, I think,' comes the reply.

Some vague kind of place where people find housing. Fuel is rationed so no-one wants to go searching. In hard times you look after your own.

In the morning, said Amos, we'd see about packing up everything of value in the house and removing it from the premises. I was too tired to argue. I'd talk to him in the morning. I went to bed and got warm, while I still had a bed to get warm in.

But I do rather wonder what Amos wants from me. And what is this 'we'?

He had to help me up. My knees had seized up. At eighty-what-ever-I am you have to keep them moving.

A Brief History Of My House

Let me make it clear that I do not want the bailiffs to take my furniture away. I want to go on living in this house until I die, with my Paula Rego on the wall, the possible Brancusi on the shelf, the Wyndham Lewis first editions, the stuff I bought in the days of my youth, and wealth. I often deny that I am interested in possessions, or am materialistic, but I deceive myself. I remember my mother Margaret saying to me that all old women end up in bedsitting rooms with a favourite ornament and a family photo if they're lucky, and I fear it was true for her, she was bedridden at the end with a mind as clear as a slightly doomy bell, but I never wanted it to be true for me. I wanted simply to stay where I was, as I was, rattling around in eight rooms, until I just did not wake up one morning. It is a tall narrow townhouse, old and draughty – quite unsuitable for someone who chills down easily and has bad knees, I know, but it is home.

You can skip the rest of this section if you want, and go forward to the ongoing story of Amos and Amy, daughter of Florrie, and their connection with the extremist organization Redpeace, an off-shoot of Greenpeace, their conspiracies, their explosives, and how they took Victor as hostage. What I say next will be boring to some, but it places Chalcot Crescent in a historical context, and projects to a world ahead which was bound to come, and so seems to me to be important to have as a background as we work out what is going to happen next in the unbottomed-out economy.

Writing is in my blood, as painting is in Venetia's, and I, like her, am accustomed to the rejection and criticism which comes when the artist tries to impose his or her will on their audience other than in the most tentative of manners. Venetia gets more stick than I do because frankly she is not very good at what she does, but that doesn't mean she gives up. I am good enough, just currently unpublished. If you have got this far, reader, you have got your money's worth anyhow. Don't even bother to skip – throw it away in disgust if this is how it takes you. Really, there is no obligation to get to the end of a book which annoys you.

I am always concerned when people, finding out that I am a writer, apologize and say, 'I'm not much of a reader actually. I know I ought but I just don't seem able to find the time' and then go on to tell me how they feel obliged to finish any book they begin. Well, of course, I say, you will be reluctant to open one in the first place, knowing what it might entail. It isn't meant to be like that, I assure them. If you begin a book and you don't like it, just throw it away. Or take it round to a charity shop. It's like going to a party: some people you linger with, knowing you get on. Some people you exchange greetings with and move on fast. It's nothing against them. They're just not your kind of person. It's the same with books. You must be prepared to discard. And though you may feel it's a waste of money not reading a book you don't get on with, that's like not opening the windows when the weather turns warm for fear of wasting the central heating. So, as I say, now is a good point to abandon the book. You have my permission – even my encouragement.

Back To The Point

Now, the lifecycle of my house in Chalcot Crescent, Primrose Hill. The terrace was built in an elegant curve around 1810, just over two hundred years ago. I have been part of its life for fifty years, a quarter of its lifespan. I know nothing about the people before me who lived in this house: why should those who live here in the future think of me? We are all temporary, and to pretend otherwise is futile.

Amos says I am being thrown out because it is a nice place for the *nomenklatura* to live. A brisk health-giving walk through Regent's Park, to Park Crescent, which now houses Victor's National Institute for Food Excellence: a little further on to CiviMedia in Portland Place, on through Piccadilly to Whitehall, and there you are, healthier but not tired out, the better to run the country. But Amos would say that, wouldn't he. I am beginning to be very conscious of his paranoia.

Areas of London go up and down but Primrose Hill has had a fifty-year run of good luck. It was built by a consortium of businessmen builders, property developers, and intended for a new breed of aspiring professionals. Space in London was beginning to fetch premium prices. Each house is only two rooms wide, but four storeys high, elegant and well proportioned, with french windows and balconies on the first floor, basement and attic rooms for the servants, and 'the family' content to be crammed into the middle. All went well until the age of railways; by 1860 smoke and smuts, from the marshalling yards needed for the trains puffing and belching out of the great new London terminal King's Cross, had driven down property prices until anyone who could possibly afford to live anywhere else, did. The proletariat crowded in, immigrant labourers from Ireland – a fixture in England through the centuries: low-paid labour to build the canals, and then the railways, and in the sixties the motorways, and with the millennium to bury fibre-optic cables so the Internet could take off.

So those who lived here at the turn of the last century were manual workers – they rented or boarded and did not own. Labourers, porters, laundry workers, shop girls, charwomen, struggling families living six to a room, the women doing their laundry in tubs in the street, sitting outside in summer, children swarming in the road. Then in the sixties the coal yards were closed, the trains abandoning steam for electricity. Primrose Hill ceased to be famous for having the highest bronchitis rate in all Britain, the middle classes returned, and the long narrow gardens out the back were filled in with kitchen and bathroom extensions, and glass conservatories. Things began to look up. The graceful Georgian façades remained untouched, protected as they were through various by-laws. And then the artists and writers and those with an eye for an attractive building crowded in – Karl bought the house in 1952 for £2,000 – and then I and Venetia moved in and Karl and I got married. Karl put half of his house in my name, an unusual thing to do at the time, and he must have loved me, at least in the beginning. He had been left money enough when he turned twenty-five: he was the illegitimate son of a wealthy businessman who wanted to do right by his son and go to heaven. Karl spent half on the house and the other half on a psychoanalysis course that went on for twenty-three years. My own went on for only eight.

The street was halfway respectable when I moved in. I remember standing on the balcony and calling down to Venetia playing in the street below, 'Venetia, come in, your avocado is ready,' and thinking at the time, what is happening to me? What have I turned into? That was in the sixties, when avocados were new on the market and exotic and suddenly instead of being poor and single I was working in advertising and making good money and well housed and a property owner. What was happening was that I was wrapping myself in layer upon layer of hypocrisy.

We in the creative arts were all socialists then, Marx or Trotsky our heroes. We were struggling for some imaginary working class who couldn't wait not to be working class. Just as I worry vaguely now about what will happen to the dispossessed – rather less vaguely now it seems I am to become one of them – then I wondered where would the poor of the Crescent go, the manual workers, the cleaners, the laundry workers, the porters, the bin men and the coal men, as the avocado eaters swept in. 'To the outskirts', friends would say vaguely, rather as in Nazi Germany, no doubt, people would say of the Jews –'Oh, I think they send them to resettlement camps, where there's more room than in their ghettos.' In those days, in our defence, cities had quite pleasant suburban outskirts, not just one vast desolate acre of business park after business park, all now empty and crumbling, left over from the Good Days when business buzzed and growth was constant.

Karl and I had a 'sitting tenant', mind you, there when Karl bought the house over her head.

Death Of A Sitting Tenant

Picture her then, this bold, handsome, energetic young woman in her mid-thirties, this Frances, who once was me, with her sexy husband and her child by an earlier liaison, and her sister Fay finally out of the picture, and her mother, too, in Australia where the gum trees weep their bark away, and a novel or two – though derided by Karl – under her belt, and the belief that all would stay like this for ever, and nothing would go wrong in Chalcot Crescent: the place was charmed, as she was, and it would move steadily up in the world for ever, as would she. The hard times were over. Just a pity about the sitting tenant, who was old and shuffled and smelt, but who had her rights, which included the use of the kitchen. And to get to the kitchen Barbara had to pass by the dining table where Frances entertained her guests.

One day she gave a dinner party for three other couples, four close friends. She was indefatigable now she was happy. Frances worked from an Elizabeth David cookbook. She prepared flaked cod with a shrimp sauce with brandy, lemon sorbet, and boeuf bourgignon with French beans and roast potatoes, and a tarte aux pommes with double cream. No-one worried about diet, or calories, and few were vegetarians and you'd have to look up 'obese' in the dictionary. People worried about status. And Barbara came shuffling through and there was a silence in the conversation –

about the effect of the birth pill upon the relationship between the genders, and whether men would simply pass on responsibility for pregnancies to the woman.

'Is that your mother, Frances?' asked a guest.

'No,' said Frances, 'it's the sitting tenant.'

And the conversation resumed, with a joke or two about how best death could be hastened. But Frances ground her teeth – so white and firm and strong – and determined that one way or another the old crone must go. She needed the room for the nursery. She was five months pregnant. This did not terrify her – it occurred to no-one at the time that babies could be born imperfect – if the midwife thought the newborn not fit for the world that was her business. But she wanted space. Karl was now running an antique business. Most of the stock was in the home, not the shop. What was Barbara doing in her life?

The 'sitting tenant' was quite a feature in the street, their rented rooms having been bought over their heads. Such tenants could be bribed, or 'bought out' so they could rehouse themselves, and the young ones would go and the old ones would stay – as was their legal right. Middle-class life would have to move around them, and the convention grew up just to ignore their presence. Barbara stayed, for Karl could not afford the sum she demanded to leave – the inheritance had indeed been spent and he declined to use Frances' earnings for this purpose – he liked Barbara as he liked many a bit of old battered furniture that had seen better days. Venetia, at the time thirteen, was on Barbara's side too – Mummy was just being snobbish and the child had even persuaded Barbara to pose while she painted her. Venetia seemed blind to Karl's hints that she should give up painting and stick to the recorder. But it was Frances who had to clear up after old Barbara – she leaked a little as she walked – and Frances' conviction that Barbara enjoyed her role as spectre at the feast, and had quantities of cash in the tin box under her bed.

'I wish she would just die,' Frances said under her breath on this occasion, as she served the chocolate mousse – six eggs, two packets of Menier chocolate – and the whiff of Barbara passing got to her and her guests. 'Eighty-eight is far too long for anyone to go on.'

Even as Frances murmured and Karl said crossly, 'Don't say that, it's wicked,' Barbara gurgled, grabbed her throat and collapsed on the floor in a heap of voluminous, smelly skirts with her dirty white laceless plimsolls sticking out. Karl reacted first, knelt at her side and tried artificial respiration while Frances hoped it wouldn't work. The ambulance came, declared the old woman dead, and took the body away. The dinner party did not continue, though they waited while Frances made strong coffee for everyone because they had drunk so much of Karl's home-made peach wine, which he made in the bath.

No relatives were traced and Karl offered to pay for the funeral, though Frances did not see why he should, and rashly said it would be she who was paying anyway, from the joint account. She was the only one who paid into it. Joint accounts were new at the time and she and Karl were not even married, because of the previous wife in the mental home. Margaret's passing words to Frances, on her way to Canberra, were, 'You can be such a fool, my dear. Thank God Fay didn't marry him.'

'You killed her,' said Karl. 'I think the only decent thing for you to do is pay for the funeral.'

'What do you mean, I killed her?' demanded Frances. 'I mopped up after her, cleaned up her burned saucepans, read her headlines from the newspaper' – she had done this too, trying not to hold her nose.

'You ill wished her,' said Karl, 'I heard you, and she died on the spot.'

He seemed quite serious: he accorded her great power when it suited him. She tried not to quarrel with him because he could sulk for days, and make her feel wholly in the wrong during that time, and lie not touching her in the bed, until lust overcame him and he moved nearer.

So she arranged with the undertaker to have old Barbara buried, and put death announcements in the local papers. It did not occur to Frances to actually go to the funeral.

'But she was like part of my family,' said Venetia. 'I don't have aunts or grandmothers like other people.'

'Yes, you do,' said Frances, 'just a long way away,' and in case Venetia started asking questions about her father she agreed to go, and took time off work, and Karl shut the shop and they all went to the cemetery in Golders Green, a dismal place where it rained, and there were no taxis, and no friends or relatives of the deceased, and the priest complimented them on their consideration for a lovely, lonely old lady.

'Do you think,' asked Venetia, as they walked back to Golders Green Underground, and Frances felt the baby churning and kicking inside her, 'that Barbara's soul will enter into the baby?'

It's House Prices, Stupid!

Surprisingly, Venetia and Karl got on well enough. That is to say, Venetia adored Karl and he tolerated her. It was all the more disturbing for the girl when he left us for the Dumpling. But all that divorce and broken-hearted stuff must be left for a subsequent chapter: it is the history of the house and the economy that matters now.

When I bought Karl out of my share in the house in 1979 it cost me £60,000. (He was bitter about that, understandably, since he had given it to me in the first place.) Twenty years later it was worth £750,000. Then came the Labour Government of 1997 and the Consumer Decade – as it is now called – and by 2007 the house next door to me sold for £1.85 million. Then came the Shock of 2008, the Crunch of 2009–11 – when house prices plummeted and still no-one was buying; then the brief Recovery of 2012, when at least properties began to change hands again, though our friendly European neighbours became less friendly, the US embraced protectionism and the rest of world had no choice but to follow. And then came the Bite, which is now, and with it a coalition and thoroughly *dirigiste* government which keeps its motives and actions very much to itself. And though a few major figures in the financial world went to prison, the *nomenklatura* still ride the middle lanes, have their mortgages paid for them, and do very well, thank you. The rest of us are presumably moving to the outskirts: fifty years on and we are back to where we began. I reckon I had the best of it.

In 1810 when this house was built there was 36 per cent inflation; in 1933, 38 per cent deflation; in 1977, 26 per cent inflation: by 2011, 10 per cent deflation and the last time I looked inflation was 27 per cent and rising. I marvel at how accurately I can remember the details of house prices and economic history, and how vaguely I recall the dates of my personal life. These seem to have their own narrative, little to do with the actual statistics of birth, marriage and death. Emotional truths are registered in the memory, clouded by wishful thinking or lingering resentments. Even at the time you live through them it is hard enough to keep up. The stroppy three-year-old looms so large in the mother's consciousness she is astonished to find it is so tiny and helpless, when the first day of nursery school arrives. When the clingy teenager declares she is pregnant the mother is amazed: she had thought her daughter was a child.

But ask me for inflation statistics and I can be relied upon to be both accurate and knowledgeable. Violent swings are commonplace, always uncomfortable for some, and comfortable for others. I studied Economics at college in the days when the Theory of Value held good and monetarism and its excitements had not yet seduced governments with their vision of infinite growth, and continuous progress, and lads like my grandson Ethan were not lured away into the City to dance, demons on the heads of pins, instead of becoming scientists, doctors, accountants, civil servants, proper people. The banksters are excoriated now, but they too were conned, like everyone else.

I could claim moral rights and demand that Amos, Ethan and Mervyn take me in to the very small house in Hunter's Alley that I bought for them in the Consumer Decade. But I wouldn't want that. And Corey and Polly and the children live in a very small apartment, and I do not think I could live with Venetia and Victor, who is too like Mr Collins in *Pride and Prejudice* for comfort. No, I will throw myself upon the State and the comfort of strangers. According to all accounts, it is usually to be had. Those who know you least well go out of their way to help. It's familiarity breeds contempt, or if not contempt, which seems far too harsh a sentiment, an awareness of the emotional complexities you bring with you.

Surely 'they' will not leave me standing in the street. And, as I say, some miracle might happen. It always has in the past – a musical made of one of my old books, the reissue of a DVD, a film, an archive bought – unexpected money in the bank, debts paid, and everything back to normal. Well, normal as far as that exists today, but at least, like old Barbara fifty years ago, permitted by the State to stay in this house until I die. I'm glad we went to her funeral and I don't think her soul went into Polly. But perhaps it did. She must have been rather angry the other side of her apparent patience, as she shuffled past our chattering dinner parties on her way to make a piece of cheese on toast, too uninteresting even to be addressed as 'the sitting tenant', which I, up to my eyes in mortgage, in effect now am. The biter bit, and serves me right.

Anyway, that is the story of the Crescent until now. I am a little worried about Amos' assumption that 'we' will smuggle my belongings to a place of safety and thus defraud the State. I have lived all my life as a decent citizen, a payer of taxes, a giver to charity – my banker's order to Oxfam now goes automatically to the CiviKindness people – but I can see perhaps none of that good behaviour has helped me very much in life. I must somehow find my inner bitch.

Breakfast With Amos

But here and now is good. I slept surprisingly well. Amos stayed the night, and in the morning seemed totally normal and offered to bring me breakfast in bed and I accepted with gratitude. I often stay in bed to write until the need for coffee becomes too great to resist – especially when Venetia has slipped me some of the real stuff from the CiviStore. After that my concentration fades and it can be hours before I return to my laptop. But this morning I got a whole lot of writing done, with nice warm toes, before Amos called that breakfast was ready. During which time I was able to fill you in very adequately on recent economic history and the rise and fall of house prices, though I daresay I lost a few readers.

Amos spent a lot of time on his mobile rather than cooking, and then it took him ten minutes to find the dried egg. He seemed to take the difficulty personally, and I wondered if his unknown father had a touch of obsessive-compulsive disorder: my side of the family being too casual and laid-back to have provided the genes which make people panicky if what they are looking for cannot be found at once. I had to get out of bed to help him to find it.

Scrambled egg using dried egg is perfectly palatable, though better if you can get hold of blue-top milk to add to the mix, and not the green-top which is more readily available. In fact I quite like dried-egg scramble, if enough time and trouble is taken squashing out the lumps.

Dried egg is once again imported from the USA: in return for our oats, as a kind of simple barter, while the international money systems wait for what is hopefully referred to as 'the restoration of financial harmony'. I reckoned this would be a long time coming: natural calamity had piled on quantitative easement to intensify both food and water shortages and continued financial chaos. On the heels of the UG99 ravages, a new strain of resistant fusarium fungus meant cereal harvests failed over the American and Russian continents in 2011–12; but at least both were spared the avian flu, which got China in a big way; a new strain of dengue fever, resistant to antibiotics, swept Africa. Most air travel now is restricted to diplomats and government officials, and everyone who sets foot on foreign soil is well fumigated the instant they arrive. This puts most tourists off: that, and the currency restrictions. Here in the UK it's £5 for every trip abroad, the same as it was in 1948. Even after the Devaluation that's the same as saying 'Just Stay Home'. No-one forbids anyone to do anything: people just know they need to be socially responsible.

America sends out its surplus eggs, China sends out its surplus milk, we have a few oats over after the needs of our own sixty million are met. Oats are a hardy crop. I say sixty million but some say at least five million have vanished off the radar over the last five years, a great chunk of them our own citizens: flotillas of little boats are said to radiate out from our coves and beaches. A Dunkirk in reverse. Government doesn't tell us, and if it did, would we believe them? Anyway, there seem to be more than enough people about, of all skin shades and divergent cultures, and just about enough food, water, warmth and power to get by.

'Only dried fucking egg,' says Amos. I explain I like dried eggs. They used to cheer me up in the austerity years after the war when we first came to England. They were a bright, bright yellow – still are – and a contrast to everything else in the country, which seemed to me as a twelve-year-old to have been dipped wholesale into some great vat of grey dye. Now of course one wonders if the hens have been fed on tartrazine to buck the yolk colour up artificially: then such suspicions never occurred to one. He asks me if I want to get up to eat or do I really want to eat in bed. I say I'll get up to save getting crumbs everywhere.

I asked Amos who he'd been talking to on the phone and he said his brother Ethan, and I said that was nice, would they be getting together later? And he said yes, and a few friends, and I asked if Mervyn was coming too, and Amos said no. Mervyn was not 'in sympathy'. I wondered what that meant and Amos said 'Oh, never mind. Waste of fucking time.' So I asked how many friends. And Amos said eight. Which seemed rather a lot. Eight, other than for a dinner party, constituted a meeting. Something else occurred to me, and I asked if Amy would be coming over too. 'She's fucking got to come,' said Amos. 'She's the life and soul of the party. It's her project.'

Oh yes. 'Now is the time for all good men to come to the aid of the Party,' sprang to my mind unbidden. That was what people used to write when trying out new pens on scraps of paper in shops. The party was the Communist Party, party of literate intellectuals worldwide in the middle years of the twentieth century. That was how the tradition of writing it had arrived, that and 'the quick brown fox jumps over the lazy dog', for the more sensible reason that it contained all the letters of the alphabet. But still 'the Party'. Life and soul of what Party?

'You'll be wanting to get on with your memoir, I suppose,' Amos said now. 'We'll be upstairs. Don't worry about it.'

In other words you are not wanted at this meeting. And I know well enough that when the young say, 'Don't worry about it,' it means you had better do so.

'We'll bring our own coffee,' he says. Coffee! A likely tale. Just as over the post-war years powdered instant coffee had come to be known as simply coffee, so now had the powdered chicory and roasted oats version of today. But it wasn't coffee as I once knew it.

With everything Amos said my unease grew. Ethan but not Mervyn? What did that signify? Ethan had settled in so easily to his new life: perhaps too easily. Amos, and his feeling of not belonging, a reject, feeling morally superior to those who lay down the ethical rules. The sign of the agitator. Ethan, converted by his big brother, the Redpeace activist, the sleeper, unsubscribing, cutting the ties in order to penetrate government, pretending to like what actually he hated and resented. This was indeed paranoia. Mervyn, the younger sibling, placatory, not wanting to get involved, or raise his head above the parapet. What poison was filtering through to their lives? Worst of all now, Amy, child of the patricide, back from the past to haunt us all.

'What exactly is the project?' I asked lightly. 'Blowing up the Cabinet?'

Amos did not laugh in return: he just pretended he didn't hear. Idealists and political romantics don't do much laughing, and only hear what they want to hear. Amy, life and soul of the party. Did she go with Ethan or Amos? I hoped Amos, Ethan being better able to look after himself, relationship-wise. But that was a stupid, passing thought: my generation was showing: any sensible person would simply want Amy out of the way. Because that would be the way my particular cookie crumbled. First Terry, whom I stole, then Liddy, then Cynthia who died as punishment, then Florrie, now Amy come to destroy my grandchild, and all because I slept with Terry when I should not have done. It was gross disloyalty to a friend.

'It's a Redpeace meeting,' he said. 'She's an area organizer.'

Well, there you are. Cookie crumbled.

Redpeace is not so much a movement as a cult, the fundamentalist spawn of Greenpeace. It is not a banned organization. It is against cruelty to animals, and is all for protectionism, free speech and the liberalization of the drug laws, in all of which policies it is in accord with NUG. It is also against human genetic engineering – an issue on which NUG are not partisan. So far so good. Myself, I rather doubt NUG's espousal of free speech; the fact is that there are certain words that cannot be said – anything fat-ist, ageist, racist, sexist, or élitist – and certain concepts that must be espoused – all are born equal, for example, that nature means nothing and nurture everything; that there is no inheritable factor in IQ scores; that to be 'middle class' is an act of will (and a reprehensible one), not like prosperity itself, more often than not a function of IQ; that so long as the motive is pure the ends justify the means – and only by co-operation and pooling resources under *dirigiste* rule (while of course preserving democracy) will the nation climb out of the pit the politicians of the past dug for us. I take care not to voice my doubts too loudly.

Greenpeace in the meanwhile has dissolved itself. The various ecology groups came together during the Recovery Years, and, in the same mood as did the charities, united to form a master organization, CiviGaia, the better to focus and express positive community and ecological indignation. Actual physical protest –

marching round with placards – was seen as laughable. Other than on Pull Together Day, when everyone came out into the streets for carnivals, best banner competitions, local tugs-of-war, and free street barbecues. A few minor groups like Redpeace were allowed to stick it out on their own – it is ostensibly against NUG's policy to ban anything or anyone – but began to seem mildly ridiculous and ineffective. Walk through the streets with a banner when it wasn't Pull Together Day and the children would hurl their shoes. And their mothers would have to run round picking them up and swearing at the protestors.

Ethan, when he was angry and miserable at being made redundant, had joined Redpeace for a time, as I have told you, but soon realized he was keeping the company of conspiracy theorists and losers in general, and had got out. But now I rather wondered whether he had. Didn't people go underground?

Surely this must be paranoia. I was leaping ahead of myself, dissolving into the fiction around which I had built so much of my life. Amy's 'project' was as likely to be finally giving in and joining up to CiviGaia as anything else. Which would be the reason Ethan was coming along. Or perhaps Ethan was 'with' Amy. The boys would do nothing to harm their poor old gran: it would not only be unkind, also impractical. My house was already under surveillance, and though Amos said the bailiffs would not be back for years, how could he be sure? But as Amos himself had pointed out, and I believed him, all agencies are one (fucking) agency. Security and financial breaches were now seen as associated threats: social irresponsibility putting the State at hazard.

'Negative thinking' has joined a list of other punishable hate crimes. *Smile and the World Smiles with You* currently goes up on posters all over London, and our exported oats are shipped in hessian sacks with red smileys printed all over them. I expect a piece of research has come out maintaining that good cheer increases productivity in the same spirit as farmers swear that playing Mozart to cows increases their milk yield.

Amos The Outsider

On the whole I devote mornings to writing my memoir, and afternoons to a strange kind of fictional fantasy, in which I write my account of what may, or may not, be going on in my children's households. The publishing industry is at the end of its tether, and is reluctant to publish any books at all. Readers have gone off the misery memoir, and want accounts of heroism and good cheer, of the kind Samuel Smiles delivered to the public with *Self-Help*, in 1859. Samuel Smiles – *Self-Help*! How could such a title and such a name not sell to the populace? In the same way as my grandfather Edgar Jepson increased bread sales no end in the First World War with his advertising slogan *Eat More Bread!* Simplicity works. The theory being that if you ate more bread you would eat less meat. Which is why the National Unity Government, or NUG (slogan: *Hug the NUG!*), had contrived that the National Meat Loaf has a lot of oats in it and not much meat. It has a rather haggis-like consistency but it's okay. My teeth are not too bad for their age; they look all right on the outside – in the days of my wealth I had very expensive veneers done, which will certainly outlast me, no matter what happens to the yellowing teeth behind them.

There were other Smiles books – *Character, Thrift, Duty*. O Samuel Smiles, thy country needs thee now!

'Gran, where did you get the blue-top milk from?'

'From your mother. She gets it from the CiviStore on Victor's card.'

Time was when low-fat green-top was all the rage. But the passion for skinniness has altogether abated. The fatter you are, the warmer you can keep. NUG is building up the dairy herds once again, as the nation strives for self-sufficiency in food – forget dangerous methane-emitting ruminants – we're hungry – and if we don't eat, and we don't have jobs, we riot and burn things down and frighten politicians so much they up and go away, no doubt taking their ill-gotten gains with them, leaving us the poorer, and searching for another leader. After NUG was elected the cult of personality simply evaporated; no statues, no public appearances, just the occasional decree in NUGNews and an illegible signature. But goodies for the *nomenklatura*, and scrapings for the rest, same as always.

'Well, she bloody well would, wouldn't she,' said Amos, and of all the things he had said lately this was the one that struck home. I realized this was a son who did not love his mother, and I felt my blood run cold. And when I say that I mean it. It was as if the stuff no longer ran merrily through my heart, but sluggishly, and thickly, and I felt a chill follow the arteries as it ran through my body.

I went into emergency gear: I did not let the expression on my face change, though no doubt my smile stiffened a little, as I worked out what was to be done. I remember the other occasions I had felt like this: when I first suspected Karl was running off with the Dumpling; when the phone rang at five one morning and it was Venetia saying Amos was in police custody; when little Polly was taken to hospital with suspected meningitis; when I waited for confirmation that Cynthia had been on the Paris flight; when the letter came from Liddy and I read that Terry was dead. The body reacts first and tells you what the mind is thinking. This was not something that could be just brushed aside and life got on with. It was real: Amos hated his mother and his smiles were lies. And if he came to Shabbat meal on Friday night (which was not a real Shabbat meal because both Victor and Venetia were atheists, and viewed religion as the source of most of the world's ills, but saw no harm in ceremony) and smiled and charmed, it was for some ulterior motive. And why? What had Venetia ever done other than love her son, cherish him, forgive him, visit him in prison, and include him in her new life with Victor as best she could? Was he mad?

It was a possibility. Schizoids turn on those who love them most. The mothers are the ones who get chopped up with the axe, not the enemies. It is something to do with neural pathways passing too closely to one another in the brain, I believe, and if you are unlucky hate and love can cross over.

It was a surprise. It was a shock I had not been expecting. There was something terribly wrong and something had to be done, and I was not sure I had the strength for it. I was old, and you lose your taste for the things that need to be done. And part of you thinks this is enough surprise for one life.

A Brief History Of My First Daughter Venetia

Venetia was born when I was twenty, without an attendant father, and brought up for her first ten years in the days of my trouble and poverty, before I went into advertising, met Karl, wrote books and became suddenly rich. Luck was on my side, and I had given birth to a blond, healthy, beaming child, Venetia, and luck was on her side too when, following in my footsteps, the child grew to conceive Amos, also out of turn. He too was beautiful and bright. I think there are some babies who are simply meant to be born: children of destiny rather than choice, their parentage being so unlikely, the coming together of the twain so accidental. Or it may just be that to seek likeness in a partner is counter-productive – you have a better chance of successful progeny if you don't know what you're doing.

Venetia was allowed to stay on at art school, became the pride of the traditionalist tutors, the despair of the conceptual fanciers, a tall, blonde, witty, willowy girl with large smoky-blue eyes and a good academic brain. Oxford wanted her, and Cambridge too, but she settled on Camberwell. I did not argue. It always seemed to me short-sighted to interfere with the children's choice of education.

'If only,' they will wail, 'you hadn't made me go to that school; everything would have turned out differently.'

If you let them do as they want, they have only themselves to blame.

Had she gone to Oxford, though, and done PPE and gone into politics – she ran the school anarchist society and was a great platform speaker – she might be running the country now and we would not be in the mess we are in. But there it goes. Like her mother, never one to live alone, being something of a sex addict, and mildly masochistic, she and Amos shacked up with first Angus Astura, the conceptual artist who wrapped up the Savoy Hotel with a red ribbon and bow, but on opening day was discovered by the media in a broom cupboard with a PR girl. And after Angus came the concrete poet Peter Patel, who bored her to tears by the clunkiness of his verse. The suitors didn't last long but were nevertheless in Venetia's bed, and sons can put up with fathers in their mothers' beds but passing uncles set off all kinds of neuroses.

I was always there in the background to support her financially, my allegedly feminist books selling like hot cakes the world over, providing both my daughters with security and, in the end, a comparatively respectable background. I'm not sure it did either of them any good.

When Amos was eight Venetia finally met someone halfway possible, and settled down with him: Victor, a biogeneticist with a respectable job, complete with pension, at the big London charity Cancer Cure. They moved into a big Victorian house in Grand Avenue, Muswell Hill, with a view over all London, and there they have stayed. Venetia did what she could to include Amos in her new family, and gave birth to Ethan and Mervyn. She employed au pairs to mind the children and found time to paint in the studio especially built for her by Victor at the bottom of the garden. He always seemed to have a little more money than his salary warranted: Amos said he took private work creating designer babies, but that was the kind of thing Amos would say.

When the Crunch hit in 2009, people stopped buying paintings and decided they could as well tear pictures out of old Sunday supplements and bung those up on their walls. Venetia went on painting and stockpiled her canvases. During the Recovery she got a part-time job with the Arts Council, but that went too, with the Bite, as indeed did the weekend supplements. (No advertising, no supplements.) NUGNews did a Saturday supplement but it wasn't much fun. The paper was low quality and the colours were dreary, and soon people had nothing to put on their walls. So now every month Venetia would complete a painting, put it against the railings outside the house and wait for someone to take it away. Which they always did.

'Art should be free,' said Venetia. 'It can't be valued in monetary terms.'

Victor, thank God, will do anything he can to please Venetia and thinks she is a genius. Her paintings are rather bright and unlikely, thick acrylic bold colours in circular shapes. I pretend to like them and have some on my wall.

They're not unlike the ones she did at her first nursery school, where she was happy. I was still an unmarried mother and walked with her to school every day and she had my undivided attention. Then I married Karl and had Polly and I think that rather put her nose out of joint, as my mother having other children before me, put mine. It's usually older siblings who cause trouble for the ones that come along next, but in my case it was the next sister up I took against. She could read and write before me, and I was envious, but I think it was being left out of that painting that really got to me.

If I go back to Amos' beginnings I can see he is the grandchild most likely to be caught up in extreme behaviour of some kind or another. He has never really belonged, any more than Venetia has.

Venetia did to Amos what I did to her, and, at around the same age, started the 'real' family as if the first child was a mistake, accidental. The others are of the blood royal, as it were, while the first and misbegotten child is a Fitz to the others' Lords, a by-blow, a bastard, through no doing of their own. Daughters are more placid and accepting, but sons will rail against fate, and look for a place to belong. William the Conqueror was known as William the Bastard at home in Normandy and had to conquer Britain to get a change of status. What will Amos do?

The doorbell rang as I was writing this, but it was quite gentle and tentative so I had no hesitation in opening up. A lean young woman in her early twenties stood on the doorstep. And I thought Terry. The same hooded dark-blue eyes, the full, slightly twisted mouth, the narrow face, and I was back in St Andrews and drunk with Cointreau and my soul was watching the union below from up there in the corner of the ceiling. I don't suppose angels get to many couplings but I daresay they do occasionally, when the consequences are of relevance to a wider future.

'Are you Frances?' she asks. 'You knew my grandfather. I'm Amy. My mother Florrie knows your daughter, who's married to Victor who works for NIFE.'

'That's so,' I say. 'You look so like your grandfather.'

'How can I?' she asks. 'I'm a girl, he was a man.'

'You're a female version of him,' I say. 'The oestrogen version, not the testosterone one.' She looks as if she'd like to argue but can't really be bothered. Terry would look like that too when he was bored or disapproving or Liddy had said something simply stupid, which she often did. She wasn't very bright, which was probably why he married her not me. Remember that was back in the fifties when dim girls were preferred above bright ones – probably because they made better mothers. Bright girls get distracted and don't concentrate on motherhood. Though I'm not sure Liddy can have made a very good mother.

'Was my Gramps your boyfriend?' she asks, straight out.

'Not in any permanent sort of way,' I say.

'It's odd to think of old people having sex,' she says.

Tact is not her strong point but neither was it her grandfather's. Why should people get better through the generations? Some do, some don't. Some families are in entropy while others are burgeoning. Yet this girl is a great improvement on wan, ethereal Liddy. I think perhaps she is Aspergery: she looks too clever for her own good. People on the autistic spectrum are often beautiful, as if the sheer capacity for emotion was harmful to the foetus in the womb, and prevented perfect, symmetrical growth.

'Anyway I never met him,' she adds. 'He shot himself before I was born.' She doesn't quite look directly at me, but I have the feeling she thinks the same ought to apply to me. But it may be nothing personal: the young are often like that. They really cannot see why the old should exist at all. I am not altogether out of sympathy: I sometimes share the feeling.

She is here to see Amos. I call him down and they go off together in her tinny little Civi run-around. I wonder where she gets the petrol. I do not think they have anything other than a friendly relationship. Perhaps she is with Ethan, who is spoiled for choice.

I am alone at last and now can turn my hand to fiction. I will give you a version of the moment of exclusion which set Amos off on the path towards social alienation. That moment when, they say, the loner instincts finally prevail, which seals the destiny of serial killers, terrorists and high-school assassins. I feel very unfair to Amos writing this: I have not the slightest evidence to support these speculations of mine. All I really have against Amos is that he swears all the time, smokes skunk, rants a good deal and means to hide my possessions in case the State gets them, and not him as in my will. (That too is probably unfair: inheritance duties are up to 80 per cent for all artworks and antiques: the money these fetch in sales these days is so pitiful that now the State just confiscates. Amos can't expect much.) But then perhaps it is my revenge upon my family, thus to let loose my fantasies in fictional form. That psychoanalyst long ago would certainly say so. I wish Karl would come back from the dead and explain things to me. It seems the least the dead can do for the living.

An Evening At Venetia's

'My God,' Venetia had said when the news of the collapse of Cancer Cure came through on Victor's email. 'How are we going to live now?'

No-one was buying her landscapes any more – or indeed anyone's – and her job at the Arts Council had come to an end. She had been working part-time, allocating public money to deserving artists – not that she thought many of them were – but in the light of the new scheme afoot – *Art for All* – that would make qualified artists direct employees of the State, her skills were redundant. Or else her views as to what constituted good art, and what did not, were now seen as reactionary. The heating bills were immense and still climbing: she couldn't paint if her fingers got too cold. If even Victor, one of the nation's leading stem-cell scientists, was to lose his job, how would they manage?

Victor told her not to panic, the Government was not going to let its brightest and best go to waste – and sure enough a posting came through from Job Direction before the end of the week. He was being offered Senior Scientist Grade 1 at NIFE, the National Institute for Food Excellence, with special responsibilities at managerial level. At Cancer Cure, Victor had been working on stem-cell therapies, in particular the implication of immuno-suppressive cytotoxic antineoplastosis: now he was required to divert them to development of new forms of disease-free edible protein. To work in the public sector was generally held to be a sensible move. The private sector was shrinking fast. The recession showed no sign of bottoming out – why should it? The public was not, as had at first been claimed, 'sensibly putting off buying until price dropped', they had just gone off buying for ever: consumerism was suddenly out of fashion. Sparse was in, lavish was out. All the same, Victor would receive almost double what Cancer Cure had paid.

Venetia was uneasy. It seemed too good to be true. There would be no more worrying about money, whether she could afford acrylic paint – the price had zoomed up and it was in short supply – Mervyn would be able to study in a warm room, she would apparently as a Grade 1 spouse have access to the CiviStore, of which wondrous things were spoken. Was there something Victor wasn't telling her? He had already, even before the interview, signed up under the Official Secrets Act 2012, so if there was he couldn't anyway.

'But I didn't marry a civil servant,' she said plaintively. 'I married someone who was going to win the Nobel Prize.'

'Well,' said Victor, 'for my part I always thought you would win the Turner prize and you haven't. So we're quits.'

But he agreed to think it over.

As for the Depression, Amos claimed, on one of his Friday visits home, at a time when Victor was still thinking it over, that it was sorting through the household waste that had started the whole thing off. While staring at an old chicken wing welded on to a sheet of oven paper, wondering if this was organic or inorganic waste, the thought had occurred to many that the answer was not to bring it into the house in the first place. A paper bag full of lentils would do for food, and later you could burn the bag in the gas-fire flame, for warmth. He was joking, of course, though sometimes it was rather hard to tell whether he was or he wasn't.

Ethan, as dark and ruddy as Amos was lean and pale, and hairy like Esau, said the recession was nothing to do with waste sorting, you had to go further back than that – but it was the fault of anorexic girls: they had started the fashion for non-consumption.

Mervyn, who was then doing A levels in classics, more like a mini-version of his father, quiet, large, hairless and stolid, said the whole recession had been deliberately contrived by Europe to bring the people under State control. Victor said it was okay to say that kind of thing at home, but he hoped Mervyn would be more prudent at school. Mervyn accepted the rebuke and asked his father about the other two jobs he had been offered. Weren't you allowed a choice of three, before direction? Victor said they only told you what the other jobs were if you turned down the first.

'Ah,' said Mervyn, 'like you're more likely to get into the college you want, if you make it your first choice.'

Victor said the first one was obviously the one they wanted you to take, and feeding the population was probably more vital in the years to come than curing it of disease. The young and healthy deserved consideration as well as the old and ill, who were taking up too much of the country's resources as it was. Longevity was now a national problem, not a national ambition.

'Disease-free edible protein?' asked Amos. 'From stem cells? Does that mean growing bulk meat in fucking vats?'

Victor, made a little tense by his situation, asked Amos if he would mind not swearing on Shabbat.

Amos said it wasn't really Shabbat, was it, just a Friday night get-together with vaguely religious overtones.

'True enough,' said Victor, his thin eyebrows raised slightly in surprise at this sudden show of antagonism from Amos. There was very little else he could say. Victor had been raised in North London as a liberal Jew, gone to Cambridge, drifted into non-observance, been infected by religious sceptics, fallen romantically in love with Venetia, taken on Amos as his own and had two sons. Since Jewishness is determined by the mother, Victor had scarcely created a Jewish family, as his mother often lamented. But he was enough of a ritualist to like having Amos and Ethan home on Friday nights and to have a residual feeling that Shabbat was special. And Venetia would lay the table with a white cloth and light candles and serve chicken, for Victor's sake. She liked it too.

'Sorry I swore,' Amos offered, relenting.

From the beginning Venetia and Victor had been conscious of the need to make Amos feel included in the family, and not trailed along as an afterthought, dragging genes of unknown origin behind him. And for his part Amos had tried to make his stepfather and brothers feel at ease, and not hopelessly naive and bourgeois, and an act of folly on his mother's part. All the same, before his mother married Victor, Friday nights had been pizza nights. And this was his dinner table as well as his stepfather's, and he could surely swear if he wanted to – he hated to be told what he could and couldn't do: there had been enough of that in his life – and it was easy enough to provoke Ethan and Mervyn into fits of hilarity, which always made Victor uneasy.

They were sitting at the table, the candles lit, waiting for Venetia to bring in the roast chicken. It would be a capon, golden brown, and sprinkled with sesame seeds according to her mother's recipe. It would be another united family triumph.

Amos said the Government had started the whole thing off back in the Good Days by making every household reduce its carbon footprint and sort its waste into organic and inorganic. Any normal person, puzzled by a piece of plastic glued to an overcooked chicken wing, would decide the answer was not to bring it into the house in the first place. Then Ethan said the anti-consumption age was triggered by anorexic girls refusing to eat. Refusal became the fashion. They giggled at their own silliness. Mervyn said if his father was going to be making disease-free animal protein in the lab he hoped he would remember the crackling.

'But does human skin make good crackling?' asked Ethan, and fell about with laughter. 'Daddy's a stem-cell specialist, after all.'

'Daddy's going to be growing "long pig" for the nation,' said Mervyn.

Victor was not laughing. He was looking quite flushed. He said that cattle had stem cells too, as did every living thing, and then Amos said, 'But humans don't get foot-and-mouth, or scrapie, or mad cow disease or bird flu – or not often – I would have thought "long pig" is a well reliable source of animal protein. And the job's inflation linked? You're being fucking bribed, Daddy-o dude. They probably closed down the entire charity network just to get you on side.'

Victor stayed silent for a little and rose to his feet. Venetia was bringing the chicken in, golden with National Butter, sesame-sprinkled: twenty food points splurged. She looked pretty: usually so pale, she was flushed from the cooker, and pleased to have all three children under one roof.

'Before we begin,' he said, 'Shabbat shalom.' Venetia, surprised, stood where she was. Victor went over to where Ethan sat and laid his hands on his shoulders and said, 'May God make you like Joseph's son Ephraim, a role model for all Israel,' and went over to Mervyn and said 'May God make you like Menasseh, Joseph's son,

117

a role model for all Israel,' and sat down again and nodded for Venetia to put the food on the table.

Amos said, taken aback, 'What about me?' and Victor just shook his head. Amos, Victor had declared, did not belong. It was a subdued meal after that.

Victor took the job. The next month Amos was in trouble with the law and would have been in prison for a long, long time, had his grandmother not intervened. Ecstasy, in which Amos was dealing, is no longer classified as a dangerous drug and, along with marijuana, cocaine, amphetamines and heroin, is all but legalized. The price of drugs, by the way, has come right down, which some say was the final blow to the stability of the world economy to which it had provided a proportion of the available investment capital, which was as large as it was unspoken. The police have too much else to do to bother with illegal substances. If people want to destroy themselves, let them. One less mouth to feed.

But I think it would have been some such act of non-acknowledgement on Victor's part that set Amos off on his vengeful path. Just as the rage of the suicide bomber, they say, is set off by some casual insult about colour, nationality or creed.

No End To The Surprises

The guests are gathering. I watch them come in from the front window and am careful not to be seen. Amy is opening the door to them. She is a gangly, but vigorous girl. If she and Ethan had babies they would be my great-grandchildren, and some of them might look like Terry. The thought makes me feel oddly guilty: I should be worrying if they would look like Karl, who I have always maintained was the love of my life. I have to believe that to retain my sense of victimhood, so important to a woman.

Two young girls come to the door, hand in hand, with the long legs and skinny bottoms girls seem to have nowadays. They are a different shape to the stumpy-legged things we were. I can't see their faces because they are wearing hoods, but they act and move with the confidence of extreme good looks. The hand on the bell is dark: I imagine they are Afro-Caribbean. They do not look like revolutionaries, just girls out for a giggle. They go on upstairs and I hear screams of excitement as they greet Amos.

When Ethan comes to the door, he uses the big brass knocker. Another surprise. Most people choose the bell instead – and the bailiffs used their fists – so heavy, antique and ornate is this intimidating fish of a knocker. But Karl would always use the knocker, should he by any chance be shut out, and the chandelier in the living room would quiver and chink in response, and he liked that. Now when Ethan uses it, he seems like Karl to be marking out his territory, almost as if he is Karl come home. But perhaps it is just he knows that the door will be opened by Amy, which it is. She seems too serious and ungainly a girl to be his type. But what does one know about one's own flesh and blood?

I could perfectly well intervene and welcome the guests in myself, and perhaps I should. It is, after all, my house. But these guests are of another, more vigorous generation. It seems to me they know what they are doing and I don't. I have been disenfranchised by virtue of age and my conditioning into the niceties of a former society, no matter how hard in my youth I tried to disregard them. The young are almost another species. Their loyalties are to each other, not to family. All the same, I could, and perhaps should, ring Venetia on her landline (another of Victor's perks: in an age of power cuts recharging mobiles became a hassle) but I don't want to be seen to be interfering.

What could I say? 'Venetia, two of your sons are in my house and making me uneasy. Did you know they may be involved with Redpeace? No, I know it isn't a banned organization, and they are adults, and I know how hard you try to make sure everything in the garden is just fine, but I have a terrible feeling it isn't.' No, I'm not going to say that. There is always a slight barrier between Venetia and me. I don't know what it is about.

Well, I do. I married Karl and gave her a stepfather and a half-sister and she could have had me to herself, if I'd truly loved her and not been so promiscuous with my affections. But she'd liked Karl well enough and looked up to him, and wanted him for a father. It was because of Karl, in the vain hope of winning his approval, that she turned her back on academia and studied art.

'For God's sake try and stop her,' Karl said to me. 'She's a nice girl but completely without talent.'

'Camberwell Art School doesn't seem to think so,' I murmured.

'Of course they don't,' Karl said. 'Bunch of talentless wankers.'

If she'd chosen to go to college he'd have said, 'For God's sake try and get her to art school. She's a nice girl but has no brains at all in her noddle.'

And I'd have said Oxford seemed to think differently, and he'd have said, 'Shower of poncy tossers. They just want to get into her knickers.'

It was by being so meanly capricious with his approval and acceptance that he kept the women around him in a state of adoration. I hesitate to say this of the alleged love of my life but show him a female and he'd try to fuck up her mind.

Mind-fucker is not a phrase you often hear these days, but when men were men and women were women, and men had the power and the money and women did not, there were lots of them. They were emotional manipulators, insidious, and why I'm still brooding about him and why Venetia is still painting hopeless paintings, which, now she has access to the CiviStore and an unlimited supply of acrylic paints, are thicker and brighter and more defiant than ever. Good for her.

What I do is call Venetia up and she answers and I ask her if she remembers playing with a little girl called Florrie. She replies, 'Yes, of course I do. Her father had just killed himself and she cried all the time. I met her again on Friends Reunited, and went round to visit her once or twice. She has a daughter called Amy. Ethan is going out with her. She's a bit bonkers but at least she has a brain. Why?'

'They've borrowed my house to have a meeting,' I say.

'They're always having meetings,' says Venetia. 'Don't worry

121

about it. It's only Redpeace. They bring their own coffee.'

'Why can't they have the meeting in your house?'

'They tried,' said Venetia, 'but you know what Victor is. He hates having people in the house he hasn't invited himself.'

Well, yes, I do know about that kind of thing. Karl was like that, and Edgar, whom I lived with in this house for seven years from 1982 to 1989. Karl filled the house with painters and antique dealers but couldn't stand writers, and Edgar filled it with Tory MPs and journalists and conspiracy theorists and couldn't stand novelists, and let me know it, even though it was my house he had moved into. Perhaps it's just a male trait. Or merely human: I daresay some women are like that about their husbands' friends.

I must get out of the habit of writing 'husband'. So few women are married these days. Correction: 'Some women are like that about their partners' friends.'

Edgar and I parted on political grounds in 1989, when the Wall came down and that was the end of the Soviet Union and the fear of war. I rejoiced, but Edgar said it was just the beginning of the Sovietization of Europe. As freedom fled east, control would flee west. Europe was just the USSR Lite: the majority of the new European Commissioners were ex-Stasis and the like from the old East Bloc. He was so far to the right, politically, that in the end I couldn't bear it, and asked him to go. That was a surprise too. He was terrific in bed but in the end principle seemed more important than sex. But I was, of course, growing older.

Venetia and I chatted a little about this and that – I didn't mention the bailiffs. Somehow I'd manage to find the money to keep them off. I always had in the past, why not again? I was not finished yet. Then Venetia said, quite casually, she thought she was converting to Judaism.

Another Surprise

I said I must just go and switch off the kettle, and by the time I came back I had composed my voice, so it sounded, I hoped, quite normal.

'Any religion is better than none, I suppose,' I said. 'But it will upset Amos.'

'What's Amos got to do with anything? He goes his own way. Actually, you're quite right, when I mentioned it he kicked your mother's old dresser so hard he hurt his toe, and then he slipped and fell over. I'm afraid I laughed, it was so funny. But he was having a real temper tantrum, the way he did when he was four. So no, I reckon he doesn't much go for it.'

I thought that was probably an understatement. Amos had put up with having one quarter of a mother for years – Victor, Ethan and Mervyn taking the other three – now his mother was betraying the years he had had her to himself, before she lugged him off to live with Victor and build a family which didn't really include him. Now she was making quite sure it didn't. No wonder he was behaving oddly. Perhaps the boy wasn't mad, just upset. I was being silly, elderly, mad myself.

There were rather odd noises coming from upstairs. A banging, as if someone was hammering. And the chandelier was clinking, as if Karl was home again, and storming about the house, complaining of the idiocy of punters, the price of petrol, the failure of governments, all the things men complain about. The house had been female for too long.

'I don't think you ought to do it, Venetia,' I said, before I could stop myself.

'Oh, don't sound so pious, Mother,' said Venetia.

I apologized for interfering. If I hadn't told Cynthia not to go to Turkey she might very well not have gone, because that's the way people are – contrary – and would still be alive today. I do try not to tell people what to do, but I am one of nature's 'why don't you?' people and it's hard to resist. Other people's lives seem so easy compared to one's own, if only they'd do the sensible thing.

'I suppose that means Victor has been taken back into the fold,' I said. 'It's quite a business, isn't it, being accepted as Jewish?'

'It's long, serious and difficult,' she said. 'But now all the children are away from home I have the time.'

I was conscious of a reproach here. My fault. I had given her three boys a house in the days when Victor lived on a Cancer Cure salary, without proper consultation, thus enabling them to live away from home. And now of course Venetia missed them and her life was empty and if I didn't like the idea of her converting to Judaism, too bad, I had only myself to blame. And Victor would think me the worst kind of interfering mother-in-law.

I said mildly that I thought all scientists were atheists and dead against the idea of an Intelligent Designer. She said these days Victor was more a management man than a scientist. It seemed he had a real logistical flair.

'But no more Nobel potential?' I shouldn't have said that.

'It's rather more important than that,' my daughter said, and the bell rang again and since Amy was upstairs I went to answer it. She'd said there was one more to come.

I opened the door to a tall, vigorous, quick-moving man with thinning dark hair, beetly eyebrows in need of a trim, and a protruding jaw which instead of making him look Neolithic and subhuman, made him on the contrary look intelligent, as if the jaw went ahead determined to search out the truth. He was not spindly tall, but simply scaled up all over, like a male hero in a fifties action film. He did not stand relaxed on the doorstep, but impatiently, like a runner waiting for the off. I stood back to let him pass. He was the kind of man I would have gone for as a young woman, which alas I no longer am. He looked familiar but I couldn't quite place him. But that is true of many people I meet these days. They look familiar and turn out to be the children, or even grandchildren, of old friends, colleagues, lovers, neighbours. If you stay in one place for long enough, familiar genes congregate.

'They're upstairs,' I said.

'I'm glad of that. The Cam on the corner's not far off being mended. They're working on it now,' he said, as he went on up. He had an Irish accent.

'I didn't know it was broken in the first place,' I said. He paused and looked down at me.

'You'll not be opening the door to anyone else then, will you,' he said.

He was accustomed, evidently, to issuing instructions and having them carried out. I resolved to open it to anyone who came.

The penalties for interfering with CiviCams had become severe. Five minutes having fun stoning them to death and, unless you were quick, because other cameras always filmed the cameras, you could end up in prison for three years. Surely the Redpeace lot hadn't dared put them out? Part of me was on their side, part of me wasn't. I realized who the tall handsome man with thinning hair was.

125

Now there was a surprise and a half. Henry, orphan son of Karl and the Dumpling; not the feeble wretch I had assumed, but a man of vigour and substance.

Son Of The Dumpling

When Karl left me in 1975 it came as a total surprise, and not a good one. Indeed, it all but destroyed me. After more than thirty years you'd have thought I'd be over the shock but it doesn't seem to work like that. Time somehow bypasses these profound personal affronts, as water will flow around and not over a stone. The current may smooth the worst of the jagged bits of hurt but not so you'd particularly notice. There's the rock, still there, harder and more obdurate than anything else. These are affronts to one's identity – and it is a matter of identity: one's very being, if you are prevented from making the connection between you now and you then, sends you off into an alternative universe not of your choice and not of your liking.

Polly, in her early adolescence at the time, and who even then saw the world through a feminist lens, maintained Karl left me because I grew too successful. He had married me as a sexy, pretty, nice little earner, an antidote to his previous wife, also a painter, who had turned out to be quite bonkers and dangerously bonkers at that, like my own Aunt Faith. Perhaps that was why I was so instantly attracted to Karl? It's not just that people with similar problems cluster together, so do their relatives – the one's who've had to cope. Or perhaps I just liked Karl's looks, short but stocky and muscular, like Picasso. The smooth olive skin, the slightly cruel, sensuous curve of the mouth, the smell of good food and wine and garlic and sex that seemed part of him. When we got together he was the serious one, the artist, the one people took seriously, And then suddenly there I was, icon of the feminist movement, treated with reverence as a writer, and the eyes of the world shifted, though only briefly, to me.

Men almost never leave a wife for an empty bed – I remember my friend Claudia saying that – and though of course Karl claimed he left for reasons of integrity, it was also because he had taken up with the Dumpling, an art student sculptor of unimaginably stolid female nudes. She had integrity. I apparently had none.

I woke one morning, late back the night before from a rehearsal, so tired I couldn't remember afterwards whether Karl was in the bed or not when I got into it. But anyway in the morning his side of the bed was cold. Nor did he ever return to it. An explanatory letter came a few days later. I would, he observed, have scarcely noticed his departure, so busy making money was I, let alone mind if he was gone; as I keep saying, he was a mind fucker. He and the Dumpling had gone to live in Somerset in a farmhouse with studio space and a good north light, where they could both work, without the disturbance of phone or newspapers, or the constant eruption of PR I found so essential in my life.

'My relationship with the Dumpling, in case you're wondering,' he wrote, 'is not a sexual one and never has been. We have a bond between us in the love, understanding and the practice of art, which, frankly, is not your scene.'

They planned a smallholding, where they would keep sheep and hens and geese, and live a country life, in tune with nature. (The return to nature was big in the mid-seventies: the price of oil had gone up to 50p a gallon and the end of urban civilization was at hand. The intellectual middle classes fled in droves to live in farm-houses, eat from the hedgerows and make nettle soup.)

Dumpling loved animals, Karl explained. He was divorcing me for adultery; the papers would be in the post as soon as he got round to it. He claimed in the letter, in the familiar handwriting that I so loved, in dark-blue ink on yellow paper, 'You have been serially unfaithful to me, and I have evidence of it.'

'Have you?' asked my friend Claudia.

She is a screenwriter and now lives and works in Hollywood. I sent for her when I received the letter. When she came round I was sitting on my bed staring into space. I stayed like that for a day or two, after she'd left. I lost three pounds in two days. Despair and anger can do that to you, can burn up the calories like nothing else, but it's not a way I'd recommend.

'Have you?' she asked.

'There is some truth in his claim,' I acknowledged. 'But nothing that meant anything.'

It hadn't either. The idea of free sex and 'open marriage' was all the rage in the progressive political and social circles I'd been moving in, especially amongst the men, though the women tended to need some talking into it. Jealousy in a woman was an ignoble and anti-revolutionary act and enough to have her discarded. It took the eighties and Aids to sober everyone up again.

'What evidence?' Claudia asked.

'I do write love letters sometimes,' I said. 'I do like to express myself in writing. I am a writer, after all.'

And I had missed the box file marked LL – for Love Letters – with all the drafts and redrafts in it. I'd thought my secretary must have misfiled it and forgotten to check up. That was before the days of computers. One made hard copies and kept them in box files.

'You're insane,' said Claudia. 'Why didn't you burn them?'

'I was keeping them for my archive,' I said.

My archive – all the writings and rewriting and memorabilia had been sold to the University of Indiana; I was proud of that. I liked to think of the future poring over my love life, and who was to know they weren't fiction anyway? Drafts for some novel?

'He's going to come back, isn't he?' I said to Claudia. 'He's not going to break up everything we have. He's gone a bit mad. He's seeing this new therapist who doesn't like me. He couldn't possibly do this to the children, to me. We need each other. We're made for each other. He keeps saying so. We were nothing, either of us, until we met. Our lives were a mess and then suddenly everything came together. He just has this rural dream about hedgerows and living next to nature. I didn't take enough notice of it. He's just trying to frighten me so we move from here and go and live in the country together.'

'No, darling,' said Claudia, 'he's divorcing you. He's found some art student he prefers to you and he's moved in with her and he's going to claim this house and try to make you keep him and his new bint on your outrageous earnings.'

'But they don't have a sexual relationship,' I said.

Claudia just laughed.

'He's been to a divorce lawyer who's told him what to say and he's saying it.'

I was silent while I took this in.

'You can put it all in a novel,' she added. 'You're a writer. Nothing's wasted.'

It was all there, I could see. How I'd failed to look after him, humiliated him in public, made him leave the house in unironed shirts, would ask his friends to dinner and then forget so he had to run out to the fish and chip shop (that happened once), was so busy with my (so-called) 'career' that I would forget to collect the children from school (twice) and so on. It all added up to 'mental cruelty'. Concepts of feminism were by no means established in the land: certainly not in the law courts. Wives in the eyes of the law were still meant to stay home and serve men. So of course Karl got his divorce, and of course he'd been in bed with her all along. The girls told me. They quite liked her.

I fought the case. I lost it, threw a lot of money down the drain and annoyed my daughters. The press got hold of it, and Venetia and Polly, not to mention a couple of passing (married) lovers, dug up by Karl's divorce lawyers, all had their pictures in the papers. Karl blamed me for that. Karl blamed me for everything. But at least the law at the time was such that I only had to support him, not, as would happen today, share all my income with him for the rest of my life. My magic life.

But my magic life stopped when Karl and I divorced. There was trouble with agents, lawyers, accountants, libel cases: money still poured in but poured out even faster. I bought Karl out of the house to his rage: he had planned to have it – the Dumpling loved it – and the house in the country too. His folly for having put half of it in my name. But in his anger he stripped the place of all our possessions – he claimed them as 'stock' from his antique shop, and got away with it – and there was nothing left of our past except the heavy brass fish door-knocker of which I am currently so conscious. I replaced everything. I spared no expense. The battered old Welsh dresser turned into Chippendale. The Hotpoint washing machine became a Bosch. If I could not have love I would have nice things. The resale value of them is precisely nothing.

And then Edgar moved in – I could not bear an empty bed –

and he and his cabal of right-wing friends engaged in some strange Pinochet-friendly scheme, which involved me becoming a Lloyd's Name. In 1993 that was more of my capital down the drain. Polly said it served me right for getting involved in insurance scams. I took her point, and held my head low in shame. I bit back mentioning that it was thanks to the scam that she and Corey and the two girls could afford a house. It was in the days before liar loans got going and they needed £15,000 for a deposit, so I helped out, and was glad to do so, although I didn't much like the house they chose. It had good high ceilings but was damp and dark. Then Corey tore a ligament in his thigh and his dreams of being an international rugby player, Samoa's pride, were thwarted. Polly's principles kept her at the coalface as a teacher, rather than moving on and up through the educational career structure into administration, where she belonged, and a more comfortable life. They needed me, and as always I obliged.

Had they shown gratitude, now that would have been a surprise. Both girls seem to have picked up Karl's attitude to me, and feel it is their inalienable right not to take me seriously, to see my success as a fluke, a symbol of the cultural degradation of our times. I have been found out. Many a lady writer feels that at the best of times: that she will be unveiled any minute as an impostor. That the review will one day appear: 'Why have we been taking this writer so seriously? She can't write for toffee.' And that will be that. It is not a worry that plagues men. On the whole, women who get bad reviews crawl under the blankets and hide: men writers roar and go round and beat up the critic, or at least think about it.

After Edgar there was Julian from what was then Czechoslovakia in my bed. He was a very family-oriented man, which I like, but which meant his brother and then his mother and sisters were living with me, and he was not, and no-one was able to work until they had visas. Which took ages. And Karl got cancer of the liver, which is terminal, and very quick. I went to see him in hospital and we agreed we should never have parted. Everything had gone wrong for us both since we did.

I should never have bought him out of his half of the house, he said. It was morally his and I should have acknowledged it.

'You made me angry,' I said. 'You and the Dumpling.'

'She was a very pretty girl,' he said. 'I like women with something to get hold of.'

'How very old-fashioned of you,' I said.

'Always ready with a smart reply,' he lamented. 'If you'd been faithful to me, I'd have been faithful to you.'

And then the Czech family finally left, and I lost interest in writing and the money dried up, but I couldn't get used to not spending it. And the credit was infinite as the offers of loans and mortgages flooded in, and the store cards and credit cards, and everyone else had money and jobs and student loans, and a million jobs were created for civil servants to micro-manage our lives, and I began to think that perhaps Edgar was right. They were purposefully stripping us of initiative, individuality and common sense – in our best interest of course – so we turned into new versions of the old Soviet citizen, controlled by our debts rather than by the KGB, dependent on the State's mercy, all thinking the same convenient thoughts, sharing the same ethics, the private sector withered away, the village fête cancelled because of Health and Safety, the churches emptied, and the shopping malls filled, and then it all stopped.

Some say this is no accident: some ask, did Prosperity fall or was it pushed? Some say this is just the next stage in the game, to crowd out private enterprise and make us servants of the State. The first bank that went belly up had its feet pushed out from under it. Some know better than to say so aloud. I have a feeling those young people in the room upstairs are saying it and it is not safe, and this is my house, and that means I am not safe either. Except I am so old it's really not going to matter to anyone what I think. I shall just nod and shrug and stare and claim Alzheimer's.

The Shock, in October 2008, and after that the Crunch, and the Crisis, and the phoney Recovery, like the phoney war – and then the Squeeze and Inflation and now the Bite, and the rest is history, or the future – and Henry, misbegotten Henry, from the loins of Karl and the Dumpling's womb, who killed his mother by being born, for which I suppose I should be grateful, is at the door, and history begins to form again as future.

For Henry too, like Amy, Florrie's daughter, comes at me out of the past, karma, come to take stock and be revenged. Amy to claim Ethan as her own, because I failed to look after Liddy and Florrie when they needed me. And Henry, for all I know, has some mad feeling that he is morally entitled to this house, which was his father's in the beginning. Then he has another think coming, is all I can say. But I feel quite panicky. What is he doing here? How can he know where I live? Except of course, I realize, he is Polly's half-brother and Venetia's too, only not directly connected to her by the flow of genes, and I have managed to deny his existence all this time. I will call Polly, to find out if there is anything I need to know.

Amos is coming into my room.

'Still scribbling away, Gran?' he asks. *Scribble, scribble, Mr Gibbon!* That's no way to endear himself to me. I sigh and put my work aside.

'Well?'

A Strange Request

'Gran, could we ask you a favour?'

Well, that's something. I am not so irrelevant to their lives that they don't feel obliged to ask. What can it be? To stay the night? Why don't they all crowd into the little house in Hunter's Alley, and foment rebellion as much as they like, without getting me into trouble, I ask him.

'Well, actually, Gran, Hunter's Alley is under surveillance, so it's not all that much use to us.'

'Why is Hunter's Alley under surveillance?'

'Because it's so central. Here we're practically in the suburbs, but not so far petrol is a problem.'

It sounds so reasonable but is obviously mad. Perhaps he's schizophrenic – the Knight's Move in chess. A sideways move between a thought and its conclusion, that at first convinces but not for long. Schizophrenics can drive their therapists nuts.

'What we wanted to do, Gran, was break through upstairs into No. 5 and settle in there, then we wouldn't disturb you.'

'How very thoughtful of you. Through the window you broke? Wouldn't the people at No. 5 be the ones to ask?'

'No, No. 5's been repossessed. They're not there. But Amy's got the plans from the Neighbourhood Watch: there'll be no structural damage; we can put it back when we're finished so no-one knows.

We just need a place to store posters and stuff. It would be safer for you to have it next door, not here.'

I am baffled.

'How do you know it's been repossessed?' is all I can think of to say.

'Uncle Henry has it on his list.'

Uncle Henry? What has been going on behind my back? I suppose it is technically true. Henry is Polly's half-brother. But no blood relation of Amos. Why should he know him as Uncle? Why does he know him at all?

'What list?'

Redpeace, it transpires, are the ones going round putting up the NUG Scum posters. Uncle Henry is a leading activist. More, they don't just want to break through my wall, they mean to unseal the back door of No. 5 and go in and out from No. 7 Rothwell Street, which backs on to the Crescent, unsealing that door too. They can get in and out across the communal garden, shielded by trees and beanpoles, without being seen.

I tell Amos not to be so infantile. What kind of games were they playing? This was not Munchkinland and no time in history to be messing about with politics and annoying authorities. A lot of people have been vanishing from the streets lately. I did not believe this: it is only rumour, but I am not averse to adding to rumour. Amos just smiles in a way that makes me think he can read my mind. I am beginning to feel cold. This is not safe. Perhaps the rumours are true?

'Why are you telling me?'

'Because you'd hear us and we don't want you running off telling anyone.'

'I won't tell anyone,' I say, 'I'm family, after all. I think you're mad but I won't tell. I suppose the camera didn't get you coming in but would catch you coming out?'

'That's about the size of it,' says Amos. 'You're not daft. We can get a lot of your nice stuff through to next door too, so if the bailiffs come back there'll be nothing of much value.'

That thought had occurred to me too.

There were already hammering and crumbling noises from upstairs. All the safe structures one took for granted were going. They had not bothered to get my assent. They were going ahead anyway. The hermit crabs were no longer solitary, but clustering.

I had a feeling if I did object, if I stood in their way, they would simply step on me and crush me, eliminate me. But that is a feeling the old do tend to have about the young at the best of times. I dismissed it. They were family. They would look after me. Amy, too, by virtue of being 'with' Ethan. Even Henry, if my life was at stake. As for the two girls, they were optional extras, as girls so often are, and did not seem the murderous kind.

Carmageddon

Talking about the universal desire to get rid of the old, other than (sometimes) one's nearest and dearest, they being such a reminder of mortality, I remember once sitting with the great and the good on a censorship panel in the late nineties. (We were not meant to call it Censorship but Classification.) A 'graphically violent driving-oriented video game' called *Carmageddon* was under review. Should it be banned, modified, given the go-ahead? There was worry at the time, it being one of the first times a game had no traditional moral values at all. If you ran down little old ladies as they crossed the road, you were rewarded. If you swerved to avoid them, you were punished. It was the triumph of amoral relativism: now, it seemed, we were all to be on Sauron's side. If you got the little old ladies there was red blood spattered everywhere: their walking sticks flew in the air. Odd that it was always old ladies, not old men, or not perhaps all that odd because it was males who devised these games, and in those days, mostly males who played them.

Unlike anyone else on the panel I played video games myself, and was as it happened particularly fond of *Carmageddon*. Amos, I think it was, had found me a pirated early copy. I failed to declare an interest; I was ashamed, just as one is ashamed in literary company to be seen reading rubbishy airport novels. But I had noticed since starting to play this absorbing game that I too, when driving, had to rein in an impulse to swerve into little old ladies. If it affected me in my female middle age like this it seemed a very dangerous toy to put in the hands of young joyriders. Still I did not speak. As it happened, the *Carmageddon* people pre-emptively censored it themselves for the UK market; they just wanted to get on with selling, and for a time replaced the LOLs by aliens with green blood. It was not nearly so much fun to play. Now I am a LOL myself I take great care crossing a road; karma waits around the corner for all of us.

For Cynthia, who took the flight to Turkey, for Terry who took my virginity, for me, who took my sister Fay's beloved, karma waits.

For the young ones I am not so sure. They don't believe in karma, so perhaps it doesn't happen. There are no elements in their self-definition that relate back to any earlier time: to the unchancy gods of the Greeks or the Romans; or the Christian God who can see into your heart; or the Buddha with his renunciation of worldly pleasures, or the Muslims, with their horror of female flesh. So many of the young see themselves as born in year zero: they have no gods, not even an Intelligent Designer. They live on a ball of rock hurtling through space and that's it. To be a good young human being now is not to play truant, to report to your teachers if your parents smoke or drink in your presence, to reproach them for anti-social thinking and to insist they sort the waste for the sake of Gaia. So dull!

The ethics of the new young come not from a vague mishmash of ancient beliefs but are dictated by the State: how can they not be? And perhaps they should be, considering how suddenly and drastically they were driven from the trashy paradise we'd prepared for them.

Amos and Ethan, Amy and Henry, two bright girls and three

more young men I didn't get to see clearly, all in the business of avoiding CiviCams, breaking through my wall, bringing in contraband 'stuff', fighting the system: in the light of NUG, in the light of the bailiffs, in the light of the family history, it was hard not to be on their side.

And yet I'll swear the god of vengeance lurks, karma is waiting round the corner for all of us, young as well as old. Be prepared to jump, and fast, in the day of *Carmageddon*.

A Conversation With Polly

After Amos left, after I had promised not to tell, I called Polly, as I had to know about Henry.

'Polly,' I said, 'it's your mum.'

She was geniality itself. We exchanged pleasantries. She asked how I was; I said, well, except for knees. I asked how she was; she said she was okay, only last month's wages hadn't got through to the CiviBank. Their computer had allegedly crashed. But probably NUG didn't dare print any more money. She'd had a nasty fright on the Underground when some madman tried to push her on the tracks, and might have succeeded only a brave, kind woman had pulled her back. In Polly's view of the universe, men are always trying to destroy you and women the ones who rescue you, and she loves to dramatize. And Corey had been darning his socks when there was a power cut and he swore and ranted, so like a man.

'But he is a man,' I was tempted to say but held my tongue.

He was very much a man, rugger players from Samoa tend to be, muscled where others have fat, skin light brown and polished, a square chin, an amiable demeanour, a delight to behold. All he wanted to be was a man, and all Polly wanted him to be, crudely, was a woman with a penis. It wasn't that she hated men so much as that she disapproved of them, and regarded them as second-class citizens in need of training.

It was as well, I thought, that she had had stepdaughters, not sons.

I told her Amos was staying with me for a couple of days.

'What does he want?' she asked.

'I don't know why you're all so mean about Amos,' I said.

'Because he's always been your favourite grandchild,' she said. 'You hardly take any notice of Steffie and Rosie.'

One thing you can say for Polly is she comes straight to the point. She starts with geniality and affection, and then suddenly she remembers a whole host of resentments. She was the same when she was a baby. I'd go into the nursery first thing in the morning and there she'd be, standing in her cot, all beams and smiles and a delight, then her face would pucker and she'd begin to scowl and stick out her chin and look furious, as if she'd start an argument if only she had the words. If she caught sight of Karl the scowl would evaporate, and the smile reappear. But I loved her to bits and still do, and when I die she will be sorry, and feel bad if we have words, so I really try not to. I forgive her in advance.

I am rather relieved that she has brought up the names of the children. I get them muddled or even forget. They are not proper names, just evidence of an unhealthy desire on the part of the parents to keep their children as pets. Who can grow up to be an Archbishop or the Prime Minister if called Rosie, or Steffie? But these were the names they came with, I suppose. Polly is bad enough: I wanted Hypatia, but was pressured by Karl, who liked his women 'pregnant at the sink and up to their elbows in soap-suds' as he once said to me – a remark that prompted me to go to my first feminist consciousness-raising group – to call her Polly. She never liked the name. I daresay 'Rosie and Steffie' could not be changed without upsetting the children.

'Polly,' I say pathetically. 'I'm over eighty, my legs are bad, and why don't you all come over and visit me?'

'Because we can't afford taxis and there's no fuel for the car, Gran,' she says.

I don't know why she calls me Gran. I'm her mother. Well, I do know. She wants me in my place as a little old lady.

She will never forgive me for not taking Karl back when I could have. Should have. Wanted to, but there was Edgar in the way by then. And I wasn't going to take on the plain dull little baby dumpling, who was obviously going to grow into the plain middle-aged man I had let into my house. Let Karl take the consequences of his actions. I had had enough.

'You should jump in a taxi and come over to us.'

Jump? Me? What planet is she on? Though that she is reluctant to accept that I am growing old is comforting. And I'm not going to say I don't have any money for taxis either, and that the bailiffs have been, because then Polly will go on and on about how badly I manage money, and how I always trusted men whom no women in their right minds would have trusted. How can I call myself a feminist, etc.

I can at least trust Amos not to tell the family about the bailiffs: I wouldn't even have to remind him: he will understand the subtleties of the situation. That is probably why he is my favourite grandchild, even though I suspect him of being a conman, a terrorist and a madman, and even now he is dismantling my house.

I will be really sorry to leave this life, as soon I must. It is so full of wonder, as well as horror. A surprise round every corner and the pace is hotting up. The GSITS is keeping very busy. The GSITS – the Great Screenwriter in the Sky – appeared in one of my early novels, *The Rules of Life*. He's the one who got the commission to script the story of the world. He is a B-picture writer by nature, that's the trouble: his sights are set low. If he gets into a plot difficulty he does something spectacular and thoroughly unlikely: sinks the *Titanic*, explodes Krakatoa, kills Kennedy, thinks up Watergate, pulls down the Berlin Wall, has Carla Bruni marry Sarkozy, and the GSITS's latest plot extravaganza is to bring capitalism tumbling down by way of the Fourth Estate – after the French revolution, Edmund Burke, looking up at the Press Gallery of the House of Commons, said, 'Yonder sits the Fourth Estate, and they are more important than them all.' I think the GSITS is on cocaine; he is so feverish at the moment. And dreadfully and dangerously easily bored. But I have my private concerns to get on with.

I casually bring my conversation with Polly round to the subject of Henry.

'You know that baby the Dumpling had, Polly –'

'Don't call her that, please, Mum. Her name was Claire. You mean my half-brother Henry, Claire and Karl's child?'

'Okay, that Henry. Do you see him? I mean, socially?'

'Of course we do.'

'Why has no-one seen fit to mention it?'

'Because you'd have hysterics, Mum. No-one wants to upset you.'

Like hell they don't. They don't think twice about keeping secrets. How can I protect them if they don't tell the truth? And the secrets always come out in the end and I am always upset. Surely they know that by now.

I ask if Venetia sees him too.

'Of course. Why wouldn't she? He's family.'

'Not by any wish of mine,' I say. 'And he isn't a blood relative of hers. I suppose you have to see him out of politeness but I don't see why Venetia has to.'

'Mum. He's a nice guy. He's Karl's child. All this stuff about blood and genes, it's sheer biologism. You've got to get over it.'

Polly goes on about biologism a lot. I am guilty of it apparently. It is the doctrine that men and women were born different, that they have biological differences that cannot be cured by Nurofen or social conditioning. It is why she goes to such lengths to turn Corey into a woman (darning, for heaven's sake!). I grant you our lot did our best to turn ourselves into men, with our bovver boots, dungarees, aversion to lipstick and refusal to smile (as placatory to men) but once we had our equal rights and equal(ish) pay, we returned to high heels pretty quickly. No amount of evidence that male and female brains are wired differently will convince her. In the beginning, according to Polly, we were all born equal in intelligence, looks, health, charm, colour and gender. If we end up unequal then it is somebody's fault. Society, or poverty, or lack of education, or racist taunts, or male oppression. In the nature/nurture debate, where most sway between the 60/40 ranges, my daughter goes for 99 per cent nurture, 1 per cent nature. She is in fact denying me.

But she may even be right. Corey makes a better mother than she ever did. A whole race of new young men coo over their babies, cook, cry, splash themselves with perfume. They are more female than their teachers, who are all tough women (male teachers may be tarred by the paedophile tendency) like Polly, who shaves her head and looks like Sigourney Weaver in an *Alien* film. Perhaps the new men are trying to restore a natural balance, like Cynthia feeling she was entitled to a good time because she had just been through a bad. And we know how that ended.

'This Henry,' I say. 'Does he come round to yours?'

'Sometimes,' she says. 'But sometimes he goes over to Venetia and Victor for one of their Friday-night things, and we go too and see him there.'

'That must be quite a crowd,' I say.

'It is,' she says. 'It's fun. And you get real chicken and not National, and real coffee, not roast parsnip or whatever it is.'

'I've never seen him when I've been over there,' I say. Not that I've been there much lately. Venetia tends to come down to me.

'Well, of course you wouldn't,' says Polly. 'Why would anyone in their senses ask him and you at the same time? You won't acknowledge his existence any more than he acknowledges yours. You refused to take him in when he was a motherless child, and you could have done, but you wanted your sex life with the fascist Edgar, so Karl his father got liver cancer and died. So he's not too fond of you.'

'That is the most extraordinary way of looking at things,' I say. 'Perhaps you ought to write fiction. It's in the family, you know.'

There is a crashing noise from upstairs and then silence. They have broken through.

'What is that noise?' asks Polly. 'Are you all right, Mum?'

'I'm fine,' I say. 'Just some people next door doing building work.'

'Lucky old them,' says Polly. She asks why the matter of Henry has come up at all. Has Amos been making mischief?

I say as casually as I can that Amos referred to an Uncle Henry, and I didn't think it could be her father's by-blow because surely he was living somewhere in the Irish boondocks, the Dumpling's mother having taken him in to rear him.

'He is a man, Mother. He is fourteen years younger than I am. He is not a by-blow, my father and Claire were legally married.'

I ask if he has large feet. I do wish the past was over, but it never seems to be.

She is baffled. I don't pursue the matter.

Three years back, she tells me, Henry lost his job in the private sector – he was some kind of pig farmer (that figures): but agricultural land is now of course communally owned and 'efficiently' farmed. He'd normally just have stayed in his old job and been paid by the State, instead of pocketing profits, but he'd run out on his own community, somehow managed to avoid Job Direction, and come to London.

'So now what? He's scrounging off you? He won't be able to get a job. He'll be on their lists.'

'Victor found him a place in the NIFE Registry,' said Polly.

So the by-blow of the Dumpling survived to really get his feet under my family's table. And now he is in my house. I am indifferent to his good looks. He used his mother to steal my husband Karl for a father. And for all I know Karl conducted much of his affair with the Dumpling in that very same room upstairs, which was my and Karl's marital bedroom, when I was off on some book tour in some other country, trusting. I feel the piercing pain in the heart that is physical jealousy, and which I can see I will never grow out of, and which I used to think would age me early and finish me off but no such luck. I keep my voice even.

'But that's pure and simple nepotism,' I declared on the way. 'Good Lord, this government. And nobody notices!'

'No more than they noticed Ethan getting to be a NIFE driver, which is one of the cushiest jobs going. Nobody quarrels with Victor, he's top dog at NIFE.'

'Venetia quarrels with Victor,' I said.

'That's what wives do,' said Polly. 'That's why I never did anything so stupid as to marry.' She quarrels with Corey all the time, but never mind.

'And I don't know why you describe Victor as a top man: he's a scientist not a politician.'

'Mum. NUG doesn't have politicians, it has management. No-one trusts politicians after the mess they made of things. Victor gave up science ages back and is now NUG Manager, Grade 1, with special responsibility for nutrition.'

'But that's like being in the Cabinet. You're joking.'

'Mum, Venetia lives like a queen up there. Roast chicken, real coffee; they have a generator and their own power supply. There's a crew from CiviFilm coming to take pictures of the family next Friday. There are security men everywhere, though, which is horrid. The houses on either side were taken down last week. There's plaster dust everywhere. Hasn't she told you?'

No, she hasn't. She only told me she was thinking of converting to Judaism. Venetia, my little atheist! I wonder what's really going on? Perhaps it's some kind of bid for family harmony, respectability? I can see my side of the family must be something of an embarrassment to Victor if he's set on political ascendancy. Well, even Bush had a brother. So does Obama.

Perhaps I should have opened the door to the bailiffs? Perhaps they came with good news? An NUG Manager Grade 1 is not going to let his mother-in-law go bankrupt. But no, no, life is not that easy. That's Pollyanna thinking. But I am still brooding about the by-blow, in my house, upstairs. If he visits Victor, has a job with NIFE, and yet slaps up *NUG is scum* posters on repossessed houses for Redpeace, is he an agent provocateur? What kind of double-double agent can he be? Mind you, everyone knows that NIHE, the National Institute of Homes for Everyone, is at daggers drawn with NIFE, and everyone is on NIFE's side because at least very few of us are hungry, just bored with our food, while many of us are homeless. When it comes down to it there is a lot to be said for efficiency.

Polly says she has to get on with her marking, she has to go. She says she's glad she told me about Henry. But the more they put it off the more difficult it had become. No-one wanted to give me a heart attack; my resentment of poor Claire and Henry was bordering on the pathological, did I realize that?

'Oh I do, I do,' I say, and ask where Henry is living.

'He's squashing in with Ethan and Mervyn in Hunter's Alley,' says my daughter, 'while he waits for housing allocation. He's been there for months. I don't know how they all manage. But the girls go over there a lot. They're all over there now. They've got involved with Redpeace. Thank God they're beginning to show an interest in something other than hair-bands and make-up.'

'Well, no, Polly,' I feel like saying, 'actually they are all in my house at this very moment,' but I don't. I have learned some prudence over the years, and that sometimes it is better to think before one speaks, even – well perhaps especially – when family is involved. This is just such a moment. My house is bigger than Hunter's Alley and at this very moment is getting even bigger, extending into No. 5, and perhaps the girls just came over here on impulse and forgot to tell their mother. But I think not. Because the pretty dusky girls at the door are of course my own grandchildren, Rosie and Steffie, and I had failed to recognize them. Polly must be quite right; I do neglect them. Mind you, they had been wearing hoods and the body language of today's bouncy adolescent girls does not reflect that of their elders. Even so. But at least I had remembered their names without difficulty.

Rosie and Steffie, now joined with their cousins in an activist cell, planning to evade CiviCams (which is a criminal offence – as,

I may say, is moving personal valuables to the detriment of the community interest) to race unseen through the potato field, and out into Rothwell Street, and no doubt use the same route to get in again, carrying with them, what? – forbidden posters, and leaflets today, leading to peroxide and fertilizer tomorrow – as NUG reminds us, in the same way governments in the past assured us, and equally falsely, that marijuana use today inevitably leads to heroin use tomorrow. All that sounds pretty active to me, the kind of activity governments since time began have not liked. I am too old for all this. Of course I am on my family's side. Of course NUG is an atrocious government and protest is necessary. I just wish they'd go away and organize it somewhere else. Revolutionary zeal still has power to move me and play me Pete Seeger on YouTube and I am flooded with nostalgia –

> I dreamed I saw Joe Hill last night,
> Alive as you or me,
> Says I, 'But Joe, you're ten years dead,'
> 'I never died,' says he…
> 'Takes more than guns to kill a man,'
> Says Joe, 'I didn't die.'
> And standing there as big as life
> And smiling with his eyes
> Joe says, 'What they forgot to kill
> Went on to organize…
> From San Diego up to Maine,
> In every mine and mill,
> Where workers strike and organize,'
> Says he, 'You'll find Joe Hill.'

I am almost in tears at the memory of youthful togetherness we found in the Labour Movement of my teenage in the fifties. Yes, but even so, this is my nice home and I have a few years left and I would like to save what I can. I don't want Redpeace damaging my prospects. If I'd bought No. 14 Hunter's Alley instead of No. 11 there was an extra room and they could have had their meetings there, but No. 11 was £75,000 cheaper and my income was dropping – even I had noticed that. Royalties were coming in with a nought missing.

But it would be good to have the valuables out of the room upstairs; the Paula Rego and the possible Brancusi and the first editions. So much for Joe Hill and the Labour Movement.

That room upstairs served as my and Karl's marital bedroom and many were the acts of joyous congress that took place there, and many the rows and reconciliations. He filled the whole house with stock from his antique shop, to my outrage, so I could hardly move through the rooms for stripped pine and old oak, and wood-worm and the smell of woodworm treatments filled the air, and I worried about little Polly breathing the stuff in, though Karl pooh-poohed the idea. We are all much more health-conscious now.

And the stairs, on which Amos and I had taken refuge. Early on in the marriage I moved twelve aspidistra plants in their green Victorian plant holders, which sat two per stair so Polly was always tumbling down them, and put them outside the house, in a row along the iron railings, to wait for Karl to take them away. It was a public demonstration of my despair. But all Karl did was put them in our Volvo and take them round to his shop, and put his mattress on the floor and live there with them until I begged him to come home. And he sold the aspidistras to his best and prettiest lady clients and reported how he'd delivered them personally and how, unlike tasteless me, they had loved and appreciated their charm and worth. So I didn't try that again.

In the back garden, where now Redpeace was constructing their rat run, Karl used to keep a chemical bleaching tank for pine furniture – we had grown the prettiest clematis, a Daniel Deronda, over the tank to disguise it, and it was covered by a safety mesh, but one night a cat jumped in and the mesh broke and the next morning Karl pulled the poor creature out; it looked like a dying rat, but Karl took it round to the vet, and fetched it back two days later, looking splendidly healthy, and parasite free, pumped full of antibiotics and oestrogens. And we set the creature free and she presumably went home and no-one would ever know the adventures she had had, other than to say, perhaps, 'My, Kitty's looking good! And her fleas have gone! Wherever she disappeared to, it was good for her!' That sticks in my mind. So much goes on behind our backs we never get to know.

The antique business had not begun when I first moved into that bedroom. I was thirty, and Venetia was seven. Karl was an artist, and this was his studio and there was a couch he slept on. When I got pregnant with Polly he moved his easel out and put it up in the attic, along with some very doomy paintings by his previous wife, which had heretofore lined the room. She had gone mad ('No wonder!' I would screech, during our rows) and was confined to a mental institution; he was in the process of divorcing her when we met.

Just my luck, the times convulsing as they currently are, if that previous wife turns out to have had a child by Karl he forgot to mention and it just so happens she or he is now also a member of Redpeace. Political agitation is in Karl's blood. Look at Henry; at Amos; Steffie and Rosie, one generation down, have caught it. Romantic radical impulse may run through my veins, but it doesn't extend to action. I blame Karl, but I think he would have told me. He loved me, at least for the time being.

He moved his easel out with some ceremony, and said he had decided to give up art and be a married man and concentrate on being a stepfather to Venetia and father to the coming baby. And I was so impressed and pleased and thought, He really loves me! And he has not picked up a brush in ages anyhow, just filled the bedroom with dustsheets and the smell of oil paint and turps and on the floor old stiff hog brushes in cloudy jam jars, and now there will be room for a proper bed, and me as a fixture and true love triumphs, and all our troubles are over for ever. Instead of thinking, as I should have, Uh oh, before long he will blame me for stopping him painting. Which was what happened in the end. He said early on a man couldn't be an artist and a family man and instead of saying what nonsense, of course you can, I took his word for it and believed it; I was a very idle thinker in those days, and if anyone said anything definite enough, I believed them, and besides I loved him and thought everything he said was wise and somehow final. I fear I still love him, even though he's dead and gone, and died in circumstances that still make me wince with pain, in the arms of another, subsequent version of Dumpling I didn't know about. Though I was with Julian by then. How can I blame him?

But now is now and there is the sound of moving furniture upstairs and from the ground floor next door the sound of creaks and bangs which make me think the back door is being freed. Amos said that Amy had the Neighbourhood Watch plans. How does she come to have these? Is she perhaps like some old Marxist and practising entryism? When you join the movement you want to subvert? Unless she is an NUG spy and practising a double bluff and checking out Redpeace? In which case I must warn Amos. But he must have thought that out for himself. And until I know more I am just going to say nothing, stay in bed and write, warn nobody, not even suggest to Polly that her children are in bad company. Well, when were one's children ever not?

What Is Going On?

I am beginning to get a fair idea of what is going on. It concerns National Meat Loaf, the very stuff Amos and I were eating, along with the last of the tomatoes from my window box, when the first surprise knock on the front door came, and made us dive for the safety of the stairs. And it concerns NIFE.

Amos is an opportunistic fellow; I do not think he had any of this planned. I think the knock on the door came as much of a surprise to him as it did to me. But he knew once the bailiffs, or secret police, or whoever they were had gone, that there was a window of opportunity, that the CiviCams on the street were out of action – no doubt the bailiffs had reported it – and seized the opportunity to host a Redpeace meeting. The Neighbourhood Watch requires prior notification of any private gathering of six or more people, with names and ID scans – all the pubs have gone out of business, most of the café chains have gone; no custom and no coffee – so spontaneous gatherings are rare. Former town halls have been converted to CiviGet-Together Centres, and they're safe and well regulated, as NUG keeps telling us, but they're too gloomy and shadowy for comfort, haunted by the ghosts of dead aldermen and their pinchpenny ways. Mind you, pinchpenny is back in fashion.

Redpeace is not a banned organization – NUG 'favours free speech' – but I did look up the Redpeace website the other day and found it simply wasn't there. There was just a 'this page is unavailable' message. Thinking back, I was pretty sure there had been nothing particularly inflammatory there. Something boring about family values – that's okay; NUG is pro-family, so long as the children are in school for most of their waking hours, and not overly influenced by their parents – and a more entertaining article about the theoretical right or otherwise of parents, sexually abused themselves as children, to be cloned and rear themselves into adulthood, thus putting right what has been spoiled by the father. Cloning stays a fairly contentious issue with the public, but NUG stays quiet on the subject. Speculation has it that livestock cloning was well under way during the Hunger – the alarming period when food prices rose so dramatically – but went wrong within the year and had to be halted. As had initially been feared, cloned animals – even once researchers were past the initial problems of inflammation of the brain and spinal cord disorders, overly large foetuses and placental problems which put the host as risk – turned out to have weak immune systems. Some new virus or bacteria was bound to come along and thrive, wiping out not only cloned animals but infecting the non-genetic stock. Which was what happened. Did Redpeace have some special interest? And NUG some new sensitivity? Was that why the webpage had been pulled? I must ask Amos, or such of the gathering upstairs who eventually saw fit to acknowledge my existence.

And talking about entryism, infiltration, what about Henry? Was it anything to do with Victor, initially working in stem-cell biotechnology, and now risen high in Food Excellence (slogan: *Devoting Resources To Your Nutritional Satisfaction*)? If Henry had been thrown out of a non-GM pig farm to make way for newer breeding methods, he was hardly likely to be a Victor fan. Yet he had used Victor's influence to worm himself into a job at NIFE. But then so had Ethan.

I knew that these days there was little love lost between Victor and Amos. Apart from anything else, having a jailbird stepson would be something of an embarrassment for Victor. Perhaps Victor was seeking revenge on Amos, and that was why the Redpeace website had been closed down. But this was surely paranoia running wild?

All the same I wish I knew at least something about the art school student who imposed himself on my innocent daughter and begat Amos. God knows what sort of villainy runs in the blood the other side of the looks and charm. Perhaps one day the father will turn up and be yet another of life's little surprises? Of course the father may not have been a student at all – Venetia implied it and I assumed it. Underneath an angular Paolozzi seemed fitting for an art student, but for all I knew it could have been a professor, or even an art critic – though they do not usually seem of the randy hit-and-run type. Too cerebral. Venetia, when she was eighteen, had translucency and innocence enough to attract any villain. She has grown quite substantial as she's grown older, and looks handsome enough but no longer breathtaking, and oozes respectability. Just right for a senior politician. He chose well.

Pity about her family, Victor may have thought, but love conquered all.

To fiction! There is too much solid text here for comfort.

Victor Getting Dressed

'Victor,' cries Venetia in alarm, 'what is all this about a show in Cork Street in March? At the Medici Gallery? I'm not an A-list painter. I've never pretended I am.'

'You only think that because your stepfather undermined your confidence,' says Victor. 'Of course you are. I've always had faith in you.'

'But no-one at the Medici has seen what I do.'

'That's neither here nor there,' says Victor. 'CiviArt thinks well of you and the Medici trusts their judgment. NUG is a great supporter of the arts.'

Venetia is washing her hair. Hers is one of the few houses down the street the water cuts seem to have missed, so although it's Saturday morning she can turn on the taps and get a pleasant, dependable flow of the precious stuff from both hot and cold taps. Not that there are many houses left in the road. This, indeed, is why she is washing her hair: the air is full of lime plaster and dust from demolished homes all around, and it wreaks havoc with hair and skin, no matter how assiduously the new maids wield the vacuum cleaners. Victor strides up and down the master bedroom and in and out of the bathroom, smiling and reassuring, looking through his recently replenished wardrobes. The tailors came to him; he did not go to the tailors. Times have changed.

He is not the man she married, she thinks, there is something wolfish about the smile, which she never noticed before. Or perhaps she just never looked, she took him so much for granted. But he admires her bum as she bends over the washbasin and gives it a little pinch. Victor loves her, she thinks, which is just as well, for men who become successful in middle age are known to decide they deserve a younger, prettier, sexier wife than they already have, and pension the old one off.

'But Victor, NUG never used to be a supporter of the arts,' she protests. 'When the Arts Council fired me the general feeling was that at a time of national emergency anyone with artistic aspirations was positively antisocial.'

'Remind me again of the name of the guy who fired you,' says Victor, as if casually, but Venetia found herself lying, saying she thought the poor man had died of a heart attack. He hadn't liked firing her any more than she had liked being fired.

'Saves a bullet,' says Victor, and of course it's a joke, but Venetia finds herself slightly shivery, and is glad of a warm towel to wrap around her wet hair. Even their towel rails stay heated all day.

'It's thanks to me, Venetia,' says Victor, 'that the Board is now persuaded that at a time like this it is particularly important to foster creativity in the community.'

'I bet you made a really good speech, darling,' says Venetia.

'I did,' he says. 'I've really become quite something of an orator.'

'Doesn't surprise me, darling,' says Venetia and then, 'but it may be a little difficult to get an exhibition together by next March.'

'Sorry, but that's the timetable,' says Victor. 'The launch of the New Venice, Land of the Arts initiative. If it's a problem we can bring in some apprentices to help you get things done. We thought we'd go with Venetia, Queen of the New Venice, or something like that. How does that strike you?'

'Sounds good to me,' says Venetia.

She hardly knows what else to say. Does she want to be a famous painter or a good painter? What is a good painter anyway? What would Karl do? She needs time to think. She used to talk things like this over with Victor, but he's someone else now. Her mother would complicate things even more; the boys aren't interested; talking to Polly about the new Victor seems slightly dangerous, for some reason; and talking to her friends would be construed as disloyal. She doesn't know why she feels she has to be very, very careful but she does.

'How are things looking for next Friday?' asks Victor.

'Same as usual,' says Venetia, surprised. 'Chicken.'

'Because we have a camera crew coming in to take a few pictures,' says Victor. 'Perhaps better if we don't have Amos around. Henry's fine: man of the soil, nothing elitist about this typical family. Don't get too big a chicken; we're a people family like Obama's, and food is short. We can have a second supper afterwards.'

'Okay,' says Venetia.

It feels safer not to raise difficulties. For some reason she remembers that she has always meant to read the autobiography of Svetlana, Stalin's daughter. Perhaps she will be able to get round to it finally, if the house is filling up with servants and apprentices, all determined they will do the chores. What happened to Svetlana's mother? Didn't she commit suicide? At least Victor doesn't have a moustache.

Victor decides on a dark brown silk shirt with high collar, which suits him well but makes him look a little military. He's standing straighter and taller. He used to have a soft kind of jaw, but it's changed, and become squarer and harder. She realizes she really fancies him, which is just as well, since he's bearing her down upon the bed, wet hair and all. He's so cheerful.

'When I am King, diddle diddle,' he says, diddling away, 'you shall be Queen.'

The car comes to collect Victor and take him to NIFE. Civi-Secure men salute him. Venetia, waving him goodbye, sees that they are all young and wear smart brown denim shirts. She calls up her sister Polly and asks her to drop by for a coffee. Polly says she's waiting for the girls to come back. She's tried to get them on their mobiles and can't get through. She really ought to stay home to supervise their homework, and anyway she hasn't got money for a taxi, and Venetia laughs and says she'll send a car. Polly agrees to come; it's fun riding in the central lanes. One of the best schemes devised by NUG, part of their Nation, Back to Work! initiative, was building the lanes: there's always a sense of excitement about them, of a nation visibly about important business.

It's tricky finding a quiet spot for the sisters to have coffee. The house is having two extensions built, one on either side, and the existing interior is being renovated, which means plasterers need to wander round putting up classical friezes and plumbers installing gold taps and fittings in the bathrooms, so wherever they go there is company. The minute Victor left the builders moved in: they are very polite but are working to plans signed by NUG's chief architect and initialled by Victor. They showed them to her when she said she didn't want the two front rooms made into one and chandeliers installed – it didn't suit the house at all, but she could see it was going to end up less like a home and more like a palace anyway, so she didn't argue.

The kitchen and dining room are being left as they were, which seems a bit strange. Though the three neat, quiet, pretty maids, who speak no English, are busy doing out the backs of the cupboards, and cleaning out the knife drawer when Venetia and Polly try to settle in the kitchen.

'Bet you've never cleaned out a knife drawer in your life,' says Polly.

'Well, I am an artist,' says Venetia. 'Tidiness isn't my forte. But I am a good cook. Mum would come over and do it sometimes, when the children were small, and she'd clean and wash behind the taps, that kind of thing. And when the children came in from school, they'd notice and say, "Gran's here! Where is she?"'

'I'm a bad cook,' says Polly, 'but always tidy. It's odd how the genes go.'

'Don't start all the gene stuff,' says Venetia. 'You're as bad as Mum. Actually, an initiative came round the school the other day saying, I quote, "In the nature/nurture debate proper attention must be given to the heredity factor in academic response." There's a lot of backtracking going on there. Some of the things NUG is doing these days are really quite worrying. Surely we are all born equal!'

Venetia moves her head in the direction of the maids to remind Polly that they can be overheard, but Polly laughs and says they don't speak English anyway and what she is saying is hardly treasonable. On Polly's insistence they decide to ignore the maids and sit in the kitchen, and Polly raves about the quality of the coffee and Venetia says she'll give some to Polly before she goes; the CiviStore has been round to deliver.

'That's a new departure,' says Polly.

'Victor doesn't want me going out until a proper security routine has been worked out,' says Venetia. 'So they come to me. I just make out a list of what I want. I'm sure if I put a Stanley Spencer painting, six feet by four feet, that would come round too.'

'But where would it have come from?' asks Polly.

'Don't ask,' says Venetia and fortunately there is a cry and a crash from upstairs and the maids run off to put right whatever needs putting right. They move as a little unit, smooth and quiet.

'A prisoner in your own home,' says Polly and laughs, but the laugh fades away and they look at each other.

'This filming on Friday night,' says Venetia. 'I think they want to get it established how simply and traditionally we live. As soon as that's done what's the betting the kitchen will be moved into one of the extensions and equipped to serve banquets, suitable for the CEO of NIFE and possibly even CEO of the Arts at NUG headquarters.'

'Things are moving fast,' said Polly. 'Feels like 2010 all over again.'

That was the year Europe began to fall apart, and the idea of the nation state to reassert itself – not that it had ever really gone away.

'I don't know that I'm cut out for a political hostess,' says Venetia. 'I'm an artist. All I want to do is paint pictures. And maybe I'm not even very good at that. Daddy was probably right.'

'Daddy always had great faith in you,' says Polly. 'He just hated acrylics and you were so stubborn about that. Anyway it's too late now. I should just enjoy. And Victor's hardly going to make you wear ball gowns and diamond tiaras. You can start a fashion in CiviKindness chic. '

'I'm not sure about that,' says Venetia darkly. Victor, who in the days of Cancer Cure had given her toasted-sandwich machines, food blenders and such for her birthdays, had last year given her a ruby necklace.

What Polly doesn't understand, she says, is why NUG, usually so low key, positively reclusive, on the subject of its top people, has suddenly decided to make Victor some kind of celebrity. Why, when it maintains it's just an efficient, well-trained management team put in to run the nation – quite unlike the greedy, self-seeking politicians of yore, with their manic squabbling – until such time as the depression bottoms out and elections become a viable option once again, are NUG suddenly putting Victor on TV? Couldn't they have chosen a woman?

Venetia says she thinks it's because NUG has decided it needs a public face – it's too somehow amorphous for the public to grasp – and Victor fits the bill. He's loyal, presentable, a bit gullible, a good family man, with a scientific background yet religiously observant but in no way extremist –

'Without ambition,' says Polly, 'but dedicated to the public good. Living simply and quietly in the same house where he raised his family, with his lovely wife Venetia, most talented artist in the land – seen here at Shabbat, all his family gathered round –'

'That's about it,' says Venetia, 'But not Amos. Amos is too, well, enigmatic, to fit the required picture.'

'Enigmatic is rather a good word for Amos,' says Polly. 'Not too negative, not too positive. Sort of wait and see. And you converting to Judaism too?'

Venetia looks startled. 'You're not meant to know about that.'

'Mum told me.'

'I should have known,' says Venetia. 'If it mattered any more that she kept it to herself, I wouldn't have told her. But NUG has decided secularism is counter-productive. The family that prays together stays together. And I don't mind. It's not as if I was an atheist, like you. Victor thinks it's less hypocritical if I receive instruction.'

'That's one way of looking at it,' says Polly. 'Victor is just so good at wishful thinking.'

The maids troop back in, and, after what amounts to a kind of brief choreographed curtsey to Venetia and Polly, silently continue with their cleaning. The conversation between the sisters becomes more casual. How Mum went mad when she heard about Henry, but was bound to find out some time. How Corey was fine, working unpaid for CiviSport; the girls liking art school and such good friends now with their cousins, round at Hunter's Alley all the time, neglecting their homework, but anything's better than drink or drugs. Polly had a fright in the Underground: the platform was so crowded that some male idiot lurched into her and nearly knocked her into the path of a train –

An electrician comes in with a ladder and starts to run a fine wire round the door frame and along the skirting board.

'What's that for?' asks Venetia and he shrugs and gestures that he doesn't speak English.

'He'll be bugging the place,' says Polly and they both laugh, but their laughs die away.

Venetia finds a couple of packets of coffee and gives them to her sister. On the way out they both hear the electrician saying, 'Oi, mate, pass over the other drill bits,' but neither woman remarks upon it to the other.

What's Really Going On

I deduced the above from a couple of remarks of Venetia's about converting to the Jewish faith, and of Polly's about how security was now tight at Venetia's and how the houses next door were being demolished. I rather hope I am wrong about all this. Victor, I know, adores Venetia and would love her to be Queen almost more than he would love to be King. But to be loved by a man of dubious sanity can be a dreadful thing. I hope she is not being frightened into too much acquiescence.

I am also worried, I realize, though I had not let this surface until now, by Polly's belief that someone tried to push her under a London Underground train. Polly is a literal girl, and not given to flights of fancy. Death by casual push is rumoured to be one of NUG's favoured methods of assassination. There is no evidence whatsoever that NUG are in the habit of assassinating people in the first place, but unless you show yourself in public rather more than does NUG, paranoia is bound to flourish. Perhaps that's why they need someone like Victor as their public face.

Since the Bite, paranoia has swept the country: we who used to be so trusting, so welcoming of immigrants, dismayed by a smacked child, hopeful of globalism, who felt loyal even to our mortgage company, are now thoroughly suspicious. Someone stumbles against someone else on a crowded platform, and Mother assumes it is a murder attempt. I must not be like this. And who on earth would have a motive for getting rid of Polly? She is no threat to Victor, even if I am right about his showing signs of incipient megalomania. Now Amos is a different matter. It does no good at all to have an Amos, a drug-taking jailbird, an utterer of profanity, in the close family of a politician – sorry, a top management man, a NUG man. If NIFE appears can NUG be far behind?

If I peer out of the back window I think I see shapes running across the potato patch under the cover of the beanpoles and through a door that leads into Rothwell Street, where no-one has fixed the CiviCam. They lose no time. Are they up against some kind of timetable, some ticking clock, some, don't say it, ticking bomb? But Redpeace is not a banned organization.

Later: I put my laptop to sleep – it has a good battery, and is eight years old, but better than anything that has replaced it since – and go to the new, sleek CiviSoft computer on the desk at my front window. There is free access to the Internet. You have to be quick; if the battery hasn't run out the wifi connections will be down of necessity to save power and the planet: local wifi is fed through the Neighbourhood Watch. (I know perfectly well William Pitt the Younger said, 'Necessity is the argument of tyrants and the creed of slaves,' but our particular NW are a cosy, companionable, potato-growing lot, hardly tyrants.) I got through to Google and looked up Redpeace. Google did its best but finally gave me the annoying message in thin print that says, 'This page cannot currently be displayed.'

I looked back through my emails to see if I still had the latest circular from Redpeace, but I had deleted it after a cursory reading, more fool me. My computer allows no time for second thoughts and has no 'deleted items' box. You either have it or you don't, and since mailboxes seem to have shrunk in size and get full rather quickly and you have to empty them to get more, paper is scarce and expensive and you have to cut it down by hand with scissors to fit the printer anyway, and who can be bothered, keeping records can be a problem. No wonder my grandchildren hide and run through the beanpole arch as dusk falls. Life has been made difficult for the conspiring classes. I am decidedly proud of them. Fearful, yes: but proud too.

So far as I could remember the Redpeace circular had contained the usual stuff about genetic engineering, cruelty to animals and something about the liberty of the individual. Nothing unduly contentious, which was why I had chucked it. We all go on about these things. But what was perhaps strange was that Redpeace had been allowed to go on for so long. Or perhaps it was a way to keep all the discontented in one place, the better to keep an eye on them. After the charities united under CiviKindness there were a lot of disturbed souls from the anti-GM food lobbies, animal rights groups, global warming deniers, homeless activists, organic prose-lytisers and every good cause you can think of, all with a grievance against NUG, who would find Redpeace their natural home. And now perhaps, finally, NUG had had enough. Delete! But surely not the living actual people, just the concept? As money had become after the collapse of the banks – a concept, a lot of noughts on com-puter file, not an actuality.

A Visit From An Ex-Husband

Someone came to the door, and used the knocker, not the bell, just
as the power was cut and the computer winked out. I knew at once
who it was, from the pattern of knocks: imperative but light. It was
Edgar, my ex-husband, the one before Julian and the Czech invas-
ion, the one I divorced for excessive right-wing thinking. I was in
two minds whether or not to let him in. He came round every few
months. I would like to talk to him but he would want to sleep with
me and I was not sure I was up to it. There are good female equiv-
alents to Viagra these days which he brings round – sex goes on to
the grave if you can be bothered, and doctors recommend it – but
I am too distracted by my family's goings-on to concentrate and
you readers won't want to know about it. Too much information.

You shall have a bowdlerized version of the meeting in script
form. I'll write it up roughly now and later edit and refine and put
it on my laptop. Julian got the laptop for me, a 2008 model, a Sony,
before they had to start laying off workers, and computers, or those
available here, have hardly got any better since CiviSoft took over.
I love this laptop of mine. It has my life on it since 1985, when I
stopped writing by hand and went over to the computer. A pity, but
you have to keep up with the times. I write less implicitly, more
explicitly, if you understand the distinction, but not so well. That's
the way it is; progress is much the same as entropy.

Imagine this man Edgar: he looks rather like Jerry Garcia in his later days, hairy and benign. He is hungry. I give him some rice and a slice or two of National Meat Loaf. Everyone likes National Meat Loaf; it is our current staple food, replacing bread, pasta, rice and potatoes. Venetia called round recently with the rice: it is hard to come by for most of us, though at least there's a trickle into the Grade 1 CiviStore. According to Victor, we produce ideas, plots and characters for computer games – the rice-producing countries have the technology, but are not hot on inventiveness. And Europe is no longer a source of food imports: everyone has their own people to feed. The European Community is in disarray and, though not formally disbanded, might as well be: it can no longer enforce its rulings through financial penalties, and has no other means of doing so. It had its own parliament and its currency all right, but had neglected to organize a proper army. Consensus is fine in a time of plenty, but collapses under stress.

Edgar: You know they put something in NML that makes it addictive?
Me: I'm sure they do. Just as well.
Edgar: Why call it Meat Loaf when it says 'suitable for vegetarians'?
Me: Everything's so convoluted these days, it's true. I'd just assumed it had so little meat in it lately it wasn't worth mentioning. Its consistency does vary –sometimes it carves smoothly, like pork; sometimes – if the oat content's high – it crumbles like a haggis. But it always tastes good. I'm sure they're doing their best. They've an awful lot of mouths to feed.

The more Edgar badmouths NUG, the more I find myself sup-porting them, trying to redress a balance that existed only in my head. I remember that's why we divorced: I would end up spouting views that were not my own, but simply the opposite of his. It was too confusing for everyone, since occasionally our views did coincide. It was just exhausting separating them out. In bed, where politics seldom entered in, we got on just fine.

Edgar: Because they're on track to ban vegetarianism, the same way they did smoking. [*He had been a forty-a -day man, until put on an obligatory aversion course*] Fertilizers have to be imported, vegetables are uneconomic and pills will do as well. Notice how the ads show vegetarians as weedy figures of fun?
Me: Well, yes, yes, it's true, I have.
Edgar: And thanks to your son-in-law in NIFE the vats will soon be producing protein from unknown sources of origin. But least said soonest mended.
Me: But Edgar, surely not like that old film *Soylent Green*? The sci-fi one where it turns out all the old people are being processed for the food factories?

I laugh but I do feel a little shivery. In these days of necessity anything can happen. Perhaps the knock on the door yesterday was not the bailiffs after all, but men coming to carry me off as an edible over-eighty. A tough old boiler. More wishful thinking. No such luck: it was my money they were after, not my meat.

Edgar: No need for that. Easier to grow human meat-mass in vats. That's what Victor will be doing, why they co-opted him. He has a background in stem-cell technology.
Me: Yuk.
Edgar: Not necessarily. Why not? It's not people. There's no brain

or consciousness involved. It's just good protein. As suitable for vegetarians as Marmite.

Me: It goes against nature.

Edgar: Spoken like a Redpeace veteran, my darling, but not exactly rational. Still, one doesn't expect rationality from a woman. That's why I love you.

Yes, he really did say that, nor did I show him the door. Edgar is one of the sexiest and brightest men I know, but does have a hard time keeping up with the niceties of contemporary thought. It's not that he can't, he won't. It's nothing to do with age: he's twenty years younger than me. He really does believe that men are rational, and women are not, and that it is for their weakness that men love women. And if he believes it, it is practically his duty to speak the truth. Why should he say anything different? He does not believe in social lies. Poor Edgar, he had a terrible mother, and needed to keep women in their place. I'd always felt the urge to somehow make up for the unhappiness of his childhood. But of course one never can. What usually happens is that the man who hates his mother tries compulsively to turn you into her and, when he's succeeded, doesn't like what he sees and wanders off with someone else and starts the whole process again.

'Well, I don't love you,' is all I say.

Really, I could be twenty again. Edgar always brings out the teenager in me, which is why I put up with him. I make him Grade 1 CiviStore coffee. The rare, delicious smell fills the room. I am in two minds whether or not to tell Edgar what is going on next door, now the subject of Redpeace is on the agenda. I decide no. There are police postboxes all over the country (labelled *Working for a Safer, Satisfied Community*), inviting people to report suspicious activities, and dangling a reward for information acted upon. Edgar always saw my family as a gaggle of what he called touchy-feely lefties, even Ethan the ex-banker. When we parted he blamed them for influencing me though this was not the case. Families tend to settle down to the status quo, and they thought I would probably only choose someone even worse in the absence of Edgar. When Julian and his relatives moved in they were proved right. I do not think for one moment Edgar would report my grandchildren, but he might tell someone who would. It would make too good a story to miss.

Me: Anyway, why bother with human meat? What's the matter with beef, pork and lamb?
Edgar: Disease.

That was convincing enough. All three short-term governments we had during the Recovery, before the sociologists formed NUG and took over – one hopes, rather more intelligently – had moved too far and too fast in their attempts to make the nation self-sufficient in food. It had become clear we could no longer depend upon European trade. Brussels was by now in total disarray, rather as the banks had been some five years earlier, before they were allowed just to go bust, and was no longer able to enforce its rulings through financial penalties. (There'd been talk of creating a Defence Force to subdue a recalcitrant Portugal but it never materialized.) So we were all independent nations again, protectionist, and feverishly looking after our own. A six-month period of extreme food shortages (known by some as the Great Hunger, though this was something of an exaggeration: nobody actually starved) meant that of necessity farms were privatized and were replaced by CiviAg communal farms. The sudden expansion had its problems.

A CiviPedia page from Google, contrary to management expectation, was not enough to communicate everything there was to know about animal husbandry. Nasty epidemics of the diseases stock is heir to ran rampant through herds and flocks, and would presumably through the vats Edgar spoke of.

Me: So that's why National Meat Loaf sometimes carves like a leg of pork and sometimes like a haggis. It's Victor, trying to get things right.
[*I laugh, but Edgar doesn't*]
Edgar: What they're after is a firm, pinkish meat, suitable for vegetarians, with a sprinkling of a substance, like oxytocin, that makes the people docile. And does no harm, or not much. Do you read Redpeace?
Me: No.
Edgar: They've got it in for Victor. They named him Dr Yuk in their last issue. NIFE is one of the most secretive of the Ministries. God knows how they found out.

Well, I think, no end of the ways they could have found out. There's Henry in NIFE's Registry, on the top floors of the old Banqueting Hall in Whitehall, where Charles I was executed, and which NIFE have taken over – that, and a great chunk of the old Ministry of Defence down the road – and Ethan in the drivers' pool, in the warren of subterranean rooms below. The Hall itself is two storeys high and for all one knows may have been converted to some great chemistry lab where any amount of pink flesh can be grown and processed, and Henry or Ethan have made it their business to investigate. Victor's laudable attempts at nepotism may have rebounded. Henry could be an agent provocateur; it would not surprise me. If he was once a pig farmer in Ireland and NIFE have put him out of business he may have latched on to the family the better to destroy it.

People talk. People are neurotic. And Victor's 'family feeling' may not be requited. Betrayal can come from inside the home. Amos is a disenchanted stepchild, and that's just for starters. Perhaps Venetia tells Polly too much and Polly spreads the word and her children find out, and that is why they are giggling their way across the potato patch even now. Then there's pillow talk. Ethan and Amy. Perhaps that's why Amy is with Ethan in the first place: to subvert Ethan to get to Victor? What kind of extremism runs in Amy's veins? Amy is the daughter of Florrie, Venetia's friend, who once committed patricide; though I'm sure I have no proof of it, only the admiral's word, and the admiral may have been mistaken, and hysterical in defence of his friend, and why one should assume admirals speak the truth I don't know.

'Friend' can cover a multitude of complexities. Ex-friends can have any kind of dangerous motives. And perhaps Venetia and Florrie are at odds and Amy has some motivation we know not of. Perhaps Victor has the drop on NIFE because what he knows about growing human nutritional protein is irreplaceable. If I was NUG I'd be looking very hard at a whole lot of security issues arising from Victor's rise to be the 'face of NUG' – and of course I have only deduced this from Polly's statement that a film crew are going round to film Victor at Shabbat and her talk of increased security. I could have imagined the whole thing: the bailiffs' knock can have wholly disturbed my mental equilibrium. I am beginning to feel too old and to want to go to sleep. Perhaps Amos is about to come down and tell me he is forming a breakaway branch of Redpeace – Blue-peace, say – because they don't agree with the attack on Victor.

Victor's security has been enhanced, according to Polly – even leaving out my elaborations on the subject.

I can hear movement in the room upstairs: they are dragging furniture. My furniture out to thwart the bailiffs, or bomb-making equipment in? Or just, again, the paranoia of old age in me? Mind you, 'the paranoia of old age' is just as likely to be the fruit of experience – a vivid understanding of Murphy's Law: if things can possibly go wrong they will – as deterioration of the brain. I think I recognize Henry's footsteps. They are like Karl's, quick but heavy, determined. I still love Karl. Why didn't I leave Edgar the minute Karl called? If I'd known what a fine figure of a man the baby Henry was to turn out to be, I'd have taken him on. Too late. Everything is always too late.

Me: [*coolly*] I'm surprised Redpeace were allowed to print it.
Edgar: It was just a small paragraph on the second page,
halfway down. Where the newspapers used to print the real
news in the Soviet Union. Those in the know would ignore the
headlines and go straight there. The censors only ever read
the first page.
Me: But why would Redpeace object to protein cloning anyway?
No-one's suffering. It's only science.
Edgar: The nature of the agitator is to prove other people wrong
in order that they can be right. It's the old irrational anti-GM
argument resurfacing with Yuk added. Meddling with nature.
Unknown forces unleashed. Who owns body parts? The citizens'
right to benefit if their stem cells are used. Etc., etc. They're all
Gaia nuts.
Me: Nobody will take any notice of them. Times are too dire.
Edgar: Don't be too sure. If the discontents are gathering, NUG

will act. Secretly and furtively, after the manner of governments, but act they will. So, alas, will Redpeace. All the hatred of the nutters has to go somewhere, it's been thwarted for so long. I hope Victor and your Venetia understand the importance of security, or are they too we-love-everyone-therefore-everyone-loves-us for that?

Now I don't know who to be most worried for. Forget Polly and the platform; forget my bloodline next door; how about Venetia? Victor, Dr Yuk, may be providing her with goodies, and she may be passing them on to me and Polly – the coffee will be smelt down the street, I swear, and that's not safe – but he is surely putting my daughter in danger. And the past keeps catching up with me. Any minute now I am going to have a knock on the door and it will be some child of the baby Fay once gave up for adoption – was it a boy or a girl? I can't remember – demanding attention and with some grievance against me. She will insist on the family having DNA tests and it will be discovered that she and Venetia are half-sisters, that her birth-mother and birth-aunt each had a child by her father and Venetia will take her in as she has taken in Henry, her half-brother on her father's side, and then Venetia will be angry with me, because she doesn't know the true facts of her parentage – a deceit I have maintained all this time simply for Fay's sake. And Fay will find out too and speak to me even less. Life was so much simpler before the State decreed back in the nineties that every child should be able to find out their true parentage: it has caused a great deal of grief and embarrassment to many, many people. I do not think it is particularly helpful to know one's genetic history: it is usually bad news.

It is normal for the child, especially the girl child, to believe she must surely have been switched at birth, and her parents are lying and she is really a princess, but it seldom, on investigation, turns out to be true. What you discover is not better than you hoped, but worse than you have.

I need time to absorb all this. I have a niggling feeling there is something yet to be revealed. Something about Polly. I will walk over to Mornington Crescent tomorrow, eighty-plus knees not withstanding, and see her and advise her not to go on the Underground for the time being. Also that she needs to tell her daughters to steer clear of Redpeace in future. It would be easier to phone but I am getting a 'no network coverage' message from my mobile phone. That usually means a power cut is on the way within the hour. The mobile masts go dead in advance. I don't know what this particular strategy is about: NUG's mind works in a mysterious way. When the ads aren't badmouthing vegetarians and threatening them with anaemia they're talking about the increase in brain cancer due to the use of mobile phones. Probably their plan is to wean us off their use altogether. The argument from health is one of their control strategies.

I put all these facts on the back burner of my brain to simmer away and come up with the answer in its own time, and tell Edgar about the time I went to a Conference of World Intellectuals in Moscow, hosted by Mikhail Gorbachev, in the summer of 1989, just before the end of the Cold War, when Gorbachev told the delegates that war was no longer to be seen as 'revolution carried out by other means' – and so declared peace, and the end of the Cold War – news I took home to the Foreign Office only to be ignored.

Edgar: You've told me that a hundred times. You were married to me at the time.

I tell him again, with the added fact that I spent most of the week in bed with an Italian journalist – this is the purpose of conferences – whose sexual skill rivalled Edgar's own, and was the real reason my return was delayed by a week. I passed out on the bathroom floor of the Hotel Sovietski, so arduous had been my pleasures. The medical staff were called; I was roughly laid on my back, naked, jabbed with a thick, blunt needle in the buttocks and didn't regain consciousness for twenty-four hours: during which time the KGB had ample time to interrogate me, or so the Foreign Office assured me. Mind you, the FO were angry with me, having warned me off going in the first place. 'Mir, mir, mir,' they'd said, 'peace, peace, peace, when all they mean is war, war, war. Iris Murdoch isn't going, and Graham Greene is, and he runs a whisky factory,' which is old Foreign Office speak for being a hopeless alcoholic.

Edgar fumes at me and calls me names, but really the sexual misdemeanours of thirty years ago have rather lost their power to shock and alarm. These days he's with a lady of a certain age, a Harriet, with a thin face, wire-framed glasses and wispy hair, who has currently broken a leg and is presumably out of play or he wouldn't be round at my place trying to revive old habits.

The conference was meant to be discussing ways of bringing MAD to an end – MAD, Mutual Assured Destruction, in which neither side dared start a war for fear of being wiped out in return – and I'd been asked by the Moscow Writers' Union, with whom I had had many dealings, to attend. It was more fun at the top table, listening to Norman Mailer, Kris Kristofferson, Günter Grass and the like, but I was delegated, being a rare female, and having rashly spoken on the subject, to the Human Rights Subcommittee, which, during the course of a couple of days, was meant to rewrite the Bill of Human Rights in simple, human terms, reflecting all views. It was my task, as the writer present, to record the deliberations of the Committee. I was sitting between an African potentate and an Iranian intellectual. The potentate asked me publicly if I would become his fifty-second wife – I couldn't rank any higher, he apologized, for I might talk too much and divert him from serious business, when lives were at stake.

'The right to have a silent spouse,' I wrote down, 'if lives are at stake.'

The Iranian spoke of his horror at cannibalism on the battle front. (This was at the time of the Iraq–Iran war.) 'The right not to be eaten after death,' I wrote down. But I was never so sure about that, and still am not. What difference would it make? So long as I am not killed specifically for that purpose, anyone is welcome to ingest me, good for Gaia-style recycling.

I excused myself from the Committee, pleading illness. I am not a sufficiently serious person to be trusted with matters of State, which require long words and obfuscations to make them work, and went in search of my journalist. Get 'issues' down to simple human terms and everything becomes frivolous, just more versions of the Watergate Tapes, in which President Nixon, once the doors were closed, spoke as he really meant – bums and crap and all, and had to go. Presidents are not expected to be like anyone else. Office itself is meant to make people wise. My experience has been that it doesn't. The people who are serious are young and usually middle class, well fed, with parents who love them, and are in a position to develop principles. The revolutionary tendency flourishes amongst the well-to-do, rather than the poor.

The noise upstairs has stopped. Edgar has heard nothing. I realize that Edgar is getting quite deaf. Men age so much faster than women. Or else he is still fuming about the journalist. Yes, he is.

Edgar: You always were an unfaithful bitch. No wonder Karl got rid of you.
Me: It was just the custom of the times, and you don't have to keep me company. Feel free to go.

He doesn't, he asks for another cup of coffee. I give it to him. But he is not finished with my punishment. He asks if I know that the son Karl had when he so understandably left me is back from Ireland working at NIFE in some lowly position.

Me: I daresay he will rise through the ranks.

Men never forget one's infidelity. I should not have told him about the Italian journalist. I don't need enemies at the moment. But I couldn't help it. I was boasting. So, how does Edgar know Henry is working at NIFE? Does Polly? I don't think so. There was no love lost between my girls and Edgar. He was their stepfather after the Dumpling had died, and Karl had decided the by-blow Henry was going to be too much for him, and neither Venetia nor Polly would take him on – I'd have killed them if they'd offered – and I'd said, with truth, I was otherwise occupied and the child had been sent off to his maternal grandmother in Cork.

Edgar: You lot were so ruthless about poor little Henry. I didn't see any reason you and I shouldn't have taken him on. We had the house, the space, the time. I could have done with a baby. But you wouldn't hear of it, self-centred bitch that you always were. Your kids were grown up; you had nothing else to do, but no.
Me: [*feebly*] I was a writer.

I could see that his upper lip had lifted in a sneer because the hair on the right side of his beard lifted and stuck out. I was fascinated. He had much the same response to my books as did Karl. Girlish twaddle. Why did I pick such men? It egged me on, I daresay, to win the world's respect since it wasn't available at home.

Edgar: That baby was part of the family, a blood relative of your children's. When he was sent off practically by parcel post, I took it on myself to check up he was okay. He was fine. I kept in touch with the grandmother: in fact Harriet is her daughter. I re-met her at the funeral a couple of years back, and we got together. So when I say what is going on at NIFE I'll have you know I'm not making it up.

Yes, but what you don't know, Edgar, I think – fuck Harriet, which you will, I expect, when her leg is better, and you're welcome – is that Redpeace's webpage is currently not available, and that your ex-stepdaughters' half-brother is currently engaged in espionage next door and I'm not telling, so shucks to you and God knows why I was ever with you. Well, I do, on the rebound. And there was the sex.

Edgar: And I can tell you this, he is not fond of Victor, and they say in Skibbereen sparks are going to fly. They say there Henry is something to do with Redpeace. There's a lot of negative feeling about the collective farms. Henry's vats are putting a lot of people out of business.
Me: Ah yes, I expect the *Skibbereen Eagle* has got its eye on Victor.

Edgar looks at me doubtfully. He hates it when I make a joke he doesn't understand. In 1889 the tiny newspaper warned the world that it had its eye on the Tsar of Russia over his expansionist ambitions. I give up.

Me: Henry is round to dinner with Victor and his family quite a lot. Or so Polly tells me.
Edgar: [*darkly*] When he goes round to sup he carries a long spoon.
Me: As one does, when dining with the Devil. I suppose for Henry Victor is a step-relative and not a half relative. Makes all the difference to an orphan in search of a family.

I decide that after all I quite like Victor. If he's to be an oligarch or President or whatever NUG decides, good for him. I wish him well. He's much nicer than most men I know, and besides, a source of CiviStore goodies. I don't suppose he's really bringing Venetia into danger, security will be tight from the sound of it, and in the meanwhile Venetia has ample access to lots of acrylic paint. The children next door will be setting up an opposition party to Redpeace and all will be well and all will be well. I'm tired. I finally get Edgar to go, back to his Harriet. I write up my notes with what's left of the battery and go to bed.

A Visit From Amos, Ethan And Amy

In the morning Ethan, Amy and Amos come pounding down the stairs in great good humour. They'd smelt my morning coffee on the Primus stove, and wanted some. I was down to my last few ounces, what with Edgar's visit the night before. I was relieved to hear that Rosie and Steffie had gone home to Polly last night, and would be going to college in the morning. I would simply not mention to Polly that they had been through my front door and out someone else's. Amy said the girls had been a great help lugging promotional material about. She had an unmelodious voice and disguised her willowy figure – so like her grandmother's – beneath shapeless, shabby, grey to black clothes, wore her thick straight hair as if she'd combed it down from the centre, put a pudding basin over it, and then scissored round the edges.

She reminded me of girls I'd known back in the seventies, who refused on moral grounds to make themselves attractive to men. As they approached their thirties they tended to relent, look in mirrors, and succumb to vanity. The cause was different but the mindset was the same. Presumably Amy thought the plainer she looked the more likely she was to bring about a world in which pink human protein grown in vats was not to enter the food chain. But she had her grandfather's eyes, as I remembered Florrie had had, in the garden out the back of this very house, a child sent out to play while the adults talked of death, those bright, hooded, dark eyes, Terry's eyes. I tried to remember that Liddy had started as a friend and only later became a rival. I offered them some National Meat Loaf, just to see what happened and they shuddered and declined.

'You ate enough of it yesterday,' I said to Amos, which was tactless, and he just said:

'I was younger then.'

'You mustn't eat that stuff, Gran,' said Amy. So, I have been promoted. Gran! We're all one family.

'It's cannibalism,' said Ethan.

Ethan was a tall, good-looking, quick-moving, extrovert lad, with thick black eyebrows beneath a thatch of curly hair, and was, I always thought, none too bright. Whereas his younger brother Mervyn was a dead ringer for Victor, a mini intellectual, Ethan was simply not. He was right for the City, for Porsches, for splashing money around, for cocaine parties and beautiful girls. He was born out of time, poor lad. And here he was with Amy, and I had to say that contrary to expectation she seemed quite right for him. They moved in unison, as lovers do: she spoke first; he then endorsed whatever it was she said. She was in charge, but they got on.

I have always noticed, when married couples gather, how often really handsome men are joined to plain women, and vice versa. I don't think it is that the plain ones – the horsey women, the fat bald men – have been married for their money. I think it is to do with wanting to join their spouses on the moral high ground, the urge to even out inequality, to return to the norm. 'Golden couples' are a rarity, usually to be found in Hollywood, where nobody started out, looks-wise, as they began. The film industry has collapsed. As drug profits failed and the need for money laundering diminished, one studio after another called in the receivers and turned off the lights. Small films in this country are made, but seldom shown: power cuts are frequent in areas where the little cinemas cluster, and Health and Safety need to see and check IDs, so it's just too much of a bother to go. *Don't be duped!* as the NUG posters say. *Originality means untrusted and untrue.* I don't know who writes these posters: some PR department somewhere, I suppose, whose message gets so tortured in committee it hardly makes sense.

I rather wished they would get on with their nefarious business, and go away, so I could start the long walk up to Polly's to warn her to be careful, without alarming her. I was not particularly looking forward to the walk: I would have to keep stopping to rest along the way, and it wasn't so much the humiliation of this that bothered me, but the rage that goes with growing old, of your body holding you up as if it was at war with your mind. Once body and mind were hand in glove – no longer so. The mind commanded, the body laughed. And soon enough the body would win, and simply die. But the Redpeacers lingered and ate all my raisins – again from the Grade 1 CiviStore – and seemed happy. Then Ethan had to be off to work so he drank his coffee, pecked me goodbye on my weathered cheek and said 'Goodbye Gran' affectionately and went not out the front door, but upstairs and presumably out via Rothwell Street where there were dud CiviCams.

No sooner had Ethan left than I heard Henry coming downstairs. I could tell his footsteps, so like Karl's it made me feel quite weak. After the divorce, when Karl stripped the house of all its contents, the court having allowed most of it to be seen as stock from his antique shop, and Karl stretching that permission to extremes so everything but the knocker went, and that stayed by accident, I sat in this very room and heard those very footsteps coming downstairs for what I assumed was the very last time. He was angry with me, and I was angry with him. He had the Dumpling; he had heard rumours of Edgar. But Karl had started it. And now this giant version of his father came into the room and looked at me, and spoke.

'You'll be Gran, my da's ex-wife,' he said. 'Sure, and I'll be thanking you for your hospitality.'

'I didn't have much choice,' I said.

'A little matter of necessity, darlin',' he said. His Irish accent seemed to me to be overdone, for my benefit, and slightly insulting.

'Why?' I asked. You have to stand up to these men or they assume you're an idiot.

'Let us say perhaps not of necessity, but certainly of opportunity.' He smiled at me in a friendly and confiding way, as Karl did when he was planning some particular devilry, and said he understood my rather basic anger at his, Henry's existence, which other members of his family had emphasized, but though his father might have technically divorced me, he himself, Henry, did not believe in divorce, and so far as he was concerned I was a family member and would be treated as such.

'I don't think anyone I know believes in divorce as if it was some kind of religion,' I said. 'It's a legal procedure, that's all. "Approve" might be a better word.'

Amos and Amy were shaking their heads at me. I was not meant to argue. Just to accept, be grateful, and shut up. Amy was certainly not in charge of this operation, as I had thought. It was Henry.

'Approve,' he conceded, 'okay, I don't approve of divorce. You had a child by my father and so you stay a family member, connected by sanguinity.' He had lost his Irish accent. It came and went as if two sides of his brain were in conflict.

187

I thought, actually, this man is mad. It was quite a clear thought, unlike so many in my mind these days.

'Rather an argument for polygamy,' I said.

'Why not,' he said. 'In the New Republic, my darlin', it will be practised, within strict boundaries. Monogamy is hardly a natural state. We do not want too many lonely and cast-off women in the new society.'

'I see,' I said. 'So, Henry, you are the new Oliver Cromwell.' He looked a little puzzled.

He did not get the allusion. That the tyrannical monster Oliver Cromwell had already laid claim to a New Republic five hundred years back had escaped him. So presumably had the fact that Cromwell had had King Charles' head chopped off on scaffolding outside the very Banqueting Hall where now NIFE reigned. There had been little history taught in the schools for years, but surely in Ireland, where Cromwell was still remembered and hated, Henry would have picked up something? Apparently not. And people are quite capable of replaying history without reference to what happened in the past. There are only so many movements to go round. The age of excess has collapsed, the age of austerity is here, and within its confines Henry will try to effect a coup, and undo NUG, to which he is not so different (I know a control freak when I see one, believe me), and employ useful idiots (my family, I fear, which unhappily is also his: Karl should not have gone off with the Dumpling) to achieve it. God knows how many others are plotting with him. And then the New Republic, with its strict polygamy and families forbidden to split and no delicious National Meat Loaf, too, will collapse and then some equivalent of Charles II will bring back Nell Gwyn and oranges, the dancing girls and the maypoles, and we will all be sexy and happy again. Till the banks collapse or whatever form it takes, and the cycle continues in sackcloth and ashes.

'Sure and I don't get you, Gran,' he said, and his tongue flickered out like a little snake's and he licked his lips.

'Oliver Cromwell had all kinds of bright ideas,' I said, 'long ago. He tried to ban Christmas.'

'You're kiddin' me, Gran,' he said. But I was no grandmother to this monster, this Cromwell reborn. No blood of mine ran in his veins. What had Karl's sexual dereliction brought down upon the world? A Cromwell who believed in the subjugation of women, who would have them all back in their box, four to every man's bed?

I could pretty much envisage the scene in Hunter's Alley, where I in my folly had allowed my family to congregate and fall into bad ways, as Henry geared up his useful fools to sticking point, no doubt to direct action. But what was it? Were his forces gathering even now? Perhaps he had recruited the Jokers to his side? Organized, they would be a powerful force for mayhem. All I knew for sure was that my grandchildren Amos and Ethan and possibly Mervyn, and my best friend's granddaughter Amy too, and Rosie and Steffie as well, whose blood I was prepared to share, so nearly mine it was – all, all in danger.

In The Name Of God, Go!

I can imagine the scene in Hunter's Alley, before NUG realized it was a problem and closed it down, so there was nowhere my family could meet. I bought the house because it was such a pretty place in such a squalid area, of storage warehouses and car-part dumps, and seemed a good investment (those were the days). I thought the boys could always make use of it as they grew older and wanted to be nearer the heart of the metropolis, and, frankly, away from what I saw as Victor and Venetia's rather stifling home life, but still near to Polly and Corey and the girls. More fool me.

It's three up, two down, bathroom and kitchen, and had stood for three hundred years or so, so why should it give up now? Or so the estate agent told me, rubbing his hands as the old fool me approached. I haven't been there for a couple of years, but Polly goes in to keep an eye on things. But her eye, I suspect, after years with Corey, is not as sharp or as stringent as it used to be. Polly and Corey live in what to my mind is squalor, but to many of their generation is common sense. Why waste time cleaning? There were a blissful couple of years when for a few months everyone could just move on as if it was the Mad Hatter's tea party, and squat in somebody else's empty house, but NUG clamped down on that pretty soon. You stay where you are so they can keep an eye on you. Stay still, stay safe, stay home – be CiviSecure!

But I reckon NUG's eye had missed Hunter's Alley. It would be housing as many young activists as could cram in the door. Middle class rather than working class, but when were revolutionaries ever not? The working class gets on with the work, the middle classes with the indignation. The activists would mostly be white British: in the great exodus the West Indians had streamed to the USA and many a Muslim, outdone in moral fervour by NUG, chose to take his family back to Pakistan where life was easier. Sunni and Shia fought it out, local enmities loomed more importantly than international grievances, and a new Wahabi imam was preaching a form of non-violent Sufism to great effect on YouTube, which was still able to flourish in oil-producing countries where the electricity supply was stable. Sweet-tongued girls now sang to you as your computer booted up, YouTube lies but NUTube knows!

And Henry would have been doing a Cromwell, sweet-talking the useful idiots of Hunter's Alley. I supposed he had spent the last few years organizing like Joe Hill, with pig farming as a useful cover. He was a born politician, an agitator, he meant to change the world for its betterment, no matter how few people agreed, and he had the cruelty – he got that from his father, whose tongue would snicker out and lick his lips when he had something hurtful to say – and charisma to accomplish it. He was working up to the dissolution of parliament. Okay, everyone wanted to get rid of NUG, who had grown intolerably odious to the whole nation, but once it was gone – and in the end all governments did go – what would be in its place? Children, hold on tight to Nurse, for fear of finding something worse.

'It is high time to bring to an end the rule of the fools and knaves, the godless sociologists and therapists who lounge and dribble in Whitehall,' he would be saying. The room would be smoky with spliff. For years it had been the drug of choice for the young who wanted to change the world. The girls would be looking up at him with adoration. He would be wearing a uniform – brown, with military overtones, rather tight trousers. He would choose one, or even two, of the girls to take to bed: Rosie and Steffie would be his choice, ripe, dusky peaches, not Amy, who looked so cross all the time. But you never knew. He might see her as more of a challenge. I hoped so. I was responsible for her for ever, but she was not my flesh and blood.

'They have dishonoured us by their lies, their contempt of all virtue: they have defiled us by their practice of every vice,' he would be saying. 'Their hypocrisy hurts us. With my own eyes I have seen them insult the Lord. They do not believe but they say they do. They live off the fat of the land while their people go hungry. They distort, they manipulate, they lie; where others sing hymns to God they sing their jingles to commerce and control. They are enemies to all good government, they are a pack of mercenary wretches, like Esau they have sold their country for a mess of pottage and like Judas betrayed their beliefs for a few pieces of money.'

It did not matter really what he said, so long as he sounded as if he believed it.

'We will not forgive them for they know what they do. We will replace these repulsive fools with the New Republic. Ethan, brother, tell us what you have seen in the back of your car.'

'I have seen all sorts of things,' Ethan will say, 'some of it rather funny. It's blow-job heaven. These old geezers on Viagra with the young girls from the food labs. If they want to keep their jobs it's blow, blow, blow.'

'Amy, sister,' says Henry, 'tell us what you have seen at Neighbourhood Watch.'

'I have seen them take the crops that belong by rights to the people, and sell them and pocket the proceeds,' says Amy. That's rather tame, but the best she can do. She is rewarded by a smile and the flash of blue eyes. Perhaps she's the one for tonight.

'Amos, brother, what have you seen?'

'I have seen what goes into National Meat Loaf,' says Amos. 'We are eating the cloned bodies of pigs, all right, but as well as those of Jokers, autistics, the insane and other enemies of the State, well laced with a new generation of tranquillizers and SSRIs – selective serotonin reuptake inhibitors – and assorted NUGNumbered flavour enhancers.'

'And who presides over this abomination?' Henry shrieks. 'Your stepfather, Brother Amos, who like Claudius crept into your mother's bed before the funeral baked meats were cold.'

Ah, so that's it. He's after Victor.

And then a squad of CiviSecure would have come roaring up Hunter's Alley and my family – always quick on their feet except for Victor, who was on the ponderous side – would have been down the garden and over the back wall and melted into the crowds, leaving nothing but a whiff of spliff behind them, and looking for somewhere else to settle in. Gran's. Naturally.

CiviSecure use battering rams to break down doors, and never mend them, so the rats come in, and dust and disease, and that's the end of my property in Hunter's Alley. It was a nice thought while it lasted.

Henry Intimidates, Or Thinks He Does

'Would it be true to say you had visitors last night, now.' It was a statement, not a question. 'And me particularly warning you not to open the door!'

I explained I had an ex-husband drop by and he said yes, he knew that, and it was not a visitor of whom he approved. I felt obliged to say that, to position myself safely. Henry was really quite a frightening man. Harriet with the broken leg was of the same family as Henry Prideaux, future Lord Protector of the Kingdom, and deserved his respect, which probably did not extend to her boyfriend, though nearing seventy, visiting his ex-wife with a view, however thwarted, to geriatric hanky-panky.

Henry said in future it would be wiser for me not to receive visitors but to stay in the house. Just until this particular operation was finished. I looked at Amos, whom I had thought so dashing and bad and fine, and Amy, who seemed so plain but strong, and they would not meet my eyes. With Henry in the room other people seemed somehow so weak. I wondered what the particular operation was, after which I would be free to wander at will.

I had my mouth open to speak but he did not let me.

'Just lock the front door and seal it with superglue,' he said to Amy.

Surprise, surprise, and not one safely in the past, like Cynthia falling out of the sky or Karl running off with the Dumpling, but here and now. And blow me, Amy went off to rummage in the drawer beneath the sink and actually found the superglue and fed it into the lock. I wondered if she shared the susceptibility of her mother Florrie that had made the poor child fall in with the Manson gang prototype in hippie California. Probably. I wondered if Redpeace had weapons, and if they did, would they would use them?

'Sure and you're blissfully self-contained in here I see, Gran,' said Henry. 'You'll be just fine. We'll make sure you're fed and watered and you can get on with your writing. Amos tells me you don't go upstairs.'

'My legs are too weak,' I said, my plan already forming in my mind.

He went to the front window and looked down into the basement area below.

'And I don't think you'll be jumping down into that, Gran,' he said. He was right. I wouldn't. In any case there was a CiviCam trained on the road and Neighbourhood Watch would be round in no time to find out what was going on and there'd be no end to it. If you called the authorities the chances were that you'd be the one to land up in prison. It was the way they worked. Saved time, trouble and paperwork, and led to far fewer complaints.

He's forgotten my phone, I thought, but no. Of course not; Henry was not a forgetful person, any more than his father had been – other than the knocker on the door which was why I valued it so. Symbol of at least a minor victory.

'Tell you what, boy,' Henry said, 'if you take Gran's phone we can charge it up for her next door. I'll be thinking there's a bit of juice left in the generator.'

Amos took my phone. If you show no doubt when giving instructions, it becomes natural for others to obey them. People like being told what to do, as Hitler said in *Mein Kampf*. So long as you tell them firmly enough they feel secure and enjoy it.

'Remind me, too, to bring in a few cans of petrol when we have a minute,' and Henry gave me the benefit of a sweet smile, Karl's smile, and it occurred to me that it was a threat to burn the house down, me included in fixtures and furnishings. Henry really didn't like me: but I daresay the circumstances of his birth gave him reason not to. And heaven knows how Venetia and Polly had presented me to him. Let alone Harriet of the broken leg. Edgar would have made a good job of badmouthing me to her, as men so often do of the women who were once in their lives. That is, if they remember them at all.

I wondered whether, if Karl hadn't disencumbered himself of Henry, how the child would have grown up. Was control freakery built into dictators, or was it acquired through childhood trauma? Stalin was well and truly traumatized as a child. His father abandoned the family, his arm withered up, he was pitted by smallpox, he was stunted in growth. On the other hand Mussolini got on well with his father, and was reckoned handsome, courageous, charismatic, and erudite – if violent as a child. Hitler had a puny kind of sex-life. I wondered what Henry's was like, and thought it was probably like his father's, kind of impulsive and frequent. I didn't want to think about it.

I know Henry was born on 5 November, a date embedded in my mind, which put his Sun in Scorpio, sign of the dictator. That figured. The emotional manipulator, the creature that stings itself if it has nothing else to sting, even forgetting it was Guy Fawkes Day, dedicated to the patron saint of explosives. Karl's birthday was 21

June. He was a Gemini. Which twin were you kissing? You never knew. That was part of the charm. If I was going to be imprisoned in my rooms I could look up the ephemeris of the planet's places on Google and cast Henry's horoscope. I bet they wouldn't like that in the New Republic; altogether too Witch of Endory.

'So see you later, Gran,' said Amos. He didn't swear in Henry's presence, I noticed. Oaths will not be a feature in the New Republic. The New Republic is going to be a lot worse than NUG. Henry must be stopped. Victor must be warned that Henry is not a desirable guest in his house, that Henry is a snake in the grass, an adder at the breast, a worm in the apple of NUG, even if Victor does grow pink ready-to-carve human meat in vats. Nobody's perfect.

'Alligator,' I say. They don't know the reference, but at least they go.

Escape

I tried the lock in the front door but it was well and truly glued. If it had been me I wouldn't have done it so well that it actually worked. Liddy, Amy's grandmother, was good at practical things. She once complained I was a bodger. It is absurd to carry these grudges, these memories back to the other side of the grave. Plan A had just been to defy Henry and leave by the front door, but no. So there was nothing but Plan B. I waited. I watched from my back window the movements between the rows of beanpoles, which during the next fifteen minutes were plentiful. Back and forth they ran, back and forth, shadowy, diving and ducking, as if they were ghostly characters in some computer game. There had been quite a wind in the night and a few more bean leaves had been swept away, so cover was not as good as it had been. Bet they hadn't thought of that. I waited until movement had ceased, the dark forms were gone, and all was quiet upstairs, when I reckoned they had all left No. 5 to set about their baleful 'operation', whatever it was, and I hoped it was minor, not major. More like a procedure.

I then set about climbing the stairs. Up to the half-landing is fine, just a bit painful, but then the stairs turn a corner and that's a problem. I have to have something to hold on to and there is nothing. My balance is not too good, and I fear falling backwards. I hate being old. I am not yet accustomed to it. If I do the stairs on hands and knees and use a cushion so the contact with knee and floor is not accompanied by dreadful crumbling noises from within, as if something internal is splintering, that might work. I try. I can. There is usually a way out. I need to get to Polly, who will get me to Venetia.

Once on level ground the passage from the landing to the room where once Karl and I had our bedroom is no problem.

I should have had my knees replaced when I could have, but I put it off and put it off and one day there was no money left to go private and the NHS had ceased to do hips and knees. All services for geriatrics had seized up. What small money there was, what few skills left after the Great Immigration, when so many in the health services went home to practise medicine in their own countries, were reserved for the fertile and economically productive. It made sense: there were fewer of us old ones left to stare forlornly into space in nursing homes, longing for an end nature had devised for us and the doctors barred to us. A long life expectancy had ceased to be a matter of competition between the nations.

And yes, the wall is a mess. They have indeed broken through to No. 5. They have not bothered to sweep up plaster, or square off the ragged hole they have made. They have taken down the painting on the wall – a Samuel Palmer fake – and leaned it against the wall facing outwards, where it could get kicked or damaged. Anyone with any sensitivity would have placed it facing inwards. But then the New Republic will probably ban art as frivolous. I wish I could remember what NUG's view of art is – I get fact and fiction blurred in my mind. Is Venetia really having an exhibition at the Medici Gallery under NUG's auspices, or was that just something I wrote? Sometimes what I invent comes true anyway. Friends say I am prophetic but I just think I'm a good guesser. Anyway I take time to put the painting so that it faces inward and is safer. It may be a fake but sometimes the skill that goes into a fake is greater than whatever went into the original: it's just the motive one suspects – money rather than art. I suppose it makes a difference. It's meant to.

I am aware that I must hurry: they may be back any minute. I go through the hole into No. 5. I need to get out of here. It's the living room of my one-time neighbours, Timothy and Sandra Croxton. I haven't seen them for some time – I thought they were away, but I think Amos was right. They are gone. The walls are bare of pictures; none of their nice Danish furniture is left. I hope it was not the bailiffs, and they managed to take the stuff with them when they skipped the moon.

Go back a hundred years and this street was full of couples who skipped the moon, that is to say failed to pay the rent and left secretly by night. Nothing changes. The rent became the mortgage, that was all. A diet of avocados and lemon veal took over from mutton and potatoes, but I daresay the sum of human happiness, human anxiety, remained about the same. I wish they'd said good-bye, though. I wonder why not? Shame? The security cameras? I wouldn't have snitched on them, warned the Neighbourhood Watch. I am a loyal kind of person, to friends, family, neighbours. I think. I wonder how much I want Venetia to stay with Victor because of my second-hand access to the Grade 1 CiviStore. Coffee and rice and all things nice.

Thinking about the Neighbourhood Watch, how did Amy come to have house plans for the Crescent in her possession? Is she one of the trusted senior watchers? Or is she an infiltrator, a sleeper, an entryist? These hard-left parties changed names and aims after the end of the Cold War, but never really went away. NUG is shame-lessly Gramsciist, its aim the destruction of the old institutions, by persuasion through redefinition rather than force, and the collapse of the bourgeoisie. The New Republic? A reflowering of Marxism, like a rose in its autumn blooming, richly fertilized by the end of capitalism as foretold by the master? No, I think perhaps, judging from Henry, something more Stalinist in its nature, favouring direct action, the literal elimination of enemies.

What I don't like is the armchair that stands by itself in the all but empty room, and the table next to it on which is laid out a few reels of that sticky stuff that my father called 'bodge tape' and the writers of serial-killer thrillers call 'duct tape', plus various lengths of cord and a pair of handcuffs. Someone, it seems to me, is going to be held here captive. Yes, indeed, things are hotting up. A kidnapping? Thank God I see no instruments of torture. I don't see Ethan or Amos standing for that, though I'm not so sure about Amy. Who? Victor? Dr Yuk, as excoriated by Redpeace? No, that is too unlikely even for me. I think the cloning business is just a diversion, for the likes of Edgar to take seriously. I think Henry has bigger plans, greater ambitions. He's like Yeltsin, waiting in the wings for Gorbachev to be deposed, so he can sweep back on a tank and retake Moscow.

Getting down the stairs of No. 5 is not easy; there's the same bend in the stairs to negotiate as at No. 3, but I realize I can put my feet at a sideways angle and stand on tiptoe as the right foot goes down, and then swing the left foot as far to the left as I can before putting it down, and thus, absurdly, descend. As I say, if you want to do something enough, there is usually a way. But I am also on the side of those *Carmageddon* makers, who aim their cars at little old ladies, the LOLs, and leave them as a splodge of red blood on the ground. That's fun: the green blood of alien life forms, legitimate prey, just isn't the same.

A Conversation With Polly

I get out through the back door of No. 5 and cross beneath the arch of beanpoles. The ground is really muddy after last night's rain. The potato plants are in flower: when they begin to die off it is time to lift the crop, before the blight gets to them. Phosphate rock for fertilizer has to be imported so the crop does tend to struggle. Neighbourhood Watch is setting up some intricate organic waste scheme which should help but does tend to be smelly. I go through the back door of 7 Rothwell Street and find that empty too, with the signs of a swift withdrawal – however will we get our potatoes enriched at this rate? Our sewers will be empty – and go out the front door. The CiviCam dangles from its wires. Out of action. There's a CiviSecure notice saying it has been reported and will be back in action within twelve hours, but nobody really believes it, or fills in the Security Postbox forms (*Working For A More Satisfied Community*) to report malefactors.

I half expect a car to come racing round the corner and down the road to knock me over and kill me, but all looks peaceful. I have an odd feeling that had I come out on to Chalcot Crescent exactly that might have happened. As it is, I escape unseen. But who would want to kill me? I'm an old lady and harmless, though unnecessarily taking up the nation's resources. I know nothing; I am from Barcelona. I am no more worth killing than is Polly. I am Victor's mother-in-law, and that should keep me safe. Unless Victor is the source of all the trouble: it is Victor who is to be sat duct-taped in an armchair at No. 5 and wait – till what? His ransom is paid? That seems possible. Though why would his family, my family, collude in the crime? Mervyn, conspicuous by his absence, might be the one to ask. And perhaps I know more than I think I do? The absence of torture implements is no guarantee that they're not hidden in a cupboard. Oh, the fevered imagination of the old! If only I hadn't had a life so full of surprises I could view it with more equanimity. It is just that in one's experience so much of what is imagined turns out to be true. It's almost as if one thinks of it, and lo, it happens. The Shock, the Crunch, the Crisis, the Squeeze, the 'Recovery', the Fall and the Bite, are in this case all my fault. The world unfolds before one in the way one expects. Perhaps we all have our own individual universe?

I will not bore you with an account of my walk to Mornington Crescent where Polly, Corey and the girls live, other than it was long, tiring and painful, and whenever I wanted someone's low wall to sit upon and rest, there was none. I got heart pains, and however much one thinks one welcomes death, heart pains, though usually indigestion, can give one a nasty turn. But they went away.

They live in the bottom third of a tall London house not unlike the one I live in, but rather darker, and with a bad damp problem. Mornington Crescent, like Chalcot Crescent, was built around 1820, but intended for a grander clientele, and should have looked out, magnificently, one-sidedly, on to the greenery, space and elegance of Harrington Square. Now it looks out on to the concrete slab that is the back of the old art deco cigarette factory, with its Egyptian motifs and its place in the guidebooks. The building has been converted to offices – which these days stand mostly empty –

but the façade has been preserved, with a great bronze cat on either side of the wide steps, still staring balefully out at passers-by. It is a beautiful and eccentric building from the front, but from the back an ugly, looming, squalid nightmare, cutting out light and air to poor Mornington Crescent. Some developer, back in 1926, got permission to fill in an available space, and the residents at the time were too poor to object, or perhaps notice.

In the days of my wealth I was always trying to persuade Polly to move somewhere healthier, but she refused the offer of my tainted wealth. I can't remember quite what it was that tainted it – I think it was because I had stuck with mainstream commercial publishers and had eschewed the feminist presses. Something like that. But there was always something, with both Venetia and Polly. As there had been with Jane, Fay and myself, when it came to our mother Margaret. Namely, why did you leave our father?

Perhaps with the New Republic divorce will be banned. Or, if not, marriage, for that seldom happens in the first place these days, but at any rate leaving your partner once you have children. But then, of course, who would have children?

I forgot to look at Henry's feet to see if they are exceptionally large. I have no doubt he will be in my life again – I have to go home sometime, somehow effect an entry – and no doubt will have an opportunity to find out.

'Mum,' cried Polly,' did you walk all this way, or did somebody drop you off?'

'I walked,' I say.

Polly is getting on for fifty. I keep expecting to see her at around fifteen, with her frizzy, fulsome hair, and her little rosebud disapproving mouth, so like my big sister Jane's, and the slight figure and the worried look, which actually is less worried now she has something to worry about – namely two daughters caught up in a dangerous political movement of which she knows nothing. If she was fifteen I'd be in my forties, with good knees, and would have been over to Mornington Crescent in fifteen minutes, not an hour and a half. Polly's on half-time, now the schools open only three days a week to save power and staffing costs. She works far less hard than she used to and is much better-tempered as a consequence. With unemployment at 60 per cent there are enough people at home to look after the children and indeed teach them. Literacy rates have soared since there's been less schooling.

'Why didn't you ring me?' she asks. 'I'd have come over to fetch you, and I would have tidied up.'

The flat is in a mess. Nobody bothers to put things away, or arrange anything in a neat pile so it gives the impression, however false, of order and good cheer. This is not living, this is home as base. There are piles of clothes everywhere and Corey has been mending his motorbike in the kitchen. It is not in Polly's nature to tidy up any more than it is Corey's. She is too busy with what is in her head and he with what is not in his. The girls attend to their bodies and not what is around them. A shortage of water and light does not help. But I fear Polly is depressed. And there is something she is not telling me. She does not quite look me in the eye.

But at least she and Corey have managed to keep the flat. Money is short for everyone, but since NUG declared the debt amnesty for the lower-income groups life has been easier for a lot of people. Alas, the amnesty did not apply to the self-employed, such as me. Amos says it is the State's intention to get rid of all personal freedoms, and the comparative autonomy of the self-employed irks them. But then I see the State as a collection of committees making difficult decisions on our behalf, which quite often go wrong, while he personifies it as an irritable, stupid, domestic despot of an individual, neurotic, stalking the land and out to get him personally.

'My mobile's out of juice,' I said. 'Amos very kindly took it away to friends who have a generator.'

'I thought Health and Safety didn't allow generators,' said Polly. 'Trust Amos. Is he still with you?'

'Yes,' I said. What else was I going to say? That actually I have had to break out of my house because Amos asked some family round, including, by the way, your daughters; Ethan's girlfriend sealed up my lock with superglue; your half-brother Henry is an embryo Mussolini; the house next door is prepared for a kidnapping; Victor is in some way involved, and Venetia must be warned? If I could hardly believe this nonsense, how could she?

'Do you have any tea?' I asked. I needed time to think. 'And then if you have any petrol can we go round to Venetia's? It's so long since I've seen her.'

Polly set out to make nettle tea. Nettles grow quite profusely at the back of the Black Cat factory. It's damp and nettles like damp. Some 'real' tea is available – there was cheery stuff on NUGNews the other day about *Cutty Sark*-style clippers racing through the Roaring Forties as part of the revived tea trade. It looked great, but I was pretty sure most of it was special effects. Corey and the girls were at Westminster Abbey, said Polly, rehearsing for a free-for-all candle-lit performance of the *Messiah*. Corey had a good voice and the girls squeaked a bit on the high notes, but they had fun. They were staying overnight with friends. I hoped all this to be true. And yes, she had petrol, and she was happy to take me: there were a few things Venetia and I ought to sort out.

'What do you mean, sort out?' I asked. I was the mother: she was the child. I was the one who was in charge. But she kept talking as if it was the other way around.

'Actually,' Polly said, finally finding the tea in the general muddle and only then remembering to put on the kettle – the power was out but she has Calor gas – 'Venetia has been rather staying out of your way. She's putting off telling you. Henry's been staying up there with her and Victor. She doesn't want to hurt you.'

'So it's more than just the occasional visit on Friday nights?'

'Yes.'

'If you don't want to hurt me, Polly, try telling me the whole truth and not part of the truth.' I was quite sharp. She snivelled, as if she were a little girl, but I could see the time must come when I would snivel when reprimanded and she would not. It was not a nice thought. So few, when one thought of the future, were.

'But he's moving out this week. I think he may have gone already.'

Yes, and living next door to me. I was right, things were hotting up. The tea was horrible, but Polly had sugar.

'I suppose Venetia brought the sugar round on one of her Lady Bountiful trips,' I said.

'Now you're being mean about Venetia,' she complained. 'What is the matter with you? You're not usually like this. You look exhausted. Why come all this way if you're just going to be nasty to me? I've had enough troubles as it is today.'

I asked her what troubles. She said she'd been awake all night waiting for the girls to get home: when they did she couldn't sleep. She thought they were lying. They said they were going to a Redpeace meeting at Hunter's Alley. But it sounded more like some kind of rally to her, Polly, which would get them into trouble with the law. And their hands smelt of glue and she thought they might have been putting up posters. She longed for the old days when you worried about things like drink and drugs. When would things ever get back to normal?

'This is normal,' I said. 'It was the good times that were the anomaly.'

And I told her about the day way back in 2005 when I'd gone to a garage for some unrationed petrol for my '05 car and they had on sale – a bargain from China, only 99p – what looked like an six-inch-long cigarette lighter with a little compass set into the handle. I bought it. 'What's it for, exactly?' I asked, and the boy stared a little and said he had no idea – perhaps it was for lighting fires?

'But why then the compass?' I asked, and he shrugged. 'Someone thought it up,' he said. 'And you bought it, didn't you?'

I knew then we were heading for real trouble. If the wealth of nations depended upon the invention and creation of unnecessary things, such as battery firelighters with built-in compasses, we were already up shit creek. If the survival of multitudes depended upon pointlessness, and those multitudes existed only because of the desperate busyness of nations 'thinking things up', why then any shock, any surprise, could shatter the globalist construct. We were nearing the end of the tramlines of absurdity, and there would be nowhere to go but back. It was a process described by Carl Jung as enantiodromia – why Saul, persecutor of the Christians, saw a great light and turned in an instant into St Paul, defender of them. A great light shone into the world of unnatural plenty, and lo, there was frugality. It was the equivalent of the principle of equilibrium in the natural world, which declares that any extreme is opposed by the system in order to restore balance. The Great Accelerator, the Hadron Collider, switched on to discover the secrets of the universe, spun so fast for half an hour it burned itself to death. The super-abundance of any force inevitably produces its opposite, and so the overcrowded world, the dog devouring its own tail to satisfy its greed, must one day abandon consumption because, simply, it could go no further. And on that amazing day, the St Crispin's Day of the new order, we happened to be there.

'You'll make a drama out of anything,' was all Polly said. 'And it's all very well, but I have a dreadful cough.'

It's true, she has. Normal life is full of coughs, colds, toothache and unreplaced hips and knees. Money used to cure these ills: now it can't. Money is nothing but a medium of exchange, after all. And I have nothing to give in exchange any more, other than a little maternal love and concern. Once I gave money and bought and sold love, I daresay.

'Things have to bottom out in the end,' Polly said.

'No they don't,' I said. 'These are the Last Times, and we are the ones to witness them.'

Well, I am gloomy, and troubled. Old ladies imagine things. As you grow older the far past seems more real than the recent past. Surely I must have imagined what happened last night, this morning. The shock of the bailiffs' knock on the door – bang-bang-bang-de-bang – had triggered some paranoiac episode. Or I have finally flipped, and cannot tell fact from fiction any more, period. Bring on the men in white coats – only now they do not come kindly, to hospitalize you, they come in brown uniforms, to throw you in jail or disappear you in some even more sinister way, into Victor's pride, the pink oh-so-sliceable National Meat Loaf, perhaps. Or perhaps passive-smoking Amos' stinky skunk has upset my mental balance. And the surprise and shock of finding that Venetia is in touch with the by-blow Henry, who is not even a blood relative, has been the last straw. Oh, surprise, surprise!

There was a faith healer of Deal,
Who said though I fancy I feel,
When I sit on a pin,
And it punctures my skin,
I dislike what I fancy I feel.

That the world is in the state it is in is no fantasy. It is real enough. The tea Polly hands me is nettle tea, not Earl Grey. Even her face puckers at the taste.

'What are you doing, Mum?' asks Polly.

'Pinching my leg,' I say, 'to see if it hurts.'

'Does it?'

'Not much,' I say. 'But then I tend to be numb in odd places these days. The soles of my feet, for example, are no longer a reliable witness to the surface I walk on. But enough to tell me, yes, it hurts. Yes, I am real, and the world of NUG is real and the days of plenty are over for good.'

She hates me talking like this. She looks at me as if to say 'No wonder my father left you. No wonder he had a baby by the Irish Dumpling.' It is the look she directs at her students, no doubt, to keep them in order when their flights of fancy disturb her. Her father was an artist, her mother was a writer, and Polly means to keep not just her own feet on the ground, but those of everyone around her. She is a literal-minded soul. In her experience, creativity leads to disaster. I am quite sorry for her students, though they will pass their exams, heads bowed beneath the burden of so much reality.

And Polly certainly cannot conceive that we are really living in the end of times, that it's goodbye to all that, all the goodies we had in the past. The easy days will not come again: they were a one-off, an abortive mutation in the evolution of civilization, as the peacock's tail is over the top when it comes to attracting the dowdy peahen, merely an over-response. If the processes of evolution were to start all over, you could wait for ever for the peacock's tail, just as you'd have to wait for ever for the rise of the froth and bubble of the hedge funds, or Paris Hilton to step again from a plane in a white fur coat. An accidental over-response, now righted. Face it, the good times are gone. They will not return.

So, farewell to it all, to the time that was, when I was rich, and safe, guarded by money, when the streets were crowded and noisy and thrilling, not quiet, as they are now, and lovers knocked upon the door, not bailiffs. When I went to smart hairdressers and fashion shows, hired limousines at will, saw something I liked and just had it, person or possession. When there were mwah-mwah-mwahs from people who had their names in the papers, when I did too, when friends used my name to get a booking at The Ivy, and one ordered Iranian caviar without a second's thought for the poor pregnant fish whose eggs we stole and ate, at great expense, on money it turned out we didn't have. When people queued to talk to me at parties. Gone, all gone.

Marx saw first the collapse of capitalism under the weight of its own contradictions, the rise of communism and then the withering away of the State. I saw it in person: I was there on those St Crispin's Days.

> This day is called the feast of Crispian:
> He that outlives this day, and comes safe home,
> Will stand a tip-toe when this day is named,
> And rouse him at the name of Crispian.
> He that shall live this day, and see old age,

Will yearly on the vigil feast his neighbours,
And say 'To-morrow is Saint Crispian:'
Then will he strip his sleeve and show his scars.
And say 'These wounds I had on Crispin's day.'
Old men forget: yet all shall be forgot,
But he'll remember with advantages
What feats he did that day: then shall our names,
Familiar in his mouth as household words,
Lehman, Madoff, and Northern Rock,
The Royal Bank of Scotland, Brown,
Be in their flowing cups freshly remember'd.
This story shall the good man teach his son;
And Crispin Crispian shall ne'er go by,
From this day to the ending of the world,
But we in it shall be remembered;
We few, we happy few, we band of brothers.

Marx got the order of events wrong. I can bear witness. I was there. Communism was the first to go. I saw it fall at the Intellectuals' Conference in the Kremlin, when Gorbachev said that war was no longer revolution carried out by other means. That was in 1988. I was there in Berlin the day the Wall came down, in 1989, when anything-goes fled East and control fled West. I saw the collapse of capitalism, the first of the dominoes falling with Lehman in 2008, then down they all went, faster and faster, click, click, click, until the old order lay flattened on the floor. And yesterday morning I saw the rise of the State when Henry the lordly misbegotten spoke in my kitchen. The State has no intention of withering away.

Just another surprise, an unlikeliness, like Cynthia falling out of the sky: Henry turning up as master of the universe, Lord of the

New Republic, handsome and frightening in equal measure. William the Conqueror was William the Bastard back home in Normandy. They say that's why he felt the need to conquer England, just to change his surname. Must all England suffer because I was unkind, such a bitch to Karl that I wouldn't house his child?

'Oh Mum,' says Polly, 'write it all down.' (I will, I will, I say, and do.)

I must have been talking aloud. Another sign of batty old age.

'I was trying to tell you about my day,' she says, 'but you weren't listening.'

How about my day, girl? Yes, how about that?

She'd had a nasty fright. She'd been walking out of the Crescent into the Hampstead Road and a car coming towards her had mounted the pavement and was making straight for her and she'd had to jump backwards into a doorway to avoid it – and it had reversed and come back at her at speed, only there happened to be a security guard – one of the new ones with the brown uniforms and epaulettes, and a CiviCam in the helmet – just coming round the corner and the car had seemed to change its mind, squealed to a stop an inch from her, and then just driven on.

'Perhaps it mounted the kerb by accident, and came back to make sure you were all right,' I say, but my voice trails away. It's a rather feeble voice these days at the best of times. And this was not the best of times.

'It wasn't like that,' she says. 'I had the same "almost" feeling I had when I nearly fell under the train the other day. Almost dead. I can't die. The girls need me. Do you think paranoia is inheritable?'

'Yup,' I say.

'Because why would anyone run me down? It was an official car and should have been in the centre lane anyway. I expect the driver was drunk. Those Ministry drivers are famous; most of them are ex-bankers.'

'Born for the thrill of the chase. Ethan is one. What did the driver look like?'

'I don't know,' says Polly. 'But it was hardly likely to be Ethan. You can be very odd about your own flesh and blood, Mum.'

'Polly,' I say, 'let's just go and see Venetia now.'

'You promise not to make fuss about Henry, or Dad, or anything like that?'

I gritted my teeth – fortunately in the days of my wealth I had a lot of work done on my teeth – crowns, implants, and veneers aplenty – so I could grit them in confidence – and promised.

Surprise

It took some time to get up to Muswell Hill. There were roadblocks at Camden Town and Highgate, and Polly's little CiviCar had trouble getting up the hill. Amos says that underpowering the CiviCar is done on purpose, to make driving so unpleasant people stop doing it, use the buses to get to work, if they have any, or otherwise just stay put and sleep like good citizens.

I remember my mother saying that the streets were so quiet when she was a child because families had only one pair of shoes between them, and so stayed home. They couldn't afford to leave the house. It is beginning to be the same now, but there are still enough cars for a tailback of miles up the Hampstead Road.

'How's the writing going?' Polly asks, at Camden. The police were checking tyres.

'It's fine,' I say.

'But will anything come of it?' she asks.

'Probably not,' I say. 'But it's what I do.'

'So what are you writing about?' she asks, politely, but already bored.

'It's a fantasy about alternative universes,' I say. 'In which I didn't marry your father but your Aunt Fay did, and had four sons.'

'But if you hadn't married him you wouldn't have had me. You're wishing me out of existence.' She sounds quite hurt.

'Yes, but then she divorces him and I marry him and have you.'

'Is that legal? Marrying your sister-in-law? Surely not.' She's so literal.

'In my alternative universe all things can happen,' I say. 'But actually no, I'm just teasing. What I'm really writing about is an elderly woman living alone whose house is taken over by an extremist terrorist gang who also happen to be family, so she's torn.'

'You wish,' says Polly. She sits at the driving wheel and her jaw juts out and her little rosebud mouth is grim and who she reminds me of is Henry. But then she is his half-sister, so why should she not look like him?

But if I'm right, and all this is something I wrote, my invention and not real, how do I know what the grown Henry looks like? I won't have seen him since Karl came round to Chalcot Crescent when Henry was six weeks old. I wouldn't let them in the door. Edgar was in bed upstairs, beneath the striped Arabian counterpane which had been at the cleaners when Karl came to do his fell sweep of our belongings.

'What does Henry look like?' I ask.

'Very good-looking,' says Polly. 'Like a taller Mussolini with a big fascist jaw, but actually he is sweet.'

Not good. I am too accurate for comfort. I want to get back into my home, and rewind the film of my life to the time I am having lunch with Amos, after which the day proceeds normally. With no bailiffs, no Redpeace meeting, no Ethan, Amy or Henry or Polly's girls, no imprisonment and no escape. The trouble with escaping is that there has to be a return and if it's true and not what I wrote, how am I going to get back in my own front door?

I feel in my pocket and there is the key. That's something.

The real test will come of course when I stick it in the lock and see if it is indeed bunged up with superglue. If it is, then it is thanks to Amy, and my memory has not been playing tricks: the Redpeace plot exists. If the key turns easily and sweetly, then I am the victim of my own overheated imagination. Polly's mention of the Mussolini jaw might just be a coincidence, a lucky strike on my part. Perhaps someone once described Polly as having such a jaw – which I suppose she has: but I would never be so unkind as to say so to her face – and I buried the memory until it surfaced in the fictional account of Redpeace's intrusion into my life and home. Because after all if the shape of Polly's jaw is dictated by the genes of her father's line, then it might be true of Henry too. They are half-brother and half-sister, so it would be reasonable for my fictional Henry to have at least some resemblance to Polly. And yet, Occam's razor. 'One should not increase, beyond what is necessary, the number of entities required to explain anything.' The easiest and simplest explanation is that what I remember happening, happened. In which case, how do I get back into my house?

'Why doesn't she just go to the police?' Polly asks. 'This woman in your book?'

'She can't go to the police, because this is now, and not the old days,' I say. 'She is frightened that if she does the police will take in perps and victims alike, put them in a van and disappear the lot of them. In these days of overpopulation, simply to be associated with trouble is enough. As the Catholics used to say when crusading against the Albigensians, "Kill them all: God will recognize his own."'

'You exaggerate,' she says. 'You've been talking to Amos. He's such a conspiracy theorist.'

The policeman lets us through. I will say this for NUG: teachers and those in reserved occupations get free car parts and her CiviCar has new tyres.

217

A Flurry Of Slippages

At the Highgate roadblock CiviSecure, in their smart brown Hugo Boss uniforms, are checking that diesel cars are not running on tax-free central heating oil. If they are, they will be confiscated, and the drivers turned out to find their own way home as best they can. CiviCars have no locks on their tanks, and Polly is worried because Jokers have been caught in the Mornington Crescent area; occasionally you hear strains of the old TV *Batman* theme drifting over the rooftops. *To the Batmobile – let's go!* and then the durdurdurdur, durdurdurdur – broadcast from some high empty building, to be abruptly cut short as they pack up and leave before CiviSecure can get there.

And very spooky it can feel, with no Batman and Robin to the rescue. The current fashion of these roaming gangs is to add heating oil to permitted diesel. They think it's funny. Amos of course says it's a scam and NUG employs the Jokers and provides the illegal oil, so as soon as a car gets on to the market it will be confiscated and up for resale again. I don't think it's necessarily the case. I can hardly believe the Jokers are organized to this extent. They work singly or in packs, young men and women who are outside the system and look for their entertainment – violent computer games and films being banned – by making a nuisance of themselves. They model themselves on Batman's arch-enemy; they love chaos and destruction, finding it hysterically funny, and will disconcert passers-by, especially young girls, by suddenly revealing Joker lapel badges, which, when pressed, peal with maniacal laughter. Then they melt into the crowds. They used to wear rouge, but it made them too obvious so they stopped. Some say the old street gangs have simply united under a leader and evolved into the Jokers. NUG likes to blame them for the occasional dead body found in the street, the ransacking of a newspaper office, the odd knee-capping, but Amos of course says NUG is playing a double game, the Jokers are a useful scapegoat. He said as much at one Shabbat dinner and Victor almost conceded that it was true.

'The ends can justify the means,' Victor said. 'Justice sometimes needs to be silent, swift and sure. These days necessity rules.'

'Necessity,' said Amos, 'when it's not being the motherfucker of invention, is the excuse of tyrants and the creed of slaves.'

Those Shabbat dinners were getting increasingly tetchy. I was not altogether sorry when the Friday night invitations ceased to be a matter of course, and became occasional. And Venetia, the loving and dutiful daughter, kept up her habit of bringing round goodies for her poor old mum. But naturally not mentioning the arrival of Henry on the scene. I could see how much the girls wanted me to be 'civilized' about Henry, and I could understand it in Polly, but why Venetia? I had brought her into my marriage with Karl: I should surely expect some loyalty when I took her out of it? Was she not my appurtenance? That is not in accordance with contemporary thinking, I know, when all emotion is meant to be mild and not raise the blood pressure – but if you can't hate, how can you love?

'I couldn't bear to lose this car,' says Polly, as we wait in the queue at Highgate. She's nervous. She bites her nails. My fault. Everything that goes wrong with my children is my fault. She turns and smiles at me. She has a lovely smile, Karl's smile.

'At least,' she says, 'I have you with me. They're not likely to turn you out into the cold. You're an old lady. They may even recognize you.'

My children delude themselves as to the power of fame and wealth. Both, though part of the outer landscape of their lives, which they see as permanent, are transitory. If I was recognized, which is unlikely – CiviSecure teams are composed mostly of school-leavers – I might well be on a list of undesirables. I talk too much, and so can only be a fifty-second wife. I am too old and add that to talkative and I'm in trouble. I have too much memory of the past. I look younger than my years, but even so, the Dignity Civi-Van might arrive, the one rumoured to take the elderly off to the National Meat Loaf vats, whenever a new input of stem cells is required. I say as much to Polly and she looks at me in alarm.

'Mum,' she says, 'there is no such rumour.'

'Only kidding,' I say, but now I have thought of it I can see it might well be true.

I realize that this bout of trouble with what is truth and what is fiction, what true memory is and what false, started when I was sitting on the stairs with Amos. I had felt unreasonably happy, and the stillness, the sense of marvel, had descended. It was the slippage into an alternative universe, the same one I had felt up the alley kissing Venetia's father: also the night I stole Karl from my sister Fay: the night I turned Karl and the baby Henry away: occasions when all life switched and split and went off in an alternative direction. I expect there was another one the day my mother decided to carry on with the pregnancy that was me. Somewhere there are other universes where I do not exist, or Venetia, or Polly, where Fay married Karl and had four sons. There are an infinite number of universes: too many to contemplate.

The slippage I was conscious of yesterday was wavery – perhaps because I am getting too old for such events; they usually happen when people are young – perhaps because I write so much fiction, which is, after all, the creation of alternative universes by other means. Just as war is the continuation of revolution by other means. Either way, I would not be more certain of the universe that I was in. I only wish the slippage had happened before the bailiffs knocked upon the door and not after. I might find myself in one where all other things were the same, only I was not in debt; that would be really nice. I feel for the front door key in my pocket, to remind me that when I next use it, I will find which reality I inhabit.

> *There was an old crone from the Crescent,*
> *Who said though I live in the present,*
> *I know more than I should*
> *About things bad and good,*
> *Which happened or otherwise didn't.*

'Did you say something, Mum?'

'No.'

Polly bites too hard down on a fingernail and lets out a little cry of pain; the CiviCar edges forward a yard or two.

'Polly,' I say. 'What aren't you telling me?'

'It's just I don't think Venetia and Victor are getting on too well.'

'But he adores her,' I say.

'That's the myth,' says Polly. 'It suits us all. Actually he's a fascist bastard and he beats her up. She's not good enough for him any more.'

221

Surprise, surprise. Another universe in which things turn out differently. I go cautiously into it. I must remember that Venetia and Polly are half-sisters and there will be envy and possibly false witness. Venetia seems to have everything. Money, power, acknowledgement as an artist even though she can't paint for toffee, and by comparison Polly has so little. But if Venetia has an unhappy marriage and a brute of a husband, then that's one up to Polly. And Venetia was always Karl's favourite, and Polly felt it, and that won't help.

'Is that what she says or what you say?' I ask.

'Twice lately she's had a black eye and twice she's said she walked into a door. That could happen once but surely not twice.'

'You're not an artist,' I say. 'You don't walk into doors but Venetia may well forget they are there.' That hurts her. Poor Polly. She hates it when I bring up her general lack of aesthetic sensibility. Karl would complain that Polly had no taste, no awareness of her surroundings, which is why she could live in a dump in Mornington Crescent and not even notice.

'I didn't want to tell you before,' says my younger daughter, 'because Venetia might not want you to know. You know how proud she is. She said Victor had changed. He wanted her to change too and to go on a diet and be more like Carla Bruni. Mum, she told me she was frightened of him. And she had this black eye. But Mum, we have to get her away from him. She could always go and stay with you. There's no room in our flat.'

'How convenient,' I say, which is not at all nice of me, but I am upset.

Nobody likes the bearer of bad news, and that for me, at the moment, is Polly. I have a lot invested in Victor and Venetia being happy together and not all of it fresh coffee. I had rather hoped I might stay with Venetia until Henry and his cohorts moved out. Revolutionary cells do move on, that's the great thing about them: they're so paranoiac they find it difficult to trust the ground beneath their feet for long. A couple of weeks and surely this nasty, unreal episode would be over. I could have asked Polly and Corey to take me in but I didn't think I could stand the mess or the noise. As for Venetia moving in with me, it is out of the question; Amos has beaten her to my spare room, not to mention my top floors, forget the house next door. Venetia is going to have to stay where she is for the time being. I say as much to Polly.

'Victor is very stressed at work, of course, and that never makes for matrimonial bliss,' says Polly now. 'It may just be a bad patch they're going through.'

If I'm not going to take Venetia in, Polly certainly doesn't want to, so she's already backing down. But that doesn't mean that Victor hasn't taken to beating Venetia up. What is this new universe I'm in, in which Victor is a monster?

'Thank God Corey's work leaves him time enough to look after his family,' Polly goes on, smugly. And then she says that according to Amy the reason Victor is in a bad mood these days is because there's a vacancy on the Prime Committee at NUG, and NIFE being such a power in the land, what with the National Meat Loaf, Victor just might be appointed to it, or he might not, so he's tense.

I am certainly being kept out of the loop. Whole tangles of loops forming and re-forming in front of my eyes and nothing I can do about it, just sit here in a traffic jam.

'Like when Stalin, the country boy from Georgia, turned up to join Lenin and Trotsky,' I say. 'Did someone die to create this convenient vacancy?'

'I think she said it was a heart attack,' Polly says. Her usually confident teacherly ways have deserted her. We both wonder if this new Victor is capable of murder.

'People do die from heart attacks,' I say briskly. 'So now it's Top Brass Number One, Top Brass Number Two, and our Victor, and if NUG is reviving the cult of personality, as the photoshoots suggest, Victor will be its figurehead and will have quite a lot to hide. His wife's family can't be a source of comfort to him. And now you're going round saying to everyone he beats up his wife. Is this wise? NUGIntel is not going to like it. If you think strange men are trying to push you off Underground platforms and mow you down in cars, can you be surprised?'

'There was only me and her in the room.'

I wonder if she is telling the truth. I ask her which room and she said the new dream kitchen. I say, well, if that was the case it most certainly was not just her and Venetia in the room but NUGIntel too, the rooms being wired for sound, as all government offices were, so should we stop this conversation now?

Polly says but we're in the car, and I say, well, perhaps Amos is right and the Jokers are in the pay of NUG, and when they're out contaminating the diesel they're bugging the cars as well. Polly snorts and complains about my imagination. I say my imagination has paid her rent for long enough so let her not insult it and if I've learned one thing in a writer's life, it's that if you can invent something, someone, somewhere else, will actually be doing it. Salman Rushdie told me so.

She looks at me and her face changes, and pales. She nods.

'I've been stupid,' she says.

'Yes,' I say.

'Okay,' she says. She looks behind to see if she could reverse. I shake my head. That would make them even more interested. We must take our chances at the checkpoint.

'It takes them a long time to get round to things,' I say. 'We're probably okay.'

But thereafter our conversation is for public consumption.

'My sister rather inferred that Victor was beating her up,' Polly says loudly, 'and I was taken in at first but then I realized she was working out a what-if scenario for a construal art piece. She's a real artist, so creative. She imagines things. Victor and she love each other dearly, and the children. I really hope they become First Family – they so deserve to!' Well done, Polly, I thought. Probably too late but a good try.

'I didn't know you knew Amy,' I say casually. Suppose Polly is more involved than I thought. Perhaps she too is part of the Red-peace conspiracy, the New Republic? Perhaps she and Corey know very well where their children go in their spare time?

'Amy works for the Neighbourhood Watch,' says Polly. 'She's very keen. She came to talk to our school about the Feeding NUGNation children's campaign. How are your potatoes going?'

'Very nicely indeed,' I say. 'No rot, no weevil. Neighbourhood Watch is a fine institution. They're so right, grow what feeds you, not what pleases you.'

Plant the veg, forget the flowers.

'So true,' says Polly. 'Amy's a nice bright loyal girl even though she doesn't quite seem Ethan's type.'

'That's what I thought,' I say. 'But it takes all sorts.'

'I hadn't realized you'd met her,' Polly says.

'I once called by at Hunter's Alley and she was there.'

I can lie fast. I write fiction. But I am not feeling too good. If Polly knew Amy as I knew Amy, oh, oh, oh, what a girl! Chances that my front door key will fail to turn in the lock rise to 100 per cent. My universes are no longer wavering. This is the real one, and it isn't nice. How am I going to get back into my home?

Victor At The Office

The queue moves slowly. One in three drivers are being turned out to make their own way home, lucky not to be prosecuted. Either the testing apparatus is faulty or the Jokers have been particularly active. No-one questions, no-one protests.

As for me I am not quite strong enough for reality yet. Better to envisage this new Victor at the office. I have an altogether different view of him now, no longer the benign patriarch: no longer the young Mugabe but the old. People do change.

Now he sits at a great desk in a large room: the man of power. I was once invited to the offices of the head of the Writers' Union in Tbilisi. He was a fleshy, handsome man with a moustache and a vain, cruel face. There was an ante-room, all tattered gold and crimson splendour, lined with moth-eaten chairs on which pale-faced supplicants sat, queuing for favours. All looked shabby, shoes thin-soled. I was led in past them. I took precedence, there by invitation. Their hungry eyes followed me. They hated me. A shuddering girl in a tattered dress crouched in a corner of his room. God knows what went on there. I doubted that the Culture Tsar had ever read a book in his life.

Instead of a background of faded baroque splendour, everything around Victor is clean and trim, modern and soulless, hard-edged. Otherwise what's the difference? The ante-room at the National

Institute for Food Excellence is also full of hungry-eyed hopefuls, on their cellphones and BlackBerries, ready to murder for a place in the queue, wanting favours, hoping for preferment. The girl in the tattered dress has turned into a Kate Moss at sixteen lookalike, but the principle is the same. The brave deserve the fair, and why does a man want power other than to have his pick of women? Come to think of it, the Victor in my vision has a faint look of Berlusconi about him.

The vats in the purpose-built labs behind the Banqueting Hall in Whitehall are a mass of heaving, pulsating rumps of flesh: rounded hare-like haunches that look all too like skinned baby limbs as they dip and surface in warm bubbling organic broth. Behind are the laboratories where experiments are perfected: dissecting tables on which flayed animals and humans are pinned out, some still sentient, some not, organs and stem cells for the asking. *NUG – Caring for the Nation! Your Health Is Our Responsibility!*

'It has to be done, how else are we to eat?' as Victor would argue. And I like National Meat Loaf as much as anyone. The many must suffer that the few may prosper. *NUG – Building Opportunity and Tolerance*. Truckloads of victims come into the yards where they've cleared space all the way down to the Thames. *NUG – Moving Beyond the Voluntary*. They arrive, under cover of night. The area is a no-go for civilians. *NUG – Discovering What's Best for You*. By day the same vans leave, hosed clean, no doubt, and now carrying delectable cans of salt-free National Meat Loaf. *NUG – Creating New Ways of Thinking*.

And here comes NUG in person into Victor's office. Two top brass: you can tell from their body language, and the smoothness in the fall of their suits. (Whatever the government, good tailors, good cooks and good cleaners will always survive. The chambermaid

228

escapes a bullet when the royal family is shot: someone has to make the beds.) Victor raises his bulk to meet them. He is nervous. Is this to be the good news he hopes for or the bad news he fears? It is the good news. Smiles all round.

The young Kate Moss clone, who must have said something out of turn and is huddled in the corner like the Tbilisi girl in the tattered dress, pulls herself together quickly and produces champagne. The men behave as if she wasn't there: she is merely an office accessory with a rapidly developing black eye. They will notice her if they are in the mood for casual sex but not otherwise. Women should never forget that men are bigger than they are and liable to lash out if provoked and unobserved: the respect that virtue brings sometimes protects a girl, but I doubt if this one was laying claim to that.

I remember at the Moscow Writers' Union back in the seventies pretty girls with writing talent were expected as a matter of course to offer sexual and secretarial services for very low wages and think themselves lucky to be employed at all. One of them told me she wanted to write a novel but where would she find the time?

'Get up early,' I advised her. 'Do it before the working day begins.' That was my advice in my own country.

'But I get up at five anyway,' she said, in her perfect English, 'and I don't get to bed until past one.'

She lived with her in-laws and her husband and child in a small apartment and they expected her to keep house and cook food and clean up for all of them, and when she got to work her boss required 'comfort' before the day began. Perhaps some day, should she have pleased him enough, she might be invited to join the Union, and be eligible to publish, but what would be the use of that if you had nothing written to publish? I gave up offering advice.

'Victor,' Top Brass Number One is saying to him now, 'the Prime Executive met this morning and agreed that the Ministries of Culture, Sport and Family Values are to be grouped under Nutrition. National Meat Loaf is an achievement of which NUG can be truly proud. A heavy workload, we know, but if all goes well it puts you in line for the Presidency. Perhaps lose a little weight, dear man? The presidential role is mainly photogenic. No reason why things should not go well? No family scandals, no hidden indiscretions?'

'Of course not,' Victor says. 'Nothing at all of that kind.'

They raise a toast to the dear departed Top Brass Number Three whom Victor is replacing. Victor is urbane and charming, his skin polished and plump. The other two are misshapen and ugly, as if they wore their hideous souls spread over their bodies like rancid butter and it ate inwards and consumed them. They need a public face.

'A fine fellow,' says Number One, 'but never quite one of us. Too much the sociologist, the theorist, not enough the pragmatist.'

'Ate and drank too much,' says Number Two, 'but the wrong food, clearly. Never touched National Meat Loaf. Moral objections.'

'A great mistake,' says Victor.

Top Brass Number Two has noticed the Kate Moss lookalike. She has managed to tear her dress a little and a section of breast is exposed. Probably the tattered nature of the Tbilisi girl's dress was contrived, and my pity wasted.

'Perhaps you'd like to lend me your secretary for a week or two,' Top Brass Number Two is saying, 'or are you very short-staffed?'

'I daresay I can manage,' says Victor. 'There's always the agency pool.'

Visiting Venetia

The queue moves forward. We have no option but to reach the CiviSecure barrier. There are eight young brown-shirted males at the booth. They are overquick and edgy in their movements and I assume are on drugs. They carry weapons, and are scarcely more than children. Everyone hates them. We get out of the car. They study our IDs for rather a long time. One of them looks at me and smiles and gnashes his teeth a little, in a nibbling movement. Once upon a time it would have been a pass, but now I wonder if he just wants to eat me. The trouble with giving birth to a rumour is that it may well come true. They wave us on. We get back into the car, trying to look as uncaring and unthinking as we can.

We pass a motorist who has been rash enough to give lip to the wrong people as he sets out on the long walk down the hill. He is in the centre of a circle of young men – and women too, I am sorry to say – and the Jokers' maniacal laughter echoes all around as they push him from one to another. Most now sport rouged clown circles on their cheeks again and some wear Joker noses. Heaven knows where it will end – badly, I fear.

We drive up towards Muswell Hill and the famous view over all London.

'Let's get out and look at the view,' I say, just in case.

There are still some things to be said which others should not overhear. There are useful gaps in the houses and shops up here, where properties were burned down in the middle-class tax riots of 2011, so at least you can get to see the view. The London of my childhood, when we first arrived after World War II, was gat-toothed like this. Hitler's bombs had done that damage. Now we did it to ourselves. Some said it was because we were allowed no enemies for so many years, but must love everyone, that we had forgotten the uses of the common enemy and had turned our innate aggression inwards, not outwards. Though you could see NUG building up resentment once more against the French. We'd moth-balled most of our reactors and gone over to wind power. The French hadn't, so still had plenty of nuclear power, but refused to share it with us. If we could all hate the French, at least we need not hate each other.

Polly and I stood together and looked across to the far towers of Canary Wharf, and I felt great affection for her. She was flawed, but so was I, and by what right did one require a perfect child? She had given me only quasi-grandchildren, true, but Venetia had given me real ones all right, and look what had happened there. Children were once seen as the punishment for sex, and if they were, why then the universe was only exacting its price for the pleasures I had enjoyed with Karl.

'It's green where once it was grey,' Polly says, and it's true.

The Thames Barrier had failed in November 2012 and the flooded area had more or less been abandoned, and foliage crept up to cover cracked concrete. As with the bombed landscape of London in 1946, it was remarkable how quickly nature re-established itself. Japanese knotweed could crack bricks, and did; bougainvillea had started a long, long, colourful journey up the sides of steel towers. Someone up here had charitably set up a telescope, the kind you used to get on seaside piers, in one of the razed sites and trained it on E14. The telescope stayed unstolen and undamaged; vandals, contrary to expectation – and if you left out the suspiciously too well-organized Jokers, who presumably did not have telescopes on their to do, ha-ha lists – were a rarity. If things are in short supply there is less impulse to destroy, though perhaps more to steal.

'I may be completely wrong,' I say. 'I'm a novelist. Two coincidental accidents don't make a murder attempt. Because CiviCars are leased out by NUG doesn't mean they're all bugged. Because a thought crosses both our minds that Victor is capable of disappearing a political rival, doesn't mean he is. Because Venetia implies Victor beats her up, doesn't mean he does.'

'How can you doubt the word of your own daughter!' complains Polly. 'What sort of feminist are you? If a man lays a finger on a woman it is her duty to leave at once. She owes it to her sisters.'

And there, on the top of Muswell Hill, she makes a political speech with only her mother to hear. She manages to leave Corey out of her definition of 'man' – I would be very surprised if he hasn't taken the odd swipe at her – so much does she like the sex. She is in denial. But then I suppose we all use our indignation as cover for the real dangers in our lives. Amos will be raging against the evils of society while he is smoking and drinking himself to death. It is not so much denial, I daresay, as a misplacement of fear. We rage because we are afraid.

In the face of her own theoretical indignation against the male, I notice, she seems to have forgotten her own predicament. It is left to me to point out that if even the remote possibility exists that political powers are out to get rid of her, her girls could be left motherless, and Corey would perhaps prove an adequate single parent, but probably not. It wouldn't necessarily be Victor doing it, I am at pains to point out – it would be NUGInform, busy building the image of Victor as the respectable, God-fearing husband and father he once was and now to all accounts no longer is.

Marking Time

It's not that I don't understand Polly's indignation. We went to a café and spent far too much money on two cups of acorn coffee with dried milk, and what they called a Spam sandwich, which was actually slices of National Meat Loaf between some rather stale National Bread, but up here tradition lingers, and vegetarians are not altogether convinced that NML is suitable for vegetarians, though the slogans say so. My vision of the bubbling broth and the hare-like haunches stayed with me a little as I lifted the stuff to my mouth but not for long. It was good, though if Victor was in charge of the nation's bread he should do something about the texture. This batch was so gritty it stuck between the teeth.

As we sit there, putting off the time when I will have to come face to face with Venetia, I realize just how much I don't want to see her. What happens next is going to be even more dreadful than what is happening now. Forget the sealing up of my front door, forget Redpeace, forget NUG, forget Venetia's putative battering, Polly's 'accidents', I will have to talk about Henry to Venetia. I have to face my own anger, my own past. And we have got along so satisfactorily for so many years without doing so.

A Story For Feminists: Skip At Will

Polly is still fuming about my lack of feminist credentials so I tell her the story of Doreen, who came to the door of Chalcot Crescent in the early days of my marriage to Karl. The girls are always glad when I manage to talk about Karl without rancour: it somehow seems to validate their childhoods.

In the winter of 1965 a pretty girl called Doreen – pretty in a febrile, sensitive, quivery, me-me-me kind of way, a fashion model from South Africa – knocked at the front door of Chalcot Crescent in the middle of the night. I left Karl sleeping in the bed and went downstairs shivering in my nightie, and there found Doreen and her seven-year-old daughter Chloe on the step. They too were in their nighties – white cotton with pink smocking as was fashionable at the time – shivering in the cold. Doreen's face was streaming with blood. Her nose was broken. They had run out in the street and come to me. Chloe held her mother by the hand rather than the other way around. I didn't know her very well but she lived round the corner and Chloe went to the same school as Venetia. I found a cloth for Doreen's face, and put Chloe to bed in the lower bunk in Polly's bedroom. She asked if I would look after Mummy and I said I would. 'Daddy shouts in the night,' she said, and went off to sleep. I put Doreen to bed on the sofa.

I knew Daddy shouted because I had been woken one night a

month or two earlier also by Doreen, calling me up on the phone, whimpering down the line and saying, 'Stop him shouting,' and this roaring sound halfway between an enraged bull and the sound of a sjambok cutting through the air, and 'Help me, help me' from Doreen. And then the phone was slammed down mid-roar. I didn't have her telephone number to call back and it was before the days when you pressed a key and it happened. Karl had woken and asked what was happening. I said I thought Saul Delpick the journalist was murdering his wife.

'Oh her,' said Karl, 'she deserves it. She's a drunk. I would murder her if she was mine. Come back to bed.'

So I went back to bed, but I can still hear the air quivering with the violence and hatred of that shout, and the sense of entitlement that went with it.

I checked out where she lived and went round and Doreen was limping and her face was bruised and she said she had walked into a door. She was courteous but distant. I went away and asked around friends, and people looked shocked at the very suggestion that someone as respected as Saul could possibly be harming his wife, and more, that if he was she must have provoked him. It was the time before sisterhood. Female loyalty was owed to the provider of money and home, not to friends. Women got the blame for everything in those days. If a man ran off with his mistress, the wife had neglected him or the mistress had seduced him, or probably both. The man stayed innocent and well thought of throughout.

Karl was angry and wanted her out of his house, out of his life, off his sofa. Saul was his friend and Doreen was going round bad-mouthing a good man: she was a neurotic slut who had trapped him into marriage, slept around and called poor Saul vile names. It was true: I had heard her impugn her husband's virility over the dinner table, and shocking it was, but then if he beat her up in private by night she might turn a bit nasty in public by day. Ranks closed against me. This was not at the time a possible scenario. Wife battering was known to happen amongst the drunken, ill-educated, work-shy classes, but not in middle-class homes. Sex-crazed women deserved a beating, asked for it, and even encouraged it, the better to enjoy the reconciliation afterwards.

Everyone said Doreen had dragged her child out of bed in the middle of the night and broken her own nose to make it bleed.

I paid for a hotel, I paid her lawyers, I paid to set her free. She divorced Saul and moved back with Chloe into the marital home. It was unheard of. Until that court case, if you left your husband you left the child. No-one forgave me, and I daresay my defiance of Karl started the rot of our marriage. The Dumpling did as she was told.

'Why come to me?' I asked Doreen that night. 'You have lots of friends to go to.'

'You're the only brave one,' she said, 'because you earn your own money.'

'I suppose now you have no money,' said Polly, 'you are no longer brave.'

'That's pretty much true,' I said.

238

Polly In Another Sulk

'You've told me all this, Mum,' says Polly. 'But it's way in the past.' How children do hate to receive instruction from their parents. I sympathize. I remember my grandmother trying to teach me to play the piano, and the boiling rage of resentment it called up in me. 'Can we get on? At this rate we'll never get to Venetia's.'

'I've never told you what happened next,' I say.

I tell her Saul never forgave Doreen and never stopped loving her. He married again and beat up the second wife in the same way. Doreen stayed lonely and tearful for the rest of her life, which was not a long one. She took to yoga and drink and had druggie boyfriends who also beat her up. She neglected the house once it was hers, died of drink and few people came to her funeral. Chloe was okay, but after the flight in the night became and stayed overweight. Nervy people can coat themselves in fat so the slings and arrows of outrageous fortune don't hurt so much when they land. I think that was the case with Chloe.

I should not have interfered. Doreen and Saul would still be together, and might even have gone to AA and no longer disturbed the neighbours; Saul's second wife would have been saved the shouting and hitting. Chloe would have grown up to be as beautiful as her mother. Fathers for Justice would not have gone on risking their necks perching on tall buildings in attempts to see their children.

I have really annoyed Polly. This not what she wants to hear about – the difference between what ought to happen and what does happen. For example, you go to Turkey because you deserve it, and come back to fall out of the sky. Justice is not built into the system, but this is a really hard concept for some people to accept.

At the third roadblock rebuilding is proceeding apace. I scarcely recognize the area. Most has been torn down: big new attractive houses – the word dacha comes to mind – parklands and ponds are being built where once Grand Avenue stood in suburban splendour. Dominating all, such has been the skill of NUG architects, is the old Victorian family home of Victor and Venetia, now with an outgrowth of steel and glass buildings, and topped by an array of spiky aerials, which means it is very much in touch with the rest of the world.

We have to line up behind rows of white CiviVans, no doubt already bringing in items of luxury and pleasure. It was like the Good Days back again, when the traffic jams would be caused by cheerful activity and the sheer volume of vehicles, not the booths of CiviSecure. The end of the road is gated, as is Downing Street, and the policemen are armed. But at least here we have proper adult policemen to check our passage, stare at us long and hard, and confiscate our IDs. They are polite to us but check ahead and we are motioned into a lay-by to wait for permission to pass.

Polly Tells The Truth

'It seems NUG is coming to Victor, not Victor going to NUG,' I say.

'Told you so,' says my daughter. And then, 'It's probably nothing to do with Victor beating her up, probably no-one minds that at all, like you: at least they have the excuse that they're men. You don't.'

I wonder what it is she objects to exactly. The truth or my refusal to deny the truth? It's a fact that in the past I never carried the story on to its proper end but wrapped it up with the successful court case. Today was different.

'It's the other things she told me,' complains Polly. I hate it when she is in this mean mode.

I blame myself for having smoked while I was pregnant with her. But perhaps I don't need to. Polly is a Scorpio and they can get moody, bitchy, self-pitying and destructive, in which case one can blame the time of birth and not the faulty, irresponsible, smoking mother and I am off the hook.

'And even then I wish she had not told me what she did,' Polly goes on. 'I don't know why she had to, since she spent nearly thirty years not, and never told a soul.'

'What is that, Polly?' I ask. 'What secret?'

Long-kept secrets are usually to do with the fathering of babies. Ethan someone else's baby, not Victor's? But I'd have known. Surely. And it's true; Ethan doesn't look much like Victor. Even I have remarked upon that. Then who? Who was involved with Venetia all those years ago?

'Tell me about it,' I say.

'We'll have to get out of the car,' she says, 'if your mad fantasies about bugging are true.'

'Okay,' I say, and get out of the car. I wish I hadn't.

Surprise, Surprise, Surprise

Good Lord, I think: surely I deserve a break. That's what Cynthia said and I denied it to her. Now it's I who deserve one. I may have been a bad girl in my youth but since then I've paid my way, worked hard all my life, been a conscientious citizen, got the law changed, become wealthy and famous, worked for charity, helped others on their way, was dubbed a Dame for my pains, had books published and plays performed, and still it has come to this.

Forget bailiffs at the door, the taxman coming, eyesight if not exactly fading, at least needing light bulbs that are bright, God help me now. Do not let me hear what I think I am going to hear, and from the mouth of my own daughter, who ought to know better than to try to kill me with the truth. The girls have always been full of blame, blaming my various lovers for my present predicament. I blame myself – for the last thirty-five years I have caught up lovers and husbands in a spiral of self-destruct and they really didn't know what hit them.

'What Venetia told me,' says Polly, 'and she was crying and bending over the sink with a bit of steak held to her eye – can you imagine, real steak? – wasn't just about him hitting her, it was about Ethan.'

'If Victor had just "heard about Ethan" perhaps that is why your sister had a piece of steak to her eye. Men get funny about that kind of thing. When your father realized I had a lover, he hit me. I didn't hold it against him. I do not suppose Venetia will hold it against Victor. I hope they sort it out.'

I add that I am glad the taps have been running because it might mask what was heard on the mikes. Polly doesn't like the thought of me having a lover – one rule for the men, apparently, one for the women, same old thing – and called me a slut.

'No, I was not a slut,' say I. 'Certainly not by the standard of the times.'

And I point out that I'd only had a lover in the first place because her father had decided he was too good for me, artistically speaking, and had already gone off with a semi-human, malformed creature shaped like a dumpling. What was I meant to do? Live on my own and mourn my loss for ever? I was doing it for their sake, I add. So I wouldn't be an emotional burden on them for ever.

'She was a perfectly nice, very attractive woman, just not too bright and a bit fat. And I don't think you're remembering things in order,' says Polly. 'Our father made a mistake, that's all, and wanted to come home. But you only cared about yourself, not us.'

Ah, there we have it, laid out clear.

'So I suppose Venetia having a baby and palming it off on poor Victor is my fault too? I like Victor.'

'Mum,' she says, 'you only like Victor because it's through him you get hold of real coffee and sugar. You are a Vicar of Bray. Victor is a monster who puts human meat stuff into the National Meat Loaf.'

I am aware that I am putting off the moment of truth, and so is she. I more or less know what I am going to be told. I want to live in a world in which I don't know a little longer.

'You've been reading Redpeace,' I say. 'It's all in there and all lies.'

'Ethan says it isn't.'

'Does Ethan know he isn't Victor's child?'

'No.'

'Then he's an ungrateful lout, biting the hand that feeds him.'

But I can put it off no longer.

'Who is Ethan's father? Tell me.'

One should never ask one's children a direct question any more than offer a direct command, it opens the way too easily to a blank refusal to speak, or act. I remember only too well an episode upon the stairs when I forgot and told Polly outright to wash her face. She had come back from Primrose Hill where she had been taking part in a protest. The conversation had gone like this. She was six.

'What was the protest about?' I asked her.

'Something about caning in schools,' she said.

'Do you have caning in your school?'

'No.' Then realizing I was questioning the reasonableness or otherwise of the protest, she added, 'But we might have any time.'

'Ah,' I said. Then because her mouth was ringed with a mixture of ice cream, chocolate and sticky sweets I said,

'Go and wash your face, Polly.'

'No,' she said.

'Polly,' I repeated. 'Your face is very dirty. Go and wash it.'

'I won't,' she said.

'Do as I say.'

'No. Why should I?'

I think hard for a good reason.

'Because I'm your mother.'

'I didn't ask to be born.' Very shrewd. Where can she have got it from? She's only six. I should have said, 'Wouldn't it be a good idea for you to wash your face,' or 'You would look much prettier with a clean mouth' – anything but the direct command. The 'no' still comes, but only to the proposition, not the command. But too late now.

'I told you to wash your face, so wash it.'

'No. Why should I?'

'Because I'm bigger than you,' I said, getting to the nub of the matter, and I slapped her across the cheek to prove it. I have never hit her before or since, or, until now, given her a direct command. She said nothing and stared at me. She turned on her heel and went to her bedroom, which was then where my kitchen is now. I stayed where I am, helpless with remorse. What had I done? She will hate me for ever. A minute later she comes out of her room. Her face is smeared with blood.

'See what you did,' she said. I was horrified. Then I remembered she could make her nose bleed at will by sticking a sharp fingernail up her right nostril.

I began to laugh. So did she. She went up to the bathroom and washed her face, from blood and ice cream, chocolate and sticky sweets, and came down good as gold, and peaceful. I do not think this conversation will have so good a conclusion this time.

'It isn't going to be easy for you,' says Polly. 'It wasn't easy for me either, I can tell you. Another half-brother all this time, and not knowing. But it's not as if they were blood relatives.'

'I told you to tell me who Ethan's father is.'

'Oh Mum, work it out. She only did it for your sake. So you and Karl would get together again, and poor little Henry would have a mother. But you wouldn't.'

So. Karl. Karl fucked his stepdaughter and Ethan was born. The square Mussolini jaw came down through the male line.

The senior policeman is coming over to us. He is smiling. We have been approved.

'I'm honoured,' he says, 'Lady Venetia's mother and sister! We'll lead you in.'

'I'm so sorry,' I say. 'I've been taken rather suddenly ill. My daughter here will take me home.'

He is all concern, but I say I feel faint and I have no doubt I look it.

Polly takes me home. There are no roadblocks. She prattles on the while. I think I hate her too.

'We should have gone on in to see Venetia,' she says. 'It wasn't good to back out like that. We should all have talked it through. Made our peace.'

Where does she think she's living? Munchkinland?

'Mother, it happened a long time ago. She's had to bear the burden of secrecy ever since.'

The burden of secrecy! The joy of deceit, more likely.

'Poor Daddy. He was so unhappy when Claire died, and he tried so hard with the baby.'

And what did Daddy think I was, when he left? Happy?

'And you know how Venetia always adored him. And she was all alone with Amos.'

Oh the poor, poor thing. I was paying for her keep, sending Amos to school. Venetia is a festering store of ingratitude.

'And Daddy had become so helpful about her art. It made such a difference to her. It's only like Woody Allen and his stepdaughter. They're very happy together.'

I don't seem to remember Mia Farrow being very happy about it.

'It's not like it was an abuse of power thing.'

'No?'

'Oh Mum, loosen up.'

Is she insane?

'Venetia didn't mean to get pregnant. When she found out she wanted to get rid of it, but Karl said keep it. It would be company for Henry. He really loved Henry. Venetia would have moved in with Daddy but she thought it would make you unhappy, so she married Victor and everyone assumed it was Victor's child.'

Oh honourable, kindly, disgusting Venetia. 'Lady' Venetia. That was quick. You are not my daughter. Every pleasure I ever took in motherhood I hereby renounce and deny.

I wish you had never been born. I envisage you and Karl together and want to vomit. You took me into another universe all right and it is hell, and ever since I've known you, always has been. I should never have been born. I curse my mother's womb, and my own, and Venetia's. And Polly's, come to that. I almost curse Rosie's and Steffie's but find I can't.

Prattle, prattle, prattle, on Polly goes. God, she's stupid.

'Mum. Please speak to me. You haven't said a word all the way down.'

'Just leave me on the corner of the Crescent. I'll be fine.'

She leaves me on the corner of the Crescent. I go to No. 3 and try to turn the key in the lock. I can't. It is bunged up with super-glue. I walk round the corner to 7 Rothwell Street and find the front door open. I am not conscious of pain in my knees but I expect it is there. I go through the house and into the potato field and across the mud, and curse the potato flowers and hope they wither and rot. No. 5 is as I left it. They have not come back. Perhaps they have been arrested and shot and made into National Meat Loaf. I hope so. I get up the stairs somehow, past the empty armchair with the still-waiting duct tape, through the hole in the wall, and down again to my own room. I lie on the bed and fall asleep.

Presently I wake up and open up my laptop and write the scenes between Karl and the slut Venetia.

Karl And Venetia

A country farmhouse, dilapidated and charming. Old copper pans for cooking hang from ancient beams, and are actually used, though badly in need of tinning. An ancient Aga, a charming old oak Welsh dresser, hung with chipped antique mugs and lined with cracked blue-and-white china. Everything is good to look at from a distance but on close inspection, rather grimy. A red hen running about the floor and shitting at will, two cats and two dogs. Paintings and drawings fill every available space on the walls. Ornaments and *objets trouvés* cover every surface. A toddler sits on the floor, wet-nappied, sticky-mouthed, untended. A slight smell of spliff and baby's poo combine to make a warm, welcoming atmosphere. An artist's home, fertile and creative.

Outside, geese chattering. A cluster of rather scraggy rare-breed sheep that probably don't get enough to eat stare mournfully towards the house. Venetia pulls up in her fetching yellow Volkswagen. The sheep scatter in alarm. She wears white and high- heeled pink shoes. She has a nice figure and a soulful look. She goes inside and snatches up the baby, takes it to the sink and starts washing its bottom. Fortunately, and surprisingly, there is a roll of paper towels available.

Venetia: [*calling*] Dad!

Karl comes down the stairs. He wears an artist's smock and practically has a paintbrush between his teeth. He is a cross between Picasso and Rembrandt.

Karl: Oh it's you, Venn. Don't call me Dad.

Venetia: [*hurt*] Why not?

Karl: Because I'm not your dad. We are not blood relatives. I just happened to be around when your spider mother caught me like a fly in her trap. I struggled for years and finally escaped. I should have gone home with her sister and it would never have come to this. Alone, a baby on my hands, a show to get ready in the next six weeks and the tank out of heating oil. I have been very depressed, Venn.

Venetia: I'm sorry. I found the baby sitting on the floor crying and covered with shit.

Karl: Then thank you for picking him up. I don't know how he gets out of his cot.

Venetia: Babies do grow, Daddy, with time.

Karl: That daddy thing again! It's perverted. Don't do it.

Venetia: It is very cold in here. The baby's nose is running. Dad, you can't live like this. And Mum can't live like she is. She cries all the time. It's too upsetting.

Karl: Your mother is perfectly happy in my house, which as you know well she robbed me of, cavorting with her lover. What do you expect me to do about it?

Venetia: Go back to her. She loves you.

Karl: Of course she loves me; women always love me, the meaner I am to them the more they come crawling. That is her misfortune, not mine. She's a selfish hard-hearted neurotic half-man of a bitch. Claire was all woman. She had at least some aesthetic

251

understanding and it's a tragedy to the art world that she's gone. Let alone to me.

Venetia: Daddy, Camberwell are giving me a joint show. Former pupils. Will you come to it?

Karl: No. Nothing good ever came out of Camberwell. Put that baby to bed and come up to the attic and see what I'm doing. Since I left your mother it's all falling into place.

Venetia: The baby needs feeding,

Karl: It can wait.

He finds a baby's bottle full of a browny-pink liquid and puts it in the baby's mouth. The baby drinks and falls asleep.

Venetia: What's that?

Karl: A herbal tea. Have some.

She says no, and then she drinks. He makes her some more. The baby is put to bed. They go up together to his attic which is full of paints and turpentine and paintings of Claire naked (he never painted me naked) and it's as erotic as hell. She flatters him and tells him he's better than Picasso and looks like Picasso too. It's so cold they have to get under the old kelim carpet – worn so thin it can be used as a blanket. She tries to persuade him to come back to me, and he says if he was feeling warmer he might consider it, so she does what she can to warm him, and because she's always wanted to since she was seven, and now she's one up on me, isn't she. And actually, oddly, now that's out of their system, he does give it a go but I turn him away. He doesn't come back to haunt me, more's the pity, but the baby does.

But that's enough of that. Why do I torment myself?

Action, Not Reflection

I shut up my laptop. I have put off life long enough, which is all writing is. I understand Venetia now: I don't forgive her. I do not want to see her or think of her again. She is too like me: a girl with round heels (the ones who with just a push fall back upon a bed), in a state of acute denial; she does exactly what she wants while believing she is acting selflessly. Karl is mad, not bad, and uses 'art' in the same way, to justify his actions. If we all fell for it and suffered for it, more fool us. And besides, he is dead – as Venetia said to me of my father, when she was five, and I was trying to explain the concept of death – 'Oh I see. One of those people who lived in the past.' But all such charming memories have been rendered worthless. I would be quite happy to be the same: someone who lived in the past. But I do not have the tablets to hand to see to it.

I had a daughter, Venetia, who, in my absence, slipped in beside my husband and had a baby by him. She reared the baby as another man's, under my nose, and hugged the guilty, joyous secret to herself. These are the facts of the matter. Forget governments, food shortages, kidnappings, CiviSecure and the like – they are what they are and change with the times – we could be living just as well through the Great Plague, or the Inquisition – the world outside the home composes just the frame for our lives, not the life itself.

Me and mine have been betrayed by my daughter, this is the nub of the matter. All the rest is white noise.

I have no idea what the time is. I have no mobile, no clock. I listen. All is quiet next door. The space is empty. The armchair and its rolls of duct tape wait for a victim who perhaps will never come. I look out the back window. It's dusk. The white potato flowers seem luminescent. I hope they have not been damaged by my curses. After all, what has changed? Ethan – my grandchild and stepchild both – is still the man he is, and not so interesting a human being, come to that. I have never been so attached to him as I have been to his brother Amos. I used to think that was because Ethan had inherited Victor's scientific bent, but no. He just lacks the creative sensibility of the rest of the family. Though he is certainly not as bright as his half-brother Mervyn. Venetia was wasting her time. Though if Ethan and Amy were to have children – is it even possible that I misremember and Venetia was Terry's child –

Women have a great propensity to forget what is inconvenient – namely, who exactly is the father of this baby kicking away in my tummy?

The song in my mind surfaces. 'I Am My Own Grandpaw' –

> *I was married to a widow, who was pretty as could be,*
> *This widow had a grown-up daughter*
> *Who had hair of red,*
> *My father fell in love with her*
> *And soon they too were wed,*
> *This made my dad my son-in-law*
> *And really changed my life –*
> *I am my own grandpaw –*
> *It really drives me wild.*

I've probably got it a bit garbled. It just makes me laugh. If I were a young woman I would whirl around the room with the baby in my arms, dancing to the tune of the universe. I cannot dance but it doesn't stop the tune. Nothing does. I forgive Venetia, who too is getting old.

I feel a change in the karmic weather. I feel the stillness after the storm. Everything waits. Something is about to happen. The universe slips.

The lights come on. The power cut is over. Mother, what would you say? 'When in doubt, do what's in front of you.' Obediently I go to the computer and look up superglue in CiviPedia. Acetone. Nail varnish remover? I find I have some in a sponge bag of yesteryear, which should have been thrown out, but never was. The bag is full of loose unnamed pills and crusted unguents of which I no longer understand the usages. But here it is. Max Factor, very ancient, from my days with Edgar, but it should be okay. There is still some grappa left (CiviStore Grade 1: farewell to all that), which I hid from Edgar when he called to see me the other night, and I mix the two up – how does alcohol react with acetone? There is no steam, no bubbling, no explosion, it is okay. There is an eye-dropper in the sponge bag – I used to suffer from conjunctivitis. I use it to squirt the mixture into the keyhole. Surplus to requirements trickles down from the lock and makes bubbly runnels in the dark-blue paint. It is certainly strong stuff. I will leave the glue to soften. My mother would be proud of me.

Before long I will be able to get out of my house, and the runnels in the paint will confirm to me that these events happened and were not the product of an overheated imagination.

It is normal for the parents of girls lost to death or disaster to describe them thus: 'she was such a lovely, bubbly girl, she had all her life ahead of her.' I wonder who tells the poor stunned parents what to say? The doorstepping journalist, I suppose. 'Shall we just describe her as bubbly? That seems to sum her up.' Venetia was all kinds of things but she was never bubbly. Polly on the other hand bubbled and fizzed away.

There is a noise from the potato patch. I switch off the light and look out. There is something happening beneath the beanpole arch and just enough light to see movement and scuffles, a cluster of bodies. Someone is being frogmarched across the patch to the back of No. 7. There are muffled noises, protests. Whoever it is does not mean to go quietly. Victor? Whoever it is breaks away, bursting through the bean plants; it is hardly intelligent; wherever he runs he will see nothing but the backs of houses, boarded-up doors and barred windows. But he runs, trips, falls face first into the muddy soil of the mulched potatoes. A glint of metal from the ground – handcuffs? No wonder he fell. The others run after him and fall upon him, drag him to his feet, and under cover of the arch. They are so inept. If there is anyone left living in the Crescent – perhaps they have all gone, and in Rothwell Street too, which is why the CiviCams haven't been mended – they will have been alerted. Though people are unwilling to call CiviSecure at the best of times. Wiser, when there is trouble, to look the other way.

'Come on now, me boy, or it might be the worse for you.'

The stage-Irish accent of Henry, Ethan's half-, no longer step-, brother, is recognizable, and Ethan's grunt, and I pick out the odd oath from Amos, and Amy's self-righteous squeak. And then they are inside.

I can no longer take any of them quite seriously. Henry is no new Oliver Cromwell come to rescue society from NUG, but an ill-informed redundant pig farmer in a world which has to live on reconstituted protein, rather than one which rings to the squeals and struggles of slaughtered, methane-producing pigs. He will find no followers.

Amos is a swearing, spoiled, stubbly druggie with too high an opinion of himself, envious of Ethan and always happy to get him into trouble; and not particularly honest. There is nothing charismatic about him at all.

Ethan is the child of an incestuous relationship and I do not want to think about him.

Amy is no relative of mine, only of Liddy, whom I should have looked after better. She is plain and bossy. An unfortunate face, as my mother would have said. Polly would not let me even draw attention to such a fact. She would say that a woman's looks have nothing to do with her personality. But then Polly is self-deluded and sees the world as it ought to be, not what it is.

In fact I have fallen out of love with my family, at any rate this generation of them. I have been shocked out of self-deception into clear thinking. Or perhaps I am being punished. Supposing I'd let Fay have Karl, out of kindness – but the divergence of the ways is too much to contemplate.

Vague noises come from next door. No screams of the tortured, thank God, just occasional bursts of speech and a rumbling of complaint. What can they want from Victor? Apologies? Money? Promises? If they know about the circumstances of Ethan's birth, can they blackmail him? Unlikely; the press is too tightly controlled for that. Redpeace speculated about what Victor was involved in at NIFE, and was promptly taken off the web.

If I try the key in the lock again it may work. Then I could run out into the street – or at any rate hobble, and wave at the CiviCam and help would come. I could turn the lot of them in. It would be an act of a good citizen, and a bad wife and mother, and a shocking grandmother. Or I could sit here like any old person, neutral, do nothing, see nothing, hear nothing, and not try the key. I decide to do exactly that. When in doubt, do nothing.

I try a little National Meat Loaf – it's marvellous how good it tastes. I am quite trembly. It has been something of a day and is not finished yet. Doors close and open upstairs and Amos comes leaping down. He seems cheerful, but he is acting.

A Useful Conversation With Amos

'Just popped down to see you were okay, Gran,' he says.

Just popped down to see you were still where you ought to be, is what he means. He rolls a joint.

'I'm fine,' I say. 'Did a bit of writing, now it's suppertime.'

'Being old has its advantages,' he says. 'I guess everything gets a bit wiped out. But don't mind Henry. He can come over a bit strong. He has his problems. We all do.'

One of them, I suspect, is that Henry doesn't like Amos smoking spliffs so he has to come over to me to do it. The New Republic will be a very drug-free kind of place.

'I didn't notice,' I say. 'A very good-looking boy, that Henry, in spite of his mother.'

'Gran, you really have to get over what happened fucking years ago.'

And he tells me everyone else has, and if his mother could accept Henry surely it was time I did too. Henry was a great leader and if I was sensible I should keep in with him. He was good to women and children. This was to be a bloodless coup. He'd promised to look after Venetia, even when Victor was in exile. Perhaps Venetia could come down and live with me, or with Polly. Henry was merciful, and didn't believe in bloodshed. There'd been no-one like him since fucking Che Guevara.

I could see Henry would look good on a T-shirt. It was the jaw that did it. Henry's jaw, Ethan's jaw. I put out of my mind the possibility that Venetia had made the whole thing up to upset Polly, or Polly had, to upset me. No. It had happened.

But Victor go into exile? Where? St fucking Helena? They wouldn't have the fuel to get him there. Men never have a satisfactory after-the-hostilities plan. They were all mad. What did they mean to do? Invade Muswell Hill? Men are even more given to pack behaviour than women. Show men a leader and they'll follow. I laughed. And then I thought of the CiviSecure guards, the young hotheads, with their bright eyes and their nibbling teeth, and it didn't seem too funny. I thought of the Jokers in their circle of torment and thought that Henry's cheeks were looking rather suspiciously red. Had he wiped off the rouge? If he could rally them all – the hosts of unemployed young male teenagers – perhaps he already had – if forces within NUG were already conspiring against it – NUG, government by sociologists and therapists, wouldn't stand a chance.

'But tomorrow we'll be through with the meetings,' Amos assured me, 'and your life will get back to normal. You can have anyone round here you like. Even your fascist ex-husband. You lost a fucking lot of sympathy when you married him.'

I asked, rather too sharply for the daft little old lady I was playing, whether Amy would be over to see to the lock. He looked blank. I mentioned the superglue and he said Amy and Ethan would be over to say goodbye tomorrow around midday, and no doubt they'd see to it then. Might not be too early because it was a big rally tonight.

'A rally?' I enquired. 'What fun! Where?'

'We're packing the Underground trains,' he said. 'No cameras down there. They get vandalized.'

And he stumbled upstairs. I thought again of trying the lock and running out into the street to freedom, but I didn't. I'm a family kind of person, and families have always stood between women and freedom. They connive at their own defeat.

Dr Yuk

I remembered what the loose pills were. Dexedrine. I'd emptied out their little brown bottle into the bottom of the sponge bag so nobody could identify them but me. They were illegal at the time. These days they would be in blister packs religiously stamped with date and strength: then they were anonymous, sinister in dark glass. These ones must be a good sixty years old, powdery but okay. Time would not have made much difference to their effectiveness. Amphetamine was a chemical.

I went carefully. I took only one. My chest is old-lady thin and I did not want to see or hear my heart pounding away. I felt no difference in my body, but I felt foolhardiness and good cheer enter into my mind. It was almost like the 'walk-in' my friend Ava in Glastonbury told me about, only her walk-in, a spirit from the Dog Star Sirius, wasn't very nice at all. It had made her steal the ten-pound note I had put aside for a night's lodging at the youth hostel. My walk-in was effective but not delinquent. Walk-ins make you do all kinds of things you wouldn't normally do, she told me – steal, cheat, sleep with your best friend's husband – possibly, even, your mother's husband. Perhaps that had been Venetia's problem? A walk-in, very useful to have around, but no use as a witness in a court of law. They evaporate when their existence is challenged. Nevertheless, naturally, they proliferate in Glastonbury and other fulcra of supposed spiritual power, where people are determined to do exactly as they please and still feel good about themselves.

The problem with Dexedrine is that while it gives you energy and speeds up your brain you feel like someone else. It was as someone else that I waited by the darkened window until the New Model Army had filed out, minus Victor. It seemed unlikely that they had left him without a guard, but when I got up to No. 5's first floor – moving faster made the pain less, or at any rate go on for a shorter time – there was Victor, pink-faced, plump and bald, his clothes and face muddy from where he had fallen in the potato patch, hands and legs cuffed to the chair, tape round his mouth but his nostrils free to breathe. I have always wondered what happens when people to whom this happens have colds in the head. I suppose they simply die. Victor was snorting away, as it was.

My instinct was to give him more air, and I found a serrated kitchen knife and cut through the tape at a point where it pulled tight. I wondered whether killing him would serve any useful purpose, but I could not see that it would. Presumably the New Model Army had felt the same.

'Not you too,' he said. 'Not you, Gran,' which was oddly moving. Poor man, he wept.

I disclaimed responsibility. I apologized for my family's behaviour. I told him what I did not believe: that they were motivated by a desire for the public good, and should be forgiven. Indignation made him more stoical.

'But so are we all,' he said.

Theirs was a properly elected government, not like the last one. NUG was determined to meet the nutritional needs of the people safely and fairly, and NIFE was doing everything in its power to provide the people with protein grown from basic meat cells other than human, but there were still technical difficulties to be over-come. And then his voice faded away as he listened to himself. The politician in him struggled with the person and the person won.

'Bugger this,' he said, 'I don't have to explain all this to an old woman. No offence, Gran, but just get me out of here.'

I did take some offence. There had been some talk over the last year of restricting the electorate to those between thirty and fifty, the one-person, one-vote principle being seen to be outmoded in an ageing population. The future was too precious to be trusted to a lot of daft old people with Alzheimer's, or young hotheads. The talk had evaporated but prejudice against the old had observably increased.

I said I didn't have the key. They were holding me prisoner too. But there was lots of time. They were off to a rally and wouldn't be back until late. We would work out something. He suggested I start sawing away at the metal chain that joined the cuffs but I said it was CiviCutlery and would work for duct tape but hardly for metal. He sighed and said CiviCutlery had saved countless lives but he personally had made a stand against it. If people were not allowed to express a degree of aggression they would internalize it, and there might be civil unrest.

'You were right,' I said. 'You should have talked more loudly. Then perhaps we wouldn't be in here.'

Now he began to cry.

'That snake in the grass, Henry. I did everything for him, for Venetia's sake. When he turned up I took him into my household, the same way I took first Amos and then Ethan. I love Venetia; I love their mother, why do they seem to hate me?'

Victor had always known that Ethan was not his? I had to sit down to take this in. He had married a woman who had deliberately conceived a child by her own stepfather, and then foisted it on him? And he had gone along with it? And gone on loving her? The odd black eye seemed a trivial thing. Fact kept outstripping my imagination. I was too old for this. Should I retape his mouth, go downstairs, let what happened happen? Go to sleep and with any luck not wake up at all. Join my mother, be at peace. I had done my duty by Mother Nature: I had fed two children out into the world, with the unique genes she had insisted on in her quest for improvement, to add to the general mayhem of life.

'I did my best to love Amos but it was difficult.' Victor had gone into whining mode. It can be difficult to respect men. I could see Polly's point. I had quite liked Victor but now I could see what Venetia had to put up, to get to the Grade 1 CiviStore, to get both of her boys housed – Amos, out of Anon the artist, and Ethan, out of Karl, my husband.

'I had my career to think about,' he moaned on. 'That prison sentence – he brought that on himself to get at me, I'll swear he did. Like posh girls take up with rough trade, to annoy their parents. And Henry – Henry used me to fight his way up in NIFE. I got him the job out of the kindness of my heart. NUG Human Resources warned me against him: the graphologists' report was very negative indeed, but I overruled them. Venetia insisted. He was Ethan's big brother, after all.'

So he knew that too.

'I can accept that. But Ethan? I loved him like my own. My own son did this to me. Brought me here by force, touched me with hands that seemed to hate me. How do you explain that, Gran?'

Perhaps Polly had been right. Perhaps Victor beat up Venetia from time to time and Ethan resented it. Saul had sworn he loved Doreen, when she came to me with a broken nose and took up residence on my sofa until Karl threw her out, and I think Saul did. And she loved him. People are very odd.

I said Ethan might be a little mad. Neurological research suggested that in the schizophrenic brain the impulse to love and the impulse to hate were too closely linked, and there could be slippage.

'Reductionist twaddle,' he said. That was rich, coming from a scientist.

I asked him how his predecessor had died.

'Of a heart attack,' he said, sounding so surprised that I believed him. 'Why do you ask? He ate too much real meat. It's freely available in the Grade 1 CiviStores. I'm trying to get it stopped.' And he told me that life expectancy outside NUG was higher than it was inside because of unhealthy eating habits. Real coffee and so on.

I asked him what he would do if he ever got out of here. He said he would move the family down to Whitehall, where there was proper security. He had just stepped into his car. Ethan had been driving, and had taken him to this dump where the others had been waiting. He would never feel safe getting into a Ministry car again. He would walk to work. He didn't care what Venetia said. It had been Venetia's insistence that they stayed in Muswell Hill. She liked the house. High ground inspired her. It had proved alarmingly expensive and the Committee had shaken their heads, but tried to get what benefit they could from it. Family man, all that. The public face of NUG. He'd managed to keep Amos out of the picture and of course they didn't know about Ethan, that was a baby too far –

'They probably know everything,' I said. 'They'll have the place bugged. They have most of us bugged.'

'That can't be true,' he said, but turned quite pale. Like many scientists, many left-brainers, he was naive to the point of stupidity. They used him as Henry used him, as my daughter Venetia used him, to their advantage. I wondered if it was better for the country to be governed by stupid men like Victor or men of principle like Henry. I thought Victor won on points.

'When you say family, Victor,' I asked, 'who do you mean? What are you going to do about Amos, Ethan, Henry and, if Ethan gets it together with her, Amy?' What would he do about the snakes in his bosom to stop them wriggling around?

He said he would see they got treatment. NUG had excellent therapeutic services for Grade 1 families. I asked if the treatment included pushing family members off platforms or running them down when they were out shopping, and he looked so baffled. I thought it probably did not. I thought Polly was simply feeling guilty about a lot of things and imagined aggressors where none existed. She is my daughter, after all. The capacity to invent must surely surface from time to time.

I said to him, but Victor, if what I think is happening is, if they have got you imprisoned here not because they hate you but as a negotiating ploy for when Henry stages a coup and storms the heights of Muswell Hill, unseats NUG and sets up an alternative government, with the support of half a million armed CiviSecure teenagers, what then?

'This is not a film,' Victor said, eventually. 'This is not the kind of thing that happens.'

'Victor,' I said. 'This is a new world we're in, entirely. There are no precedents.'

He replied that he wanted to pee. I could have said, 'then do,' but my maternal urge was still there. He had to put up with me finding a bowl, unzipping his fly, dragging out his limp penis, and holding it while he used it. I reflected on how this pathetic piece of flesh in the possession of men makes so much difference to so many lives.

I emptied the bowl down the sink – a yellow and pungent stream. Victor did not drink enough. Venetia should make sure that he did. The water was off but Redpeace had left a half bottle of beer behind, so keen were they on revolution, and I used that to rinse out bowl and sink. My mother, always one to rise to eventualities, would have done the same.

I made a decision, as does a Booker Chairperson when the vote is split between two possible winners. The top judge, the fifth, weighs up the judges, not the book, and tilts the weight of judgment accordingly. The desire to hide my head under the blankets and sleep the rest of my life away was very great, yet to do nothing was not, when it came to it, an option. In favour of a coup was the end of NUG, its humourless bossiness, its endless interference. Against the coup – well, the devil you know tends to be better than the one you don't. There is nothing in the natural world, other than our hopes, that suggests that if one thing is bad there must be a balancing good. Yet you have to hope – or what kind of person are you? What tipped the balance, it seemed, was family. Bloodless revolutions usually end up very bloody indeed. Victor as a hostage was bound to wind up dead, having provoked both sides to irrationality. Friendly fire from CiviSecure would like as not get my grandchildren and their mother too. CiviSecure were a frightening lot. At least under NUG we were all still alive, ate, and had shoes. I went with NUG.

I did what it was so simple to do. I got a cushion to shield my arm, and broke a window that looked out over the Crescent. I put my head out and in a voice once so strong but now lamentably shrill and weak I called out to the CiviCam, 'Help, help, we have been kidnapped.'

Then I went back to Victor and pulled up his zip, to protect his dignity, and we waited for rescue.

The Battle For Muswell Hill

In spite of his frequent Friday visits to Muswell Hill, Henry had failed to take much notice of its topography. He had travelled there only by car. Ethan was in the habit of giving his half-brother a lift up from Hunter's Alley, from where he had been organizing the New Republic. A good meal is often hard to find, especially for a busy revolutionary, and Venetia could always be relied upon to provide one. A proper sit-down meal with many courses had been a feature of Henry's grandmother's household in Ireland, and a man always relishes a comforting return to culinary childhood. The visits had also, of course, enabled Henry to understand the configurations of the house as it grew around him, its security arrangements and its communication systems. 'Victor's Palace', as it had become known down at NIFE, was rumoured to be part of NUG's new headquarters. Whitehall had survived the floods of 2012 but might not be so lucky next time. The whole government establishment, bureaucracy, nutritional labs, supply depots and all, would have to move to higher ground.

It was Henry's plan to establish his forces – the Jokers and such CiviSecure guards as had come over to his side, some two thousand men and women in all – in the Tube lines, and on a given signal to take them over forcibly but peacefully. The New Republic was to be responsible for as little bloodshed as possible. The triumphant forces were to make their way from stations all over London to Muswell Hill Underground, there to muster, and converge on Grand Avenue. Victor was to be held in a secret location to serve as a hostage in negotiations. The rallying call to action, when it flashed up on mobiles up and down the city, was *To the Batmobile!*

But warned in time that an attempt was being made to seize the Muswell Hill heights, loyal NUG stalwarts easily beat back the invaders, using new vehicle-mounted CiviCalm sprayhoses, which induced extreme nausea in anyone unfortunate enough to be in the vicinity. Poor Venetia, for one, had her kitchen door burst open by a couple of hideously masked NUGIntel officials who tried, for her own good, to put a gas mask on her. She declined to wear the unsightly thing, and as a result suffered severe bruising, but, worse, had a whiff of the gas, which kept her in bed vomiting for days.

Henry's rebels might well have won the day, but, finding there was no such station as Muswell Hill, were obliged to make for Highgate, Bounds Green or East Finchley stations instead, and, exhausted by the long, hot walk up the hill, straggled to the meeting point. They were not there in force when Henry needed them. There was a moment when they could have taken over the hoses and gassed the enemy rather than themselves, but the moment was lost. The New Model Army of the New Republic limped down the hill again, boots splashing in vomit.

Meanwhile, a proportion of those loyal to NUG – and during the skirmish many decided to rejoin the winning side – had been shuttled in CiviSecure helicopters to help restore order at the Banqueting Hall. Amos, Ethan and Amy, leading a cell of activists who had secretly infiltrated NIFE and other NUG departments over the last year, had occupied the building.

Little resistance had been offered. Transport, Registry and Lab staff had lately become seedbeds of discontent: a good 30 per cent, it transpired, had been turned. Word had got round – or indeed been deliberately spread – that a lab worker had recognized his deceased grandmother's ring on what looked like an elderly human hand as it was sucked into the mixer from which DNA was extracted. Another was said to have recognized the hennaed pigtail of Brass Number Three (in whose heart attack no-one quite believed) under a brain-dissection slab. It was rumoured that a happily married chauffeur had been ordered into the back of his stretch limo to provide an extra penis at an orgy. Ph.Ds in psychoanalytical studies were apparently being handed out gratis to favoured Committee members. Worse, access to the CiviStores was being limited to all but the most senior grades, and acorn coffee served in the canteens as a matter of course. And no-one had had a rise for two years.

By the time CiviSecure arrived, to find doors and windows barricaded, and the strikers inside, activists had the sluices and water supplies to the labs cut off. But the moans that issued from the life broth tanks – though probably only the sounds of suction and plumbing – as the water drained were enough to persuade the tender-hearted to grapple with the hard-hearted, and the former won by a good majority. Water supplies were resumed. News came down that the Muswell Hill attack had failed. Heart and zest fizzled out of the occupation. The barricades were taken down and CiviSecure entered in.

Victor appeared briefly in person, and Top Brasses Numbers One and Two called a meeting in the canteen, and addressed the strikers: *NUG – Making Peaceful Choices Easier*. Workers were promised that real coffee would be back on the menu and a 5 per cent wage increase, backdated three months, would be granted.

So the coup dissolved without bloodshed. The ringleaders were identified and led away. Life at NUG continued as normal as all prepared for a move up the hill to where the air was fresher and cleaner. A state of emergency was, however, declared and elections put off for the time being.

In The Facility

No end indeed to the surprises. What NUG possesses in great measure is gratitude. Now there's a turn-up for the books. They even gave me an award lately, a framed certificate on which was inscribed: 'For contributing to the assuagement of misunderstandings within the community.' A carpenter arrived to hang it on the wall: a carer to put the flowers in water.

NUG are grateful to have their Victor back. Why I cannot make out, but there it is: I think they have taken a leaf out of the New Republic's book and are moving towards abolishing the monarchy. It won't be long before Victor is made President, a post where dignity and little else is required. He appears on TV from time to time, wearing suits that are ever more expensive, smiling and benign, explaining the necessity of some new restriction on our consumption or freedoms.

I try not to think of his helpless cock: it makes me laugh. I try not to think of Amos and his 'necessity is the argument of tyrants and the creed of slaves' because it makes me cry, being true. Victor and Venetia and Mervyn the Dull have moved up to a house in Belgravia, where I believe the attics have been opened out to give Venetia a good northern light for her studio. I believe she is moving from acrylics to watercolours.

I am living in NUG's Regent's Park therapeutic community, in their 'Protected Housing for Deserving Seniors' facility. It is a cluster of rather ugly but mostly comfortable bungalows in what was once Queen Mary's Rose Garden. I live with no stairs and all mod cons. We get broadband, electricity and water twenty-four/seven. I am very happy.

Now I am in a different place, having been wrenched forcibly from the Crescent, the marriage to Karl and its attendant problems have faded into the past. Staying in the Crescent after the divorce, which I thought so clever, was probably the worst thing I ever did. I had nailed myself into the past. New ways of life demand new homes. NUG offer to replace my knees, and even to tighten my vocal cords so my voice returns to its former strength and youth. This they can do, apparently. I am thinking about it. The 'Deserving Seniors' get an automatic chance of being cloned, but I am not sure I would wish to inflict myself on another human being.

When CiviSecure arrived with their sirens, vans and armaments to rescue Victor they broke down all the front doors at my end of the Crescent just to be on the safe side, though they promised to make good and repaint, and even spend money restoring the whole Crescent to its former glory. Indeed, I heard an official remark that it was a pretty street and would make good housing for NUG Grade 2s. I still own my house. My mortgage and store-card debts have been repaid. I have a civil pension that is more than enough for my needs. For the time being I prefer to stay where I am, and am welcome to. Death no longer seems so inviting.

Nothing is for nothing, of course. I told them everything I knew. I handed over my laptop and they made good use of it. Fortunately for me the wife of the interrogator – 'Just a formality, Dame Frances' – was a fan and former reader of my novels, and longs for me to write a new one. NUG wives are powerful, it seems. Their whims are often taken as official directives. It is not exactly the triumph of feminism but it is something. NUG's policy is to incorporate aggression, not meet it head-on. They invite me on to their many quangos to discuss the motivation of their opponents. I have even encountered Henry at one of them, putting forward his views on the value of a new ethic. We were perfectly polite to one another. He is more closely supervised than I am, in the Hyde Park Facility for Rehabilitation.

This was where I was first taken, after Victor and I were hustled off in the ambulance. I told them everything I knew, but only on condition my family would not suffer. On the night of the coup NUG had cleared the Underground of antisocial forces. I intimated to the interrogator that I knew where a lot of bodies were buried – Ethan's parentage, for one thing; Victor's lack of judgment at taking in Henry for another. Bargaining with authority is always a risk. I do not forget Oliver Cromwell's sack of the Irish town of Drogheda in 1649, even while negotiations were under way for its surrender: three and a half thousand people died at the hands of the New Model Army. I could see it might well be a toss-up between whether my whole family, grandchildren included, would join the National Meat Loaf mix (how NUG deny that scenario: never such a loathsome rumour!) or whether I could be relied upon as a trusted ally. Fortunately the decision was made in my favour.

Amos, Henry, Ethan and Amy stay in the Hyde Park Facility and are undergoing psychoanalysis. All have been given positions of responsibility within NUG. Ethan is in charge of the limousine unit and is responsible for the safe road transport of Ministers; Henry in NIFE works on the problems of getting sufficient calorie content into the daily diet of forty million citizens; Amy is really high up in Neighbourhood Watch; and Amos works on the fair allocation of recreational drugs. I am not sure that this is the wisest method of dealing with social recalcitrants, but so long as I say so at meetings and am overruled, everyone seems happy.

The interrogator has studied the first draft of this memoir/fiction/diary. He is full of helpful suggestions. With the leisure and comfort I have now, and in the absence of quite so many surprises, I have been able to get on quite fast with the second draft you are reading now.

'Just tell us more about Amos and Ethan,' he says. 'Everything you know.'

Amos is my flesh and blood – apart from some dollop of genes from a stranger, which I can't be responsible for – and Ethan even more my flesh and blood, he being so very much in the family – so everything I know about them includes everything I know about me. Therefore this text.

The psychoanalysts here seem less interested in Henry and Amy: I think these days they are focusing more on nature than on nurture in their assessment of personality types: the flow of the genes rather than the weight of upbringing. It's the way the world is going.

I have always used fiction to get to the heart of the matter, to discover what it is I know. It is up to the facility analysts, when they finally get round to reading this text, to decide what is memoir, what is fact, what is truth (Pilate-like, I wash my hands) or some embroidery of the truth.

Venetia calls round every couple of weeks. We are distant and friendly, and talk about nothing that might disconcert either of us. Once a month I am asked round to a Shabbat-style dinner. Photographers and film-makers are often present, as we talk about social issues. As for Polly, I suggested to her the other day that she and Corey and the girls moved into Chalcot Crescent, where there is more light, air and good cheer than in Mornington Crescent. When I pointed out to her that the girls would get fewer colds, she capitulated. So a new generation of Prideauxs moves in. It's good. I am all for continuity. And perhaps Rosie and Steffie will have daughters.

Sometimes I see myself like Job, whose 'latter days God blessed more than the beginning.' God and the Devil fight it out over Job: he loses his possessions and is visited by every calamity under the sun. Job challenges God, God accepts his rebuke, and Job says okay, he'll stop whining. By giving in to the system, he gets everything. He ends up with fourteen thousand sheep, six thousand camels, a thousand yoke of oxen and a thousand she-asses – something of an overkill, one might think, suggesting a biblical writer eager to get home to his dinner. *And in all the land were no women found so fair as the daughters of Job*. That's what it feels like to be me. Blessed, but only at the very end.

I wish Cynthia were here so I could tell her all about what happened next. So contrary was she, had I told her it was okay to go to Turkey she'd probably have stayed home and not fallen out of the sky. But there you are. One does what one does.